It's in His Kiss

By
Vickie Lester

I am the author of It's in His Kiss.

Let's start with a little background on how I came to write my first novel. I used to write screenplays. Horrid, arty, little things, that were praised for their characterization and literary tone, and were optioned again and again, but never made into movies. Perhaps, because they were neither commercial or cinematic? That's a pretty good guess, if I don't say so myself.

My people came from Moscow and a London slum called Whitechapel. When the British portion of the family arrived in New York they headed out to Seattle by train, way before the plane was invented. Finding only rain, and more rain, mud, and wooden planks for sidewalks (a segment of which appeared to be an orange crate from sunny California) they immediately booked tickets south… Or, so the story goes. And thus, my father's grandparents came to L.A. Thanks for stopping by, and thanks for keeping an eye on Hollywood.

vickielester.com

Acknowledgements

For their guidance, savvy, and notes, I thank Carl Pritzkat, Tony Travastino, and Robert Winter: for her grammatical prowess, Ellen Tarlin. For their creative input, impeccable taste, and dab hand at design many thanks to John Myhre and Shirley Kawabuchi. And to my husband, Kirk, there are no words to adequately describe a life spent together, so I'll simply say thank you.

It's in His Kiss

By
Vickie Lester

There's no mistaking death. What is remarkable is how it differs from life. In fact, the moment of recognition is always bluntly apparent. A corpse is merely something immobile, emptied, and almost entirely inhuman. Ruben Martinez nudged his van down Belardo Road tossing *New York Times* and *Desert Sun* Sunday editions to the curb. The rhythm of man and machine was measured and slow. The papers hit the pavement with a substantive thud. It was 5:30 a.m. Palm trees spot-lit from below pushed up against an inky sky. Mount San Jacinto rose pinnacled and dark over Mediterranean and Mid-Century estates. It was quiet. The air was faintly scented with minerals, eucalyptus and sage. Then, as the van's headlights swept over a parked car, he saw it: a body, its complexion the palest marble white veined with green and purple. Ruben stomped on his brakes and stared. A lapsed Catholic, he wondered if this man's soul—if such a thing existed—had simply disappeared, or if it had departed and was now traveling someplace untold and unearthly. He doubted the latter, but hoped, ardently, that he was wrong. Ruben, at the age of forty-six, was frequently troubled by questions of mortality.

The body sat upright, tightly belted behind the steering wheel, eyes closed, head lolling to the side, facial muscles slack, neck blackened by bruising. He reached for his cell phone and dialed 911.

Elsewhere in Palm Springs there were several people who had been tethered to this life by various bonds of affection: a studio head, two actors, a director, a screenwriter, and a novelist who organized her thoughts through fiction. One of them was awake and remorseless; the rest were asleep and if not precisely innocent, at least unaware.

Chapter I

START ME UP

Death is a sidewinder. It strikes from a place concealed and unthinkable, triggering a reality completely unexpected. Anne was in-flight from Manhattan to Los Angeles, trying to piece together a childhood cracked by the continental United States, father in California, mother in New York, and time, a whole lot of time, in between. Dad was currently eighty, Mom was fifty-seven, her half-sister was roughly the age of her mother, and Anne was thirty-four.

Flying over the Rockies, Anne thought of the old three-story colonial on Crescent Drive that one of her parents called home. Beverly Hills was a place Anne always associated with Bob Brown, her now elderly but only slightly less lionized father. It was where she was foisted into his care. Usually this occurred when her model mother, Jill Shayes, was sent on location for a photo shoot. That is, long-limbed, green-eyed mother Jill was a high-fashion model photographed by the likes of Bailey and Scavullo, not that she was in any other way a *model mother*. These glamorous forays into print happened less and less frequently as Anne's mother approached thirty. In retrospect, Anne realized her mother's consumption of cigarettes and alcohol increased exponentially with the passage of each year, while her bookings plummeted.

Anne shifted and tried to get comfortable. The studio had sprung for business class. The seat was large; the neck rest made an angle that nudged her awkwardly near the top of her head. She continued to reminisce.

The one and only time Anne was in California for Halloween, her father had said, "You're a city girl; city girls don't go trick or treating." In response nine-year-old Anne looked up at him glumly. "Tell you what," he continued, "I'll phone next door and see what's doing."

Next door lived Gene Kelly, an old man with eyeglasses that made him look literally bug-eyed and an unconvincing sickly brown-colored hairpiece. His favored opening gambit to almost any conversation with a stranger was to bark "I'm Gene Kelly. Not *that* goddamned Gene Kelly!" Even though he did, in truth, resemble an embalmed-then-reanimated ancient version of "*that* goddamned Gene Kelly." When an intimidated Anne knocked on his door, Not *That* Gene Kelly opened it and wordlessly handed her an outsized candy bar—as he had apparently arranged with her dad—then hollered over his shoulder, in a tone reserved for his son, "Carl, move your goddamn truck! You're blocking me in!"

Later that Halloween Uncle Manny, ever-dapper and silver-haired, arrived toting a piñata. After saying a perfunctory "hello" to his brother and a much warmer one to Anne, he instructed Bob to fetch him a broomstick with which to violently open his gift. On receiving the broom from a stone-faced Bob, he brought it down on the piñata with a resounding *THWACK*, littering the entryway with its candy-filled guts. "Never forget, pumpkin, your dad might have the face of a damned druid, but, luckily, some Browns know how to party." At the time it may have been worth considering that her uncle's proclivities were partly responsible for Bob Brown's unvaryingly stern demeanor. However, Anne was a child and such thoughts were beyond her. Anne's father surveyed the chocolates on the shining parquet, Mars bars, Baby Ruths, Reese's Pieces, and Mounds. He scowled and, taking back the broom, intoned, "Imagine my joy, Manny.

Next time why not just bring a five-pound sack of sugar?"
Anne, more than slightly puzzled, reached for Uncle Manny's
hand. He was her closest equivalent to a grandparent: doting,
somewhat flamboyant, and constant.

While her father ran a media conglomerate, Uncle Manny
(once a medical student whose aspirations shifted in the gore
on the beaches of Normandy) drafted up skyscrapers, Spanish
galleons, spaceships, and transformed them all into movie sets.
As a child, Anne was under the impression that her uncle
made the magic happen and her father merely bossed people
around. Now nearly ninety, he had left the film industry far
behind and filled his time with Viking Cruises and flight
attendants.

Anne looked out the window and into a bank of clouds.
Her reasons for a winter return to California were many: her
beloved uncle's birthday, the task of retrieving his car keys
(last she'd heard from her half-sister he'd taken out a rank of
newspaper kiosks somewhere near his favorite deli on Sunset),
and sorting out an option renewal on a novel she had written.
It was her first novel, a novel that had been remaindered at
bookstores years ago but for some reason, after the project had
languished for nearly a decade in turnaround, the rights were
about to lapse and her agent had received a call. In the first
flush of publication, at the age of twenty-six, she figured the
option had been an indirect gift, due to her father's enduring
influence. He had retired at seventy. One year out people still
owed him. The money from the studio was triple what she
eventually made from her book sales. Now the studio was
offering to renew and it put her in a quandary. Her dad was
old. His sway was a thing of the past.

Anne, as a writer, had never been very well-known. She wrote
the kind of literature that was discussed and debated hotly by

graduate students at the University of Iowa and U.C.–Irvine; she was, in a word, obscure. Or, as her mother liked to put it, setting a sweaty glass of gin and tonic down squarely on Anne's second literary effort, "Honey, they pay you for this?" The answer was always: *just barely.*

Anne continually assured Jill Shayes she hadn't given up her day job as an instructor at City College, and her mother would peer at her, trying to discern the flash of her runway model genes in her mystifyingly cerebral offspring, then she would shrug and wander into the recesses of her Upper East Side apartment, clinking ice cubes as she went.

Anne was somewhat small and bespectacled. She was pretty in a subtle, stealthy way, and one had to be paying proper attention to notice. Her gamine appearance tended to put people subconsciously at ease. She wasn't in any way challenging: she listened; she kept confidences; people told her the most extraordinary things and she would file their secrets away. "Still waters," her Uncle Manny would say. Later, she would twist the secrets into unrecognizable forms and it came out as "spare, lapidary prose, highlighting the hypocrisy, pain and political unease of the 21st century," that's right—her very low-paying area of expertise was fiction—and she was about to reenter Papa's bailiwick, Hollywood. Or, as her half-sister Natalie was fond of saying, "Nepotism central."

Whatever, or whoever, was the cause of her sudden twist of fortune, Anne wasn't disembarking in Los Angeles. The travel itinerary from the studio specified her arrival in Palm Springs. Having flown in from slushy, dingy, frigid New York City in the middle of February she walked outside the terminal. She felt her shoulders drop and her neck loosen. It was warm. It smelled good—just like the cosmetic counter at Barneys. She looked up, a clear unobstructed shot of the sky, which was an uncanny shade of blue. Magenta flowers spilled over white stucco walls.

To say Anne was stunned when she was summoned to the winter home of Becky Nelson—head of production at a very well-known studio—would be an understatement. Becky had cut her teeth working for Anne's father: nepotism, there was that inconvenient word again. Was this a real deal? Had it ever been? Or could she just do as she was inclined and take her first flawed effort back home with her and forget about it? Anne kept wondering how somebody was going to turn a novel—all interior monologue, about a schizophrenic psychiatrist—into a movie. To her, it didn't seem cinematic. It never had. However, she heeded the words of her friend and agent, Danny Nero ("What? Are you crazy? Get your ass on that airplane!"), and headed where she was bid.

Dutifully, Anne navigated her hired Prius through a terrain at once dusty and opulent; Palm Springs is, after all, an exorbitantly irrigated pile of sand. Her destination was a taupe Mid-Century house, all angles and vertical glass walls. Anne parked the car by the curb and buzzed at the gate. A Spanish-accented voice answered her call and directed her poolside, where she appeared in her now irritatingly scratchy earth-toned turtleneck sweater. She thought she had stepped boldly into a new palette when she abandoned her Manhattan black, but to her mounting embarrassment she instantly saw she blended in perfectly with the scrub and rocky outcroppings covering what is known as the movie colony, an old area of town right under the hills, once home to Elvis and Frank and an ill-fated honeymooning couple of the thirties, Carole Lombard and Clark Gable.

In contrast, the other guests glistened in tanning oil. There they were, half-naked, with implausibly buoyant bosoms and supplemented bums and biceps, radiating a carefully constructed beauty; all of these individuals were in the film business or married to it. The women were skeletal; Anne assumed they had all stopped eating in about 2004. Skittering around this august company, weaving around feet and in and out from under lounge chairs, was an ugly little hairless dog with a tufted mane like the result of a hairdresser's tragic mistake—a Chinese crested. It shuddered as it ogled Anne, and she was equally appalled by its alien appearance. The animal was working up the nerve to lunge when a woman who had appeared to be asleep admonished, "Gwyneth!" and the dog cowered and shivered under her chair. Immediately Anne felt a pang about causing the creature so much angst and was just beginning to reach out to pet it when she saw her host, Steve Nelson, tall, expensively groomed husband of Becky, making his way toward her with a frosty highball in each hand. He silently mouthed the words *she bites* very, very emphatically. Anne tucked her hand behind her hip and smiled.

He smiled back—a flash of laser-bright teeth. The more Anne focused, the more improbable he appeared: so youthful. He had that round-eyed look that spoke of the surgeon's knife and made Robert Redford, Michael Douglas, and Sylvester Stallone all look vaguely like Beverly Hills matrons. He stopped briefly by the lounge of a man wearing swim trunks and a straw hat—he was shaped like a young Gary Cooper and had incandescent marine blue eyes the likes of which Anne had never seen. Mr. Nelson shook his head and *tut-tutted* as he handed the hunk a drink as it became apparent by his vacant, beautiful gaze that the man in the hat was talking intently on his headset.

Later, Anne would learn the man who had set her senses tingling was a talent agent at William Morris Endeavor and doing deals poolside at Becky's was strictly prohibited. However, cold drink firmly in hand, the man's attention shifted and he winked at Anne. She hadn't been winked at since she was seven. It was oddly endearing and she blushed at the attention. Then Nelson turned his eyes toward Anne, and her gaydar shrieked. She knew he was married, but this was deafening. As he approached she could guess exactly what he was thinking.

You poor thing! Quick! Lasiks! Highlights! And those clothes, ugh, they're, so, absolutely Bostonian! Instead, what he actually said was, "Anne Brown! Now I'll have someone to talk to this weekend. I love your books. You know it was me that made Becky read *Was That a Castle?*" Then he took Anne's hand and continued, "You're just as tiny as a minute! I didn't get that from your dust jacket. Come on, there're some people I want you to meet." With that, he led her around to meet all the beautiful people, who would have to be gently reminded of Anne's identity once again at dinner, apparently having been dazed by the afternoon sun.

Steve Nelson, loving the part of genial host, cruised the supper table refilling wineglasses, pausing for a moment here and there to exchange a confidence or provoke a laugh. As he topped Anne's Cabernet he said, "Doll, if you could get these characters to talk," he sighed appreciatively over his A-list guests. "Now, that would be a book!"

Anne smiled up at him sweetly. "Could you be angling to be my muse, Mr. Nelson?"

"Angling? I insist!"

The only one at the dinner table who remembered Anne seemed to be her West Coast counterpart, Keir Bloomfield, swaddled in layers of dusky linen, a portly bald man who told her he was allergic to the sun and that he had observed Anne's arrival from the lanai. Then, he proudly told her that he would be adapting her novel into a screenplay. "I envision," he gesticulated broadly with his fork, "a cross between *Sybil* and *The Fugitive*; we have to talk!"

"*The Fugitive*? But nobody's murdered in my book; nobody jumps off any waterfalls; it all takes place in a doctor's office," she protested.

"And, Sybil was a multiple, not a schizophrenic," interjected Cliff White, the built WME agent and winker.

"That's right!" she said, relieved to have an ally.

"If you'd done any research, Keir, you'd know a multiple personality couldn't make it through med school, or any kind of residency; their minds are just that, too fragmented, too disorganized. Whereas it is conceivable that a schizophrenic, with proper medication, could be a doctor—although, I think you're missing the point. It's a satire," Cliff continued. Anne was charmed by his knowledge, not to mention his good looks. He must have noticed. "You know" he said in confidential tones, "you know, Chief, your Dad's the original hard-ass."

"I know!" she concurred.

He leaned over to whisper to her, "Don't ever expect Keir to pollute his imaginative mind by reading any source material, and besides—take it from me—he's got the intellect of a head of iceberg lettuce." Anne couldn't help it, her jaw dropped open. *If you haven't anything nice to say about anybody, come sit next to me,* she thought of the immortal words of Alice

Roosevelt Longsworth and wondered why she was always drawn to men whose comments tended toward the dickish.

"Yeah, it's great!" Keir said ignoring the pair completely. "When Dr. Shelby goes on the lam after the murder all his identities have to emerge to evade the police, the FBI, all those marshals, all those uniforms…"

"Murder? Who? On the lam?" Keir wasn't listening. He looked unnaturally delighted. Anne remembered the paycheck Dan Nero had said the studio had offered to renew the rights, more money than she could conceive of, enough money to take a sabbatical and spend a year abroad, and she nodded politely, but something still wasn't quite right. Maybe it was the dollar amount for something she was sure would be re-shelved.

Anne caught a glimpse of Keir's shoes beneath the table; his legs were crossed at the knee and he was twitching one foot up and down compulsively. She wanted to grab his ankle and tell him to cut it out, but she just smiled. "Have you met my significant other?" Anne shook her head, expecting him to introduce a strapping young man, possibly, most likely, in the acting profession. Instead he blew a kiss to a taut, angular woman in her late sixties/early seventies wrapped in an Indonesian sarong. She smiled serenely. She was stunning. Anne tried to place the face, and then she realized she was looking at a bombshell from the fifties—Toni Todd.

Oh my god. She's my father's age—eighty, Anne marveled silently at an image from the screen come to life and almost perfectly preserved. Keir was smiling at her expectantly. He was probably around forty, maybe forty-five. "You're married?" She inquired out loud.

"Sixteen years," he replied.

Anne knew all about the May–December thing. Her father
had impregnated her mother in Cannes when he was forty-
four and she was twenty-two. That was about the extent of
their relationship, aside from the transfer of title on a New
York apartment and a grudging monthly check for Anne's
upkeep until she turned eighteen. (Her father sent checks
to *the woman*—that's how he referred to her—who had
produced his surprisingly precious little girl, not that he dwelt
on that much. He did what he could for Anne, but he was
very busy. Her uncle, perhaps because he wasn't compelled,
perhaps just because she—a tiny precocious thing fascinated
him—made time for his niece and would frequently appear
in Manhattan. Visits with her father always took place in Los
Angeles.) Anne was Bob Brown's second child, his first was
twenty years her senior and legitimate. He had still been
married to wife number one when Anne was born. She
always believed her arrival had precipitated their divorce.
However, that development didn't faze her mother at all,
"Don't do me any favors, Bob," she fairly spat at her sperm
donor. "And, don't count on me to change your diapers when
you're a hundred." Maybe Keir and Toni really were in love.
Well, at least they appeared civil.

"Congratulations," was all she could think of to say.

"Say, what's going on in that noggin of yours?" asked Mr.
White. Anne was tickled by his use of *noggin*.

"Oh, I was just thinking how different it is to be back out
here after all these years."

"Don't see your Dad much?"

"No," she said.

"How about your significant other?"

"The last significant date I had, the guy, he paid a twenty-dollar tip in silver dollars. Then, when we said goodnight he handed me a two-dollar bill instead of giving me a kiss and told me to hold onto the money because a two-dollar bill was very rare. I haven't had a significant other in years. Almost two years."

Cliff laughed; something in her manner had caught his attention. "I think I'm going to have to look out for you."

"That's awfully nice—but I have been looking out for myself for a very long time."

"When's your birthday?" He asked.

"February 12th."

"Year?"

"1974."

"No fucking way! That's my birthday! We're exactly the same age!"

Coincidences aside, brainy and brawny was paying an inordinate amount of attention to Anne so, she supposed, it could only mean two things, 1) obviously, he was a warm, delightful man or, quite possibly, 2) he was trying to poach Anne from her New York agent. Although the latter, considering the previous earning power of her books, seemed highly unlikely.

"I should fix you up with one of my friends."

"Do any of them work outside the industry?" she stumped him.

He changed the subject, "Have you ever been to Musso & Frank's?"

She shook her head. "It's a restaurant, right?"

"Where have you been?"

"Mostly in Manhattan," she responded.

"It's the oldest restaurant in Hollywood. Unbelievable! It's an institution! It's where I first saw your father." Now Anne was hooked and Cliff was warming up to tell a story, which he semaphored by flicking out his fingers like asterisks. "Musso's. Built late teens. Two big rooms. One all red leather and dark wooden booths and the best grill in town with this crazy big copper hood where we, you and I, are going to sit and watch them fire up our steaks and eat mashed potatoes and creamed spinach."

Anne frowned.

"Trust me, you'll love it. The other room is just tables and a bar. A set of booths run the perimeter and the one in the corner—the one that looks out over the entire room—is the power spot. It's where Eisner and Clint Eastwood and your father used to sit. When we were kids—me and my friends— we were all, you know, assistants. We worked in mailrooms, walked dogs, whatever, any jobs we could muster. But we all had this," he growled, "thing going on where we wanted to BE, you get it?

"I get it."

"Right. Players. So we would dress up in suits and ties once a month and pool our money, you know, because normally all we could afford was Denny's, and we would reserve a table right in the middle of the room, right in the eye line of the power booth. We called ourselves The Cannibal Club, and we even had a motto: *Entertainment or Death*."

Anne laughed. He leaned forward and tucked a hank of her hair behind her ear.

"Really. All we did was pretend we were important and drink so much we didn't notice the waiter was padding the bill. Jesus, it took us two years to figure it out and get the rat-fucker fired. You like classical music?"

Interesting segue. "Yes, I do," Anne replied.

"Check out the hands," Cliff said, proudly displaying his. "Big bear paws just like Brahms. There's a concert grand in the living room. Come on."

Anne followed him happily into a room with a soaring ceiling and low-slung couches; they were a design statement, and even she, small as she was, found them dwarfish and slightly painful. Cliff played Beethoven impressively; Anne couldn't name the piece but it was very dramatic, Germanic, the whole nine yards. When she unfolded herself from her seat and asked him why he wasn't a pianist he said, "My assistant logs in at least a hundred calls a day for me. I'm too social; if I were up to performance level that would be a minimum of six hours of practice every waking day of my life, too much discipline, too much solitude." Anne cocked her head up to listen more closely. She liked the sound of his voice.

He liked the serious, questioning, intelligence in her eyes, although it was a little unnerving. He wondered if those eyes were even bigger and more penetrating with her glasses off. Cliff, looking down into her upturned face, recognized a moral imperative forming in his frontal lobe that had to do with full disclosure, while something he wasn't immediately aware of was brewing deep in his medial temporal lobes that resulted in a distinct snugness in his pants. "You can tell I'm off my game. When Chopin played, women would faint."

"Like The Beatles?" Asked Anne.

"Like Sinatra!"

"Like two-hundred and fifty kids out of their minds on X at Coachella?"

Cliff laughed. "You're a funny little twisty. I like you." Anne felt an ember deep down in her core, one that she had buried with years of emotional ash, and let it ignite.

After the impromptu concert, Becky and Steve showed an old screwball comedy in the most comfortable place in the house, the screening room, and afterward people drifted back to the living room to chat and sip on post-dinner drinks. The Academy Awards were only weeks away, and Anne was informed by Cliff that two of the guests were nominees: James Johnson (actor) and Bill Aagard (director). She learned all these facts in short order, including the fact that the actor, like Mr. Nelson, credited himself with bringing her book to the attention of the studio. Also in attendance was one more couple, significant for the fact that they were barely out of their teens and recently married. He was Ben Haber, star of a popular TV series (primed to make his leap to film, he assured Anne), and she was the extraordinarily pretty Penny Scott (somebody Anne's father would refer to as a "bit player"). Only her new friend, Cliff White, and Anne, were flying solo. James Johnson was apparently telling an uproarious story while his wife, Shamari, smiled pleasantly. Bill downed his third scotch on the rocks as his wife, Tessa, gave him the stink eye.

It was an uneventful evening. Anne had the distinct impression she had been invited as an afterthought. At some point she got separated from Cliff. Conversation tended to focus on the industry. Only Shamari was the exception when she cornered Anne and asked earnestly about the homeless situation in New York. Anne told her what she knew, that there were about twenty thousand living spaces allocated to keep people off the streets, and Shamari sighed and said, "We have a couple hundred spaces, and our homeless population is approaching one hundred thousand. I'm on the board of B.L.A.H."

Anne couldn't help it, "Blah?"

Shamari retained her poise, "It stands for Bring Los Angeles Home."

A very worthy cause with a really unfortunate moniker, Anne thought. Points for Shamari; she was the only one there who seemed to be aware of a world beyond the screen. "Mr. White's amazing, isn't he?" Anne interjected.

"Cliff? You two have a lot in common. His dad's huge in the music industry. Sorry—correction—*was* huge."

"Cliff White?" Anne said blankly.

"Hm! He changed his name. Unlike your dad, Cliff's dad

is notorious for waving guns at his ex-wives. Five ex-wives. Soon to be six. Oh, and there was that time he was busted on Hollywood Boulevard for trying to buy crack. Hard to believe he ever owned a record company."

"Shit!" Anne exclaimed, a montage of remembered headlines flashing before her eyes.

"Exactly. Cliff prefers to operate behind the scenes."

"What's his father's name?"

"Starkey."

"And he isn't in jail because…?"

Shamari sang her response, "Money, money, money!"

Chapter 2

FEELING GOOD

Anne turned in at quarter to ten. It had been a very long day. Her room was decorated, like the rest of the house, with an elegance intended to inspire awe. The sheets were Frette, the lighting flattering and subdued; the view of the pool and the snowcapped mountains beyond through the sliding glass doors were surpassingly lovely. Anne drew the curtains automatically and was half-questioning why, considering that spectacular vista, when she heard a tapping at the window. Startled, she opened the curtains to see Cliff standing on the other side of the glass. Bathed in moonlight, face etched in silver, his white oxford shirt seemed to pulse with light and his navy jeans dropped off into black. He was beckoning to her to step outside.

Anne felt a sudden rush of heat from the tips of her toes to the top of her scalp and thought, *Oh, get a grip! He's exactly the kind of man who never takes me seriously, too good-looking, way too good-looking, too glib, too connected; I'm always the girl you confide in but never sleep with, and if you do sleep with me then it's because you know I'll sit there hour after hour listening to your relationship issues, offering chipper advice until you find somebody else who, you're happy to tell me, just clicks—like magic! Gee, thanks, Anne! If it weren't for you I never would have fallen in love.*

Well, that exact scenario had only happened once, with a visiting professor from Montreal, who last she heard had married his Quebecois goddess and spawned several munchkins. Then there was the triumvirate that had sent her into celibacy: the lawyer that could only climax if he was restrained, the broker who kept up a running commentary through the sex act as if he were broadcasting a sporting event, and the poet from Bennington who, after pontificating on the merits of single malt scotch and an inebriated night in snowbound Vermont, treated her to a sticky, spongy, flaccid nudging that didn't actually qualify as intercourse but did leave her feeling completely slimed. Never again, she resolved.

She slid the door open and walked into the cool, sparkling night. Immediately she regretted the impulse as it occurred to her that her pajamas consisted of a nearly see-through clinging T-shirt and a pair of sweatpants with something unseemly inscribed in bold over her bottom, like, *jama*, or worse yet, *juicy*. She folded her arms over her bustline and resolved not to turn around while Cliff could still see her.

"Hello, you." Three syllables uttered by Cliff and Anne felt light-headed. Was it the time change? Was it the six hours she had spent in a metal tube hurtling above the earth at thirty-two thousand feet? Was it the timbre of his voice? Or was it the fact that he had come to her and placed his arm around her waist and she could feel each of his five fingertips pressing into her skin? Suddenly, she didn't care. For once in her life she felt compelled to respond to chemistry and the novel sensation that she existed in hyper-reality. She was thirty-four. It was time.

She inhaled jasmine carried on the breeze, heard the night-scented wind's susurrating whisper, and watched it ruffle Cliff's hair. How could anybody have poignant eyebrows? There was something about him that quickened her pulse. So what, if his father was about to dump a sixth wife? What did it have to do with her? Why was she obsessing over some *acorn and tree* scenario when he was obviously just being sociable, although, there he was, touching her, and very nicely. "I want to show you something." He turned her around and planted himself behind her, one hand resting on her hip, the other pointing up at the sky. She craned her head back and looked up to see a dark heaven so vast and glittering and bright it didn't look real. She felt anchored to something strong and secure and thrilling, dangling her on the edge of a star field. "It's the desert."

"Hm?"

"No city lights, no smog," he wrapped his other arm around her and hugged her snugly to his chest. "That's good." Anne shivered. "Cold?" He held her tighter.

"Oh, no. I'm fine," Anne murmured. Anne wasn't really fine; she was convinced she was careering way beyond good sense but it felt undeniably wonderful, as was his desire, pressing against her.

Cliff nuzzled her ear. "Stop thinking so hard."

Now he was reading her mind. "Fuck!" She squirmed around so she was facing him.

"Okay," said Cliff. Anne stopped breathing. Cliff took her gently by the shoulders. "You said it, Goofy. Not me." He lifted her glasses off her face and put them in his breast pocket, palmed the back of her head and bent to kiss her. She felt the firm curve of his lips against hers. The edges of her body melted away, her heart surged out to meet and meld with his, and the sky itself seemed to cascade down and wash through them as if they had no bodies at all but were just a highly excited, happily swirling mass of strange molecules. Anne had never experienced anything remotely like that kiss, and apparently neither had Cliff. He stepped back. "What? Did you say something?"

"I didn't say anything."

"I—I heard..." stumbled Cliff. "Anne?"

"Yes," said Anne.

"Anne. I'm just going to say it." Anne anticipated another spark of magic. Her pulse quickened. "Your option's already lapsed. You own *Was That a Castle*," whispered Cliff to the top of her head. Anne was nestled beneath his chin. Suddenly her spine stiffened and she stepped back.

"What?"

"You're here because you're under the impression your contract is still under force and the studio has the right of renewal but they don't. It lapsed."

"*Why*...why should they care? I...have you read the book? It's one continuous interior monologue. Shrink goes off his meds and can't tell his patients from his hallucinations."

"They care because Becky's most bankable star waltzed into her office with an original script, a little art film he wanted made, and ten seconds later she gave it the green light. Only it turns out James Johnson lifted it almost word for word from your novel. Your novel, which they no longer own."

"What about Keir Bloomfield? He said he's the screenwriter."

"This is the land of smoke and mirrors, Anne."

"But they can't do that!"

"It doesn't mean they won't try," said Cliff.

Anne was astonished to see they were holding hands, four hands clasped like a pair of figure skaters about to execute a spin. She didn't feel in the least like letting go. "Who here knows about this?"

"Well, James Johnson, Becky, and…me. I'm James' agent…" Cliff tugged Anne in close so her head was resting against his chest. "I can feel your heart beating. Shh. You have to figure out what you want to do. And if you let me, I can help you fix it."

Anne pulled away. "Why wouldn't I fix it myself?

Cliff thought and then he said, "Because it's unbelievably hellishly complicated. Relationships. History. Shitloads of money."

"I don't care about that," insisted Anne.

"I can tell. Please let me help."

Anne felt drawn, but, "Why would you tell me all this?"

"Can I show you?" said Cliff, kissing the bridge of her nose.

"Why?" Anne inquired as she took his hand and turned to go inside. Standing in the bedroom they shimmied out of their clothes. To Anne, Cliff's legs looked like they were sculpted in the heroic style of the Greco-Romans. Tracing her hands up his body she marveled at the human personification of what she thought previously was only an ancient ideal. Everything about him was polished and firm and muscled and upright, including his erection. "You're beautiful," she exclaimed.

Laughing, he picked her up and set her on the edge of the bed. "You're beautiful; I'm handsome."

"No, you're beautiful," she insisted.

He kissed her mouth then knelt between her legs and ran his hands searchingly over her body—holding and caressing, brushed his lips against her neck, then her nipples, and then her belly. Anne pressed against him and murmured his name and curled her arm to cradle his head, and he held her tight. "Let me...tell you about...gender-specific adjectives," he whispered into her hair.

"You talk an awful lot."

"Make me stop," he responded, and she did.

When Anne came, pelvis joined to Cliff's, back arched, mouth open, eyes closed, she saw continuous bursts of blue-green Arctic light behind her eyelids, as her body contracted and released over and over on the length of his cock.

When Cliff came, sheathed inside aqueous, velvety Anne, his giving body shuddered and stretched and he heard something ringing, peeling out, soaring and lighthearted, and he realized it was the sound of laughter, his, and he couldn't stop until Anne placed her mouth over his, as they rocked together and then slipped apart.

Euphoria, for the lucky, usually induces sleep. For Anne it

caused something different. She should have slept soundly but instead she sat up in bed, purposefully still, and watched. She watched the shadow of palm trees play across the drapes. She watched the rise and fall of the sheets over her stomach as she breathed under them. She watched Cliff as he slept. She thought about what he'd said, the endearments and the warnings. When he woke and reached for her and pulled her down on top of him she let go, and fused her body with his, and existed only as a bundle of ecstatically firing neurons for another blissful, endless, oh…five to fifteen seconds. Then Cliff slept and she watched, a cycle repeated again and again.

In the wee hours as Cliff dozed and Anne tried to figure out how to extricate herself from under his arm without him waking so she could go to the bathroom, that annoying creature, Gwyneth the Chinese crested, set to yapping under the moon. Cliff opened his eyes, "Jesus, Bill and his freakazoid four-legged pseudo baby."

Anne ran her fingers over Cliff's forearm, "Should I get up and let the dog in?"

Cliff sat up, shook his head, took Anne by the chin and tilted her head up so he could kiss her. "I should go back to my room before everyone gets up." Anne nodded. "See you at breakfast and then we'll start to figure this out," and, with that, Cliff put on his shirt, pulled up his pants, found his watch on the nightstand, and picked up his shoes. He walked over to the sliding glass doors and parted the curtains just a bit to check outside. "Hey," he stage-whispered, "check this out!" Anne heard Gwyneth baying, or perhaps squeaking would be a better term, and what sounded like tumbling, bumping, scraping patio furniture. She hopped out of bed, naked, and peeked around Cliff to investigate. The dog was barking and skittering back and forth on the concrete as if it was hot coal while the Aagards, flapping their long arms, and mouthing huge, silent, obscene curses, tried to chivvy the beast back in.

The dog was ridiculous, so exaggeratedly petite, and her owners so much larger than life. Bill Aagard smoked cigars, spoke brusquely, commanded attention, and stood about six-foot-four. Tessa Aagard was scary-skinny with logic-defying balloon breasts and she talked rat-a-tat in a series of one-liners. Listening to her was exhausting.

"Looks complicated out there," said Anne.

"More than you know. Didn't I tell you you'd better go to bed?" replied Cliff, and he turned and hugged her up off the floor so only her toes touched the ground.

"You told me you were going to fix me up with one of your friends!" giggled Anne.

"You!" and he carried her back to bed where she summarily removed his clothes.

When Anne woke at six a.m. (her time-lagged body clock was insisting it was nine in the morning) she realized that she had, amazingly, slept for an entire two hours and that she was alone. After padding back and forth to the en suite bathroom she opened the drapes and saw Toni Todd swimming, doing laps in the dim blue dawn, with tendrils of steam rising off the heated pool. It really was enchantingly beautiful in the desert. She thought of Cliff and couldn't help but grin. Talk about complicated. She scanned the room until she spotted her sweats and T-shirt neatly folded on a chair. Cliff must have done that. She slipped outside in her pajamas and breathed sage in the morning chill. Toni saw Anne, swam to the side and motioned her quietly over. Anne crouched beside the pool. "You should get in before everybody gets up. I swim a mile every day. Have for the past sixty years. It restores the soul," she whispered.

"I didn't bring a suit," Anne whispered back pushing her glasses up the bridge of her nose.

Toni shrugged and said, "It's just us Injuns," before she sliced beneath the surface and was away. *Injuns?* Anne pondered, and then she chalked it up to a generational difference in language. She was tempted to get in the water, but she truly hadn't brought a swimsuit; she didn't even own one so she could always avoid the embarrassment of exposing her body in public. That was a funny thought, about exposing her body, after what she'd been doing only a couple of hours earlier. But Toni, streamlining through the water, made it all so appealing. Anne plucked at her flimsy pajama top, thought better of it, and went back inside to brush her teeth and collect herself before she saw Cliff and they faced "the fix." She didn't know why—well, that wasn't exactly right—she'd just had soul-deep sex for the last six hours, but she trusted him. She trusted him completely.

Between seven-thirty and eight, Anne, stationed by the pool under an umbrella with a vapid magazine in her lap, saw that people were beginning to stir. When she observed a freshly showered Cliff walking toward her she had to restrain the compulsion to launch herself from the chair toward him, and instead acknowledged him with a tilt of the head and a smile. He sat down next to her and dragged her chair over so their knees were bumping. "Hello," he said.

"Hello," she replied.

"Did you know you talk in your sleep?" Cliff asked.

"I don't." Suddenly self-conscious, Anne glanced around to see if they were alone.

"You do. Yes. You do. Hey, are you okay?"

"What did I say?" Anne demanded.

Cliff leaned in close, "You said, *more sex now, please!*"

"I said, what?"

"More sex now, please."

"I did not," said Anne.

Cliff crossed his heart and held up his hand like a Boy Scout. "Are you hungry? I'm starving. So, I'm taking you out for breakfast," Cliff continued. "As a matter of fact, we'll be gone all day, so we can talk."

"Is that okay with Becky and—" flustered, Anne tried to remember her host's name. It was unlike her to forget anything.

"Steve, the Nelsons, approve of hearty outdoor activities. I told them I was taking you hiking in Tahquitz Canyon." Anne's face fell. "Don't worry. I lied. Come on!" and he was up and out of his chair with Anne's hand held firmly in his. He waved brightly to Becky and Steve, who were just rounding the corner from the kitchen, and led Anne out to the driveway where he opened the door of his Ferrari Scaglietti and, with the courtly manners of another era, ushered her in.

Anne lowered herself gingerly onto the leather seat. "I think this car cost more than my apartment."

"It was a gift," said Cliff.

"From who?"

"My dad."

"My dad gave me a Civic. Once."

Before they could explore this scintillating topic any further, Ben Haber, the young TV star, came running up to the gleaming Ferrari almost vibrating with excitement. "Hey, is this your new car?"

"It sure as hell isn't mine," thought Anne.

Cliff lingered by the passenger door. "Hey, Ben. What's up?

"Whoa, this car, bro, sweet," words failed Ben. He shook his head in mute appreciation.

Cliff clapped him on the back. "Back for dinner, then you can take it for a spin."

"That is baller, boss! Baller! Thank you! Thank you!" Ben looked on with an unabated lust for polished steel and forward motion as Cliff drove the car through the gates and then accelerated down the street.

Anne, mulling over the past twenty-four hours and the last ten specifically, tried to maintain her equilibrium by grasping for the obvious. "So, that kid—dishy but dense as a box of rocks?"

Cliff replied, "Ben? He's fine. For somebody who was raised by wolves."

"Wolves?"

"His parents are high-ranking Clientologists."

"That's big out here?"

"Unfortunately, yeah. Very big."

"Wait, let me get this straight," Anne said as they drove through a low-rent district outside Palm Springs called Desert Hot Springs. The view was making her wary, red rocks and cheap pink stucco motels, "You said when you were starting out all you could afford was Denny's, but your dad gave you this car?"

"Well, it's more like he registered it in my name a couple of weeks ago."

Anne couldn't let it go. "Why would he do that?"

"It's an asset he doesn't want to lose in his divorce," Cliff said as they turned down a dirt drive that led through a grove of orange trees. This was a slight improvement over the previous landscape.

"Where are we going?"

"Aren't we inquisitive this morning!"

"I'm inquisitive *every* morning. It's one of my defining features."

"I could get used to that."

Anne pondered the significance of this statement, dissected it, prodded it, poked it, and searched it for clues that would reveal the vector of their relationship.

Cliff was thinking about how lithe and flexible and surprisingly sexually responsive Anne was and how he never wanted anything bad *ever* to happen to her. He smiled at the thought that she was right there, seated so close he could kiss her, as they were waved past a gatehouse and pulled up in front of what looked like a red brick country club but that turned out to be the entrance to Las Palmas del Rio, a spa renowned for its mineral spring grotto, mud baths, and scented massages under thatched cabanas. They collected a key to a casita and Anne was impressed to see when they opened the door to their little cottage that not only was a full breakfast laid out but also two thick, plush bathrobes on the back of a chair; swimsuits, his and hers on the bed; and slippers tucked alongside the bed skirt. *What the...?* wondered Anne.

"I come here a lot," said Cliff, opening his arms to hug her. "Come here." Anne, mind awhirl, came. He cradled her head against his chest. "Sleep deprivation. It's made you all squirrely and distant. Let's get reacquainted."

"My apologies," Anne mumbled to his breastbone. "How do we do that?"

"Well, here's my plan," he said as he began to kiss and caress her. "Let's see if you like it."

"Wait a minute. How do you, I mean, you always seem to know what I'm thinking—"

Cliff interrupted. "As somebody said this morning, it's one of my defining characteristics. I'm an agent. Figuring out what's in your best interest is what I do."

"I have an agent. This is not what he does."

He laced his fingers through Anne's. "Here's the plan. Eat; soak in the grotto; sleep, sleep, sleep; then we do anything you want."

"Like what?"

"You can get a salt glow."

"What's a salt glow?"

"It's a massage."

"A salt glow?"

"Or we just stay in this room and relax."

"That one. That's the plan," confirmed Anne. "Is today really only Saturday?"

"Only Saturday," he said, kissing her and reaching for a croissant. Cliff offered her a bite and they spent the next twenty minutes consuming everything except the tableware on the room service cart. Replete and groggy, they stretched out on the bed. Cliff's hand was resting on Anne's stomach when he said, "Look at that. Wait, give me your arm." Anne lifted her arm toward the ceiling. Cliff placed the bottom of his palm at her elbow and extended his fingers. "See, that? My hand is bigger than your forearm. How is that possible?"

"Testosterone."

He scissored his leg over her and propped himself up on an elbow. "Aren't you glad?"

"Thus far, no complaints."

"Hey," Cliff said.

Anne felt warm and full of light.

"Hey, I like you. Do you like me?" asked Cliff.

"Yes."

"What if I more than liked you?"

"Then I'd more than like you back," laughed Anne as she wrapped her arms around his neck. Less than four minutes later, after slipping into each other, they had slipped into sleep.

When they woke Cliff coaxed Anne into a swimsuit and, bathrobes draped over their shoulders, they walked out to the grotto, an enormous lagoon-shaped cement pond, painted blue, fringed with palms and ferns, fed by a hot lithium spring. They staked out a cove of their own and sank down in the water until it lapped at their chins. "God," Anne said with pleasure.

"Pretty great," Cliff agreed and then began to rattle off an itinerary of plans for Anne once she arrived in L.A. He'd call Dan Nero; she needed to set a new price for the novel, if she wanted to sell the rights at all. Anne wasn't really listening. Something had gelled in her mind and it was this: she was completely unaccustomed to feeling this good, and she wanted the feeling to last.

"Hey," she said. "Did you know that it takes the average person thirty seconds to fall in love? And, the over-the-top passion lasts no longer than three years."

"That Italian study. We read the same things," said Cliff. "You're still thinking too much." He began massaging her neck.

Anne hadn't realized how stiff she was until he started kneading her muscles. "Oh, God."

"You keep saying that!" chided Cliff. He put his lips by her ear. "Too much sex, not enough practice."

"Hey!" said Anne.

"I'm just saying it could be the best three years of our lives."

Anne twisted around to see his eyes. He looked perfectly sane. Perhaps she'd misinterpreted.

Cliff cupped Anne's face in his hands, "Who knows what could happen in three years? There'll probably be a baby, and then we'll be too exhausted for the passion."

She hadn't misinterpreted at all. This man intended to continue having sex with her for a very long time. "Oh... my..." Anne exclaimed as he kissed her full on the lips.

When they broke for air he gazed into her eyes while he stroked her hair back from her forehead. He meant to be soothing, but there was a certain look in Anne's eyes, the moment he touched her, that was unmistakable.

"Maybe we should go back to our room and test out your theory," suggested Anne.

Cliff clasped his hands and cast his eyes toward heaven. "Oh lord, I know she was sent here to try me—but couldn't you just send frogs instead?" Anne exhaled a laugh, inhaled fragrant air and felt a kind of buoyancy that had nothing to do with the water she was floating in, and wondered if this was love. "You," said Cliff as he kissed her neck.

In their casita, they peeled off their bathing suits and climbed straight into bed. Eventually, when they disengaged, Cliff, hand around the base of his penis, said, "Annie?" She looked up at him with a serene smile and stretched. "The condom broke."

Anne, still buzzing with endorphins, sat up to take a look, "I've never seen that happen before."

Cliff removed the torn condom and wadded it up in a piece of tissue from the box on the nightstand. "I don't want you to worry. I haven't been in a relationship in six and a half months but when we get back to L.A. we'll get tested for HIV and—"

"I haven't had sex with anyone for almost two years," she said placidly.

"And we'll get a pregnancy test."

"You're such a responsible citizen; I love that," she said, calculating her odds of pregnancy at slim to zero since her period had ended two days ago.

"Nothing seems to faze you. Nothing! I love that," he said, hugging her close. He was promising her blood tests; this was a level of commitment she hadn't experienced in a very long time.

They returned to the Nelson's at half past five. At the dinner table it became apparent Anne's social status had changed. The dynamic was beginning to remind her of high school. She wondered if getting laid, getting a February tan, or having the skinny on a tainted business deal was the cause. Tessa, seated to her right, expressed awe at the size of Anne's pores, "Look at that skin! It looks airbrushed… You're glowing!"

"Sun," Toni Todd interjected, "the ultimate laser facial." She peered at Anne knowingly and smiled.

Becky extolled the virtues of sunblock. Shamari commented on the relationship between vitamin D and calcium, and Penny Scott announced she was lactose intolerant, to which Toni added that so was everybody else over the age of five.

Anne was wondering if all the women had, somehow, intuited she had recently had sex, and a lot of it, when Cliff dispelled any doubts by draping his arm around her shoulders and carelessly brushed his lips across her forehead. Curiously, she felt marked, like a coyote's territory.

Becky's eyes narrowed for a nanosecond, and then she smiled radiantly and instructed her husband to pour more champagne. Bill Aagard got sentimental and proposed a toast. James Johnson, observant actor and perfect mimic, patterned his behavior after Cliff's and put his arm around Shamari. Keir looked politely bored, as if he were watching a good friend's very bad off-Broadway play, and Ben Haber frowned, wondering if this was an inopportune time to bring up the promised spin in the Ferrari.

After dinner, the Nelsons lit a blaze in a stone fireplace. The flames reflected in the pool and the hosts and their guests once again lounged poolside on couches and chaise longues with drinks in hand. Cliff and Anne were the only ones actually touching the water, as they had both removed their shoes and were sitting on the cement coping with their feet dangling in the water. They sat side-by-side, chatting oh-so-casually to all appearances. Every once in a while when they laughed their shoulders bumped, and if anyone had been observing closely they would have seen their palms spread on the concrete at their sides with their pinkies interlocked.

Anne was in a pleasant, wonderfully disorienting, state of disbelief. How could anyone so, so funny, handsome, and aware, be so into her? Cliff was in a similar state of bewildered bliss; how could someone so funny, beguiling, and lovely be sitting there sharing a secret caress? He felt that within the last twenty-four hours he had developed a million new nerve endings. He whispered in her ear, "Let's get out of here."

They stood up and flexed, like a pair of cats, and walked barefoot away from the pool. The Nelsons' estate sat on a comfortable acre. Cliff and Anne, holding hands, kept walking over lawn and through garden, and eventually circled around into what appeared to be a service area on the opposite side of the house. Gravel covered the ground, and citrus trees, heavy with oranges and grapefruit, grew in orderly ranks. A laundry line arched over an old lawn chair. "Ouch!" Anne yelped as she attempted to cross the gravel. Cliff laughed and scooped her up in his arms and carried her to the chair and sat down there with Anne in his lap, and they kissed, nested together under the intensely dark blue desert sky.

"Hey," said Cliff.

"What?" said Anne.

"Where're you staying in L.A.?"

"At my dad's."

"I don't want to spend any more nights away from you," murmured Cliff.

"You mean any more nights than the one we've had, total? Count it! You mean the Friday that we spent together? Almost all night, but not really," laughed Anne.

"Oh, you're such a comedian. Why don't you stay at my place?"

"Ah," Anne hesitated; she wanted to, but there she went, careering again.

"Or I could get the studio to book you a suite at the Mondrian," suggested Cliff.

"Yuck."

"Okay. Why don't you tell me how you really feel?"

Anne laughed again, giddy, and wrapped her arms around Cliff's neck and looked up at the stars.

Cliff persevered. "Will you at least think about staying with me?"

"I'll think about it."

At midnight they made their way back to the group, which

was now breaking up and heading for bed. Anne and Cliff parted with exaggerated decorum. "Don't forget your shoes, kids," said Becky.

On Sunday morning everyone congregated for breakfast at nine, everyone, except Cliff White. "That's weird," said Becky, the gracious hostess. "Honey? Would you mind checking on Cliff?" she asked her husband. Steve excused himself, put his napkin down, and got up from the table. A few minutes later he returned carrying an armload of carefully folded sheets.

"Well, that IS weird!" he said.

"What? That you're stripping beds? Leave it for Clothilde!" said Becky.

"He stripped his bed and left. And if I leave these for Clothilde, I might as well just throw them in the pool and beat them with rocks."

"Fine." Evidently it wasn't fine. Becky went on, "Did he say anything? He must have said something."

"Not to me, he didn't," Steve answered on his way out of the dining room.

Becky was exasperated, "I didn't hear him leave. Where's his car?"

"Gone, I presume," said Toni, spooning up a very tiny, very sweet, strawberry.

Anne looked down at her plate, steaming pancakes piled high with berries, slathered with butter, dripping with maple syrup. She looked up; everyone was looking expectantly in her direction, as if she had the answer to this mundane riddle. Anne froze. Without Cliff seated beside her she felt awkward, like an outsider, like somebody who showed up to a pool party in Palm Springs wearing two layers of wool.

Shamari jumped in, "Maybe he went to get the paper?"

James said, "Why wouldn't he just read it online?"

"I don't know, James. I don't know what his personal habits are. Some people still like to read the paper," Shamari snapped.

"This is ridiculous; we get the paper. We get five papers. I'm going to call him and find out where he is," said Becky. She reached for the cordless on the side table and jabbed in a number. Becky was not one to hide her irritation. A cell phone rang somewhere down the corridor. "Great!" she barked, "He forgot his phone."

Ben Haber loaded his plate with an extra helping of pancakes. His wife giggled. Keir Bloomfield was twitching again, but Anne saw he was subtly trying to detach the Aagards' dog from his ankle. Bill was holding what appeared to be script pages over his plate as far away from his eyes as he could, and scowling. Attentive Tessa quietly handed him a pair of reading glasses that were hanging from the V in her blouse. Anne, ever the observer, noted all this and thought everyone here had settled into fairly obvious patterns, with the exception of herself. Thus far, her days in California had passed in a series of intense impressions and attenuated moments of joyful discovery. She felt a quickening in her core that was part sense memory and part sexual. He wasn't even in the room and… Cliff had mentioned stopping at a place called Hadley's for a date shake on their way back to L.A., maybe he went to pick one up instead? Becky was looking at her, her expression tight, imperious, and inquiring.

"Don't let this spoil your breakfast! Eat!" Becky insisted.

Anne thought she should interject with a plausible explanation for Cliff's absence. However, the moment evaporated under the power of Becky's glare. The table did as it was told, and they ate. "I'll track him down on his other line," she said slapping a pancake onto her plate.

But she didn't. Ruben Martinez had already found Cliff White a couple of hours earlier: belted in his car at the side of a road not a mile from the house, dead. The face that had entranced Anne hours before now alabaster and unrecognizable, the man so full of life now emptied of purpose and meaning.

Chapter 3

YOU ONLY LIVE ONCE

Cliff White's funeral mass was held at the Church of the Good Shepherd in Beverly Hills just after news of the coroner's report was leaked. The *Los Angeles Times* obituary cited the cause of death as a heart attack; it also stated the services were private with the family requesting that in lieu of flowers donations be made to the Coronary Care Facility at Cedars-Sinai. Anne arrived at the funeral with her father, uncle, and half-sister, Natalie. They made their way past a police cordon. The sidewalk on Santa Monica Boulevard was free of paparazzi. In Los Angeles, this was considered private.

Although the atmosphere inside the church was appropriately dejected there was a pervasive sense of something else lurking underneath. What was it? Anne glanced around. A prominent actress was in attendance with her female partner and their four children. They never appeared in public together, ever. An action-movie icon was openly weeping on the shoulder of his male companion. Two very clean-cut young men were standing stoically in their Paul Smith suits holding hands. Everyone in the church appeared to be "out." But there was something else; Anne looked again, downcast eyes, disapproving frowns, murmuring voices. Cliff's friends were angry. Angry, and that wasn't all. People stared at her with blatant, undisguised, and tacitly hostile curiosity.

Then Anne saw her father shaking hands with a tall,

cadaverous yet bronzed man, who had the most startling deep blue eyes. If he wasn't distinctive-looking enough already, his short silver hair haloed his head like he had received an electric shock. Uncle Manny leaned over to tell her it was Cole Starkey—Cliff's father. Bob Brown motioned her over. Cole turned to see Anne and released her father. While murmuring her condolences, Mr. Starkey, reacting to his son's name, stared at Anne's face as if transfixed and made a sound like none she had ever heard before. The ambient hum of voices seemed to cease in the background. Regarding his dilated pupils and distraught expression with apprehension, she realized he had asked "*Why*?" in tones so deeply afflicted, so heart-torn, so wounded, she couldn't, at first, discern the meaning.

Her eyes stung with tears. Her throat closed. All she could do was nod and, before she knew it, she had reached up to touch Mr. Starkey's leathery cheek.

After they were ushered to the pews, Natalie whispered in her younger sister's ear, "Did you hear the coroner's report?" Anne had not. She spent the morning sitting in her old room at her father's house, staring at a *Serious Moonlight* poster still pinned to the wall even all these years from her childhood. "He said Cliff had Viagra and Ritalin in his bloodstream." Ritalin? Cliff had Ritalin in his bloodstream? Anne doubted Cliff had attention deficit disorder. Things were getting bizarre; some supremely weird shit was starting to roll in. Ritalin was related to amphetamines and, when crushed and snorted, it was used to intensify orgasms, but it also made it impossible to achieve an erection; that's where the Viagra came in. You didn't indulge like that to spank the monkey; you dosed like that to satisfy, really satisfy, a partner. Was what they had together incendiary passion, or was it something illusory, artificial and chemically created? Anne was startled by a sudden ripple of

nausea. Wouldn't she be able to recognize it if someone was
strung out on uppers? That didn't add up. He wouldn't have
slept like he did when he was with her, fully relaxed, if he had
been abusing Ritalin. He wouldn't have had such an appetite
either; come to think of it, he ate like a horse. Then there was
the nagging, persistent, sickening thought. *Was he with someone
else between midnight and 5:30 a.m.? Someone who would leave
him dead in his car?* Or—she found herself speculating—*DID
he die in his car?* Anne could feel the blood pulsing behind her
cheekbones and through her skull. She tried to spot the other
house party guests in the growing crowd. All of them—like so
many others in the congregation—were wearing sunglasses,
lending their faces a blank, obscured appearance. Natalie laid
her hand on her sister's arm.

She said, "Annie, did you hear me?"

"Were you talking?"

Natalie nodded. Anne's eyes involuntarily blurred with tears.

Cliff had died of a heart attack brought on by Viagra and uppers,
Anne thought as the choir began the requiem. His friends
were pissed because he'd overdosed. She pondered the exact
circumstances of his death as the priest discussed eternal
rest, perpetual light, and something about a lamb of God
and the removal of sin. Listening, she wasn't comforted; she
felt broken, confused, empty. She had known Cliff only a
brief time, but his sudden death had left her inconsolable,
and she wondered if the sensation would ever pass. There
was some small comfort in the fact that she was feeling
something. Since being informed of Cliff's death—upon her
arrival back in L.A.—she had felt somehow not altogether
present, so detached that it was as if she was inhabiting a
space outside her body, merely observing it from six inches

away. She looked at the hands folded in her lap. They were hers, emphasized by the fact, she saw now, that her uncle had covered her hands with his palm and somebody was holding on to her while she was drifting, numbed cold to the core, in a sea of tears.

The eulogies were many; one in particular seemed significant to Anne. The female star with the four children and same-sex partner said, "Cliff White was my best friend. He was the first to know when I fell in love with Celeste. The first to know when our children were born. The first to know and share our—" Finding it difficult to speak she resorted to a focusing bit of business, unfolding a piece of heavy stationery with unsteady hands that she read from: "In a world of make believe the truest thing you can do is love who you love, to keep the love growing. Congratulations on number four." She set the sheet of stationery down on the lectern. "Our loss is unfathomable, but he inspired us. He kept the love growing. And we will never forget."

Anne was descending the church steps after the service when a stranger approached her holding his card in front of him like a shield. She took it calmly and barely had time to register that he was a homicide detective before—as if on cue—she was surrounded by her father and uncle on one side, Becky and Steve Nelson on the other. Bob Brown's hand tightened slightly on the back of Anne's neck. Becky and Steve removed their sunglasses. Becky, artfully dyed blond hair professionally smoothed, makeup perfect, made the introductions. "Anne Brown, this is Detective Vasquez of the Palm Springs police."

The detective extended his hand, "Phil." He had penetrating brown eyes in a face that had seen way too much sun, and he wore a navy jacket mismatched with charcoal trousers. "You've made a big impression."

Bob Brown's hand was still on the back of Anne's neck. "Me?"

"Cliff White's last phone call Saturday night was to his father. Seems all he could talk about was you."

Anne was about to attempt a reply, but before she could, her father interjected with fake joviality, "Phil! Should we have an attorney present?"

"No, sir. Not at all." Then Vasquez turned his attention to Anne, implicitly ignoring Bob, "Ms. Brown, if you could come down and speak to me at the station in Beverly Hills at your earliest convenience? You know where it is? It's right next to the library on Rexford."

She was eager to follow the detective. She wanted to give him any help she could. She needed more information. She needed to know so much more. She remembered Cliff atop her, his hand in her hair, his voice repeating her name as the length of him surged inside her and how their eyes had locked and she had felt overwhelming love…

"Tomorrow's fine. I'll be here a couple more days wrapping things up."

Anne stuttered something incoherent in reply.

"We're going to the cemetery. We'll see you tomorrow, detective," Bob said.

"Sir. I just want to have an informal talk with Anne. Just Anne."

"Very good," said Mr. Brown curtly, unaccustomed to being

excluded from anything. He marched away toward his car with his daughters. When he was out of earshot, Bob swore a mean blue steak, "Starkey! Fucking rock-'n'-roll burnout, teabag-happy limey junkie SCUM!" Uncle Manny shook his head ruefully at his brother's temper.

"Teabag?" Anne asked.

"Cock-sucking Brit! Higher than a kite at his own son's funeral," he muttered angrily by way of explanation.

"*Teabag* doesn't mean what you think it means, Dad."

"Just get in the car, Anne. If that prick thinks he can implicate my daughter in this dirty mess, then he's got—"

"I don't think he's trying to do anything, Dad," Anne interrupted. "And I'd like to talk to the detective."

"We'll see about that!" her father replied. He was recalling a Thanksgiving dinner in the mid-seventies with Cole Starkey and Mick Jagger. As Bob Brown stood carving the turkey at the table he noticed Starkey was kissing his leggy socialite girlfriend while completely unaware that Jagger, swallowing a straight whiskey, had his hand up the socialite's skirt. "Disgusting!"

"What?" Anne said.

"We'll talk about this later!" Bob answered. He looked to his other daughter, Natalie, for support. She responded by frowning at her father and wrapping her arm around her sister. "All right! All right! Just everybody get in the car!"

"Want me to drive?" Natalie inquired.

"Do I ever?" her father bellowed.

Uncle Manny smoothly injected himself into the mêlée, "Bob, Annie'll ride with me. You take her home from the cemetery." Natalie cringed and widened her eyes like a cartoon character; Manny's driving was the stuff of nightmares, like a twenty-four-hour marathon of Michael Bay movies. She looked meaningfully from Anne to her uncle's car keys and back, giving a mock-horrified and imploring shake of the head. Anne took Uncle Manny's hand, just as she did when she was a child. Manny gave her a peck on the forehead.

Chapter 4

SOMEWHERE, THERE'S A PLACE FOR US

Anne climbed into her uncle's old Jaguar. It was as finely maintained as Manny. Burl wood dashboard polished to sheen, leather seat oiled to suppleness, high design everywhere she looked. Anne unrolled the window and took in a gulp of air. "Uncle Manny?"

"Pumpkin?"

Anne thought. What could she tell her uncle and her father, without unnecessarily upsetting them? What exactly did she know anyway? She wiped her puffy, rid-rimmed eyes with the back of her hand; when she looked up she noticed her uncle was going barely twenty in a thirty-five-mile-per-hour zone and was beginning to get anxious when she realized he was inching along in a cortege flanked by motorcycle cops. He was driving—or creeping—along just fine. "You know those people in Palm Springs?"

"Some of them," said Manny, one gnarled hand resting casually at the bottom of the steering wheel.

"What about Becky Nelson?"

"She's your dad's girl all the way. Took her out of legal and made her a studio head."

"But what's her story?"

"What's her story? In other words, what's her motivation?" Uncle Manny reached for the pipe in his jacket pocket. He tapped the bowl against the steering wheel and reached into another pocket for his tobacco pouch. Anne was concerned about her uncle's diminished capacity to multitask. She knew he considered Wilshire Boulevard his access route to nearly any location in the Los Angeles basin; he shunned the freeways as scars on his beloved city, using instead a variety of once well-known surface routes of the 1930s and 1940s for destinations ranging from Santa Barbara to Pasadena. She eyed the curb warily for newspaper kiosks. She would find another time to talk him into giving up his car keys before he put himself—or others—in danger, though quite how she'd do that, she wasn't in any condition to decide. While her sister showed no interest in the industry and her father employed an overarching professional discretion about the business he was once so integral to, Uncle Manny always had choice commentary on anything or anybody that had to do with Hollywood and its ever-tangled web of public and private relationships.

"Well, on the level, angel heart; I hear your little house party in the desert—the Nelsons' little party in the desert, I should say—was born out of a very…scandalous situation."

"What kind of a scandal?"

"Some incident on the set where agents were called in and a whole lot of feathers went flying," said Uncle Manny.

"Was Cliff White one of those agents?"

"He certainly was."

"What happened?"

"From what I hear somebody was so drunk, or maybe so stoned, they couldn't stand up—or even lie down—straight."

"Who?"

Uncle Manny replied, "That, I don't know. But I do know who was on set. And it's rumored that on Ms. Nelson's very first feature—some indie thing that got your Dad's attention back in the eighties—the whole damn crew was coked to the gills."

Anne thought for a moment, "So, was this scandal on set about somebody providing the drugs or somebody getting hammered or high on the job?"

"Beyond hammered, beyond high."

"And who was on set?"

"Well, it was Bill Aagard's picture, made for Becky's studio; James Johnson was the star and Cliff—

"And Cliff was called onto set," Anne finished the sentence. "Is that a big deal?"

"Is what a big deal?" he countered, chewing on his pipe stem.

"An agent being on set."

"Let's just say there's always a natural antagonism between management types and creative types. Your father would call it something else, but we'll call it a natural antagonism."

Chapter 5

CRY FOR LOVE

There aren't any graveyards in Beverly Hills. Cliff White was buried at Holy Cross Cemetery in the flatlands of Culver City. Standing next to the neat rectangular hole in the ground was Cliff's mother, Dawn White. The coffin sat perched on emerald turf, white stargazer lilies and roses cascaded over the lid and spilled down the polished wooden sides. Anne smelled the perfume of a multitude of imported blossoms, the peatiness of freshly turned earth, and—far less pleasantly—the heady whiff of petrochemicals drifting down from the 405.

She saw Cliff's mother was dressed in a lavender suit that made her seem to glow in the sea of black mourning clothes. Dawn's hair was salt-and-pepper gray and fell to the center of her back; Anne guessed she must have been just barely sixty. Lustrous pearls hung around her neck while her clasped bony hands were bare. Two women who looked vaguely familiar to Anne separated Dawn White from Cole Starkey. They seemed territorial, guardians of the distance between the bereaved mother and her ex. Anne suddenly realized who they were: these women—Dawn included—were folk singers from the late sixties. She flashed on images of kohl-lined eyes, blunt-cut bangs, paisley clothing, and acoustic guitars. They must all, at some point in time, have been involved with Starkey either emotionally or professionally and the bitterness between them was palpable.

The woman stood statue-still as Cliff was lowered into the earth. Cole hugged one arm to his body and with the other shielded his weeping eyes from the descending coffin.

And then it was over. The mourners dispersed. Starkey was finally led away by a huge Samoan chauffeur. Anne seemed rooted to the ground. The man who was promising her blood tests was gone. She felt a gnawing ache from her throat to the pit of her stomach. Her middle-aged sister tugged at her elbow; their father stood waiting by the car. Her uncle had already started the Jaguar.

"Sorry, Annie. I've got class at three." Strangely, Anne had followed in her half-sister's footsteps as opposed to her parents'. Natalie was a tenured professor at UCLA.

"Okay," Anne replied.

They walked toward the car. "You all right staying with Dad?" Natalie asked.

"Sure."

"You can always stay with me," Natalie prodded.

"I'm fine."

Bob Brown's house was a glorified Colonial on Crescent Drive designed by Wallace Neff sometime in the forties and purchased by Brown in 1964. The entry hall had a curved stairway and the walls were hung with Pop Art. There was a Jasper Johns—an embossed print of two "mouths" (where eyes should have been) behind a pair of glasses—a cartoon image by Roy Lichtenstein depicting a teary blonde—a repeating silkscreen self-portrait of Andy Warhol—and, a weird painting by Mel Ramos of a naked and busty brunette pinup embracing what appeared to be a tube of Colgate toothpaste, though what the iconic white word spelled against the red background on the upright tube was *comfort*. Suddenly, Anne couldn't get past the pictures. "Dad, what's with the artwork?"

Bob Brown was ambling back toward the kitchen, "Huh? You want a sandwich? I got egg salad."

"No, what are these?" Anne persisted.

Her father paused and blinked at the walls and then retraced his steps into the gallery-like foyer.

"You like 'em? I'll write your name on the back," said Bob.

"Write my name on the back?"

"Right. After I die you can have them. When your sister was your age, they were in my study. You remember," he said gesturing at the art, "she told me they were misogynistic pieces of crap. Something about dead white men." He patted his pockets for a pen.

"Daddy! You can't write on these!" Anne was appalled.

"On the back!"

"No, what are these?" Anne persisted. "Dad, I just want to know what they are."

"Are? They *were* a deal. Leo Castelli, he repped all these guys. Around the time I got the house in, I don't know, sixty-four, sixty-five? He couldn't move them; nobody wanted to buy. So

I made an offer and got all of 'em, everything you see here, in a package deal. Two hundred dollars apiece. You got any idea what they're worth now?"

Anne shook her head.

"Let's just say a helluva lot more."

"Dad, I don't want to talk about…" The words caught in her throat; she was overcome by the thought of her father dying and didn't want him talking about it because even if he was at ease with the idea, she wasn't. She could feel the sting of tears welling even as she tried to smile.

Her father looked at her quizzically. "Now look, Anne, I know you and Natalie are independent, grown women, but I'm still your father and I want to support you in any way I—"

"That's not what I meant."

Bob *harrumphed* (Anne's father was one of the vanishingly few people she'd ever heard "harrumph" in real life), "Suit yourself. You want that sandwich or what?"

"Yeah."

"Anne, I want you to have the paintings."

When in her father's company she felt frozen at twelve years old. "Daddy, are you responsible for my movie deal?" Even as she said the words she realized how peevish and immature they sounded; even worse was how inappropriate and solipsistic the question was considering Cliff had just died. Bob didn't seem to notice. Or care. Social niceties never meant much to him. Instead he launched into a patented Bob Brown tirade.

"Jesus Christ! Everybody thinks Hollywood people are godless, degenerate, bottom-feeding philistines who wouldn't know quality if it kicked them in the ass. Moviemaking is the single greatest culture of creativity the world has ever known. And, no doubt, the biggest fucking employer of artists, ever!"

Anne was confused at this seemingly off-topic rant, "I—"

"You wrote a good book," her father interrupted. "Somebody noticed. Then somebody noticed again. End of story."

Anne took a breath, attempting to understand where he was coming from. In his ranting non-answer Anne had detected a note of praise, not something her father gave out frequently. Overwhelmed, she let her tears flow. She hadn't the heart to tell her father that his handpicked successor, Becky, and the studio's biggest star, James Johnson, had been trying to buy her silence. They had plagiarized her novel and then flown her to the coast to collect a fat check. But the things that were truly preying on her mind were to do with Cliff—and his death. No, *more than that*, the *nature* of his death. Those thoughts, and what Uncle Manny had said about the drug-related on-set whatever-it-was, were tornadoing through her consciousness. Even though she had no proof, something about the proximity of those events seemed meaningful to her. It was no doubt crazy, but she had the nagging feeling that they were connected, that Cliff's death wasn't what it seemed. Had she watched too many movies? She didn't know. It was all...

"Pumpkin?" Bob prompted, and in response Anne sobbed.

"For shit's sake! Look at that! Your blood sugar's dropping again!" For the past few days Anne's father had been handing her an endless supply of water glasses and small snacks. His angle was simple: he knew if you were busy swallowing it was impossible to cry. "Did I ask you if you wanted a sandwich, or not? Come on, already!" He turned to go into the kitchen and Anne followed.

In the kitchen Anne set two plates on the counter as Bob toasted four slices of whole wheat and meticulously constructed the sandwiches. His attention didn't waiver as he said, "So," and patted some lettuce dry, "you and this Starkey kid."

"White, Cliff White."

"Whatever. He took his mother's name."

"Was she—she was famous?"

"Yeah, she had her day, sang some syrupy stuff in the sixties about..." He thought briefly, "Parking lots, clouds, that kinda shit. But this kid, Starkey..."

"Cliff."

"People are sayin' you were quite an item."

"I just met him, Dad."

"So?"

"I don't kn... It just all seems like a... I can't make any sense of it right now."

"I met your mother four hours before you were conceived. You know what I'm saying?"

Anne's face crumpled, "Dad, it's hard to explain."

"Yeah, and even harder now that he's dead. That's called shock, kiddo." Bob Brown peered at his daughter and handed her a paper towel. "Here, wipe your nose."

Anne swiped at her nose and then clung to the paper and let it absorb her tears.

"You want me to make an appointment for you today with my doctor?" asked Bob.

"What...kind of doctor is he?" Anne asked warily.

"The kind that'll give you something to make you feel better."

"Somebody I lo..." Anne gasped back more tears; her purchase on reality was rapidly vanishing and the rest of what she wanted to say came out in a disassociated rush, "He... he...just died! I... I'm... I think I'm *supposed* to feel like this!"

Bob, blithely missing the point said, "That's fine." He took the paper towel from her hand and dropped it in the trash. "You know when I was thirty-five I had my first kid, and in 1953 I was considered an old father. Thirty-five. And for women it's worse."

"Dad, you were forty-five when I was born. Is this supposed to make me feel better? And besides, weren't you twenty-five when Natalie was born, not thirty-five, and what does—"

"That's right, forty-five. That's what I said. I was forty-five when you were born and I didn't do any of the heavy lifting. Your mother was twenty-three."

"Help me out here, Pop. Is this still a pep talk?"

"Christ!" Bob admonished. "Don't be a smart-ass. Natalie is fifty-four. You think she ever tells me what's on her mind? I'm just saying, considering the circumstances, it couldn't hurt if you did." Shaking his head he sliced the sandwiches on the diagonal, just the way his daughters liked them. "All I'm saying is that for me, now that I'm up in years, the real stuff doesn't have to do with a spouse, or a partner, or a whatever-you-call-'em these days. What's really important to a person is their kids and how they're doing, no matter how old they are. You get me?"

"Okay, Daddy."

"You want a soda or some fizzy water?" The subject, apparently, was closed.

Chapter 6

ALL THESE THINGS THAT I'VE DONE

The morning after the funeral, determined to put a lid on the crying and think things through rationally, Anne sat on the edge of the bed. Was she feeling sorry for herself...for Cliff... for a missed...? Her eyes spilled over. So much for rational analysis—Anne wiped away the tears quickly. She pulled on a pair of jeans, cowboy boots with stacked heels, and a very soft sweater. Dressing for the West Coast always tried her and, given recent events, making up her mind what to wear was proving particularly bothersome. However, after anxiously calling her sister at seven a.m. pleading to know what was suitable to wear to both a police interview and a lunch meeting—requested by a tearful Keir Bloomfield—she calmed down, decided she was trying too hard, and attempted to relax. However, she hadn't reckoned on her father. She saw Bob Brown sitting at the kitchen table eating a bowl of berries, cottage cheese, and wheat bran. He was wearing a tartan cap, cardigan, sweatpants, and he had a white gym towel draped around his neck, having immediately sat down to breakfast after his morning walk.

The kitchen was a nearly untouched artifact from the forties—original black-and-white tile floor, marble countertops, an O'Keefe and Merritt Town & Country gas range with six burners and four ovens—Anne remembered *if it ain't broke don't fix it* was less a hackneyed phrase than it was a guiding principle. The only recent purchases were a refrigerator, which dated from the nineties and a Chinese toaster that Bargain Hunter Bob (the not-so affectionate nickname his friends called him but never to his face) had picked up at the grocery store for an astonishing nineteen dollars.

"Good morning, sunshine!" he greeted her. "What's on tap for today?"

"I've got lunch with Keir Bloomfield," she answered.

"That writer guy?"

Anne nodded. "And then I've got an appointment with Detective Vasquez at four."

"That, you'll probably make, but lunch you should reschedule."

"I can't reschedule."

"Sure you can. It's expected. Makes your time appear more valuable. Anyway, I'm taking you to the Nominees Luncheon today, and that thing you got going with Mr. Bloomfield, that's just a bullshit courtesy thing."

"No, Dad, it's...wait! The Nominees Luncheon for the Academy Awards?" she asked, remembering what Cliff had told her—that James Johnson and Bill Aagard were both nominated for awards.

"I'm on the Board of Governors," he said, taking in her scoopneck sweater, jeans, and boots with a glance. "You bring a dress or a suit?"

"Both." Anne surprised herself. She had never previously attended an industry function, nor wanted to, but suddenly she needed to go to this one. Her mind made a strange leap; from remembering her uncle's comment on the antagonism between management types and talent to fixing on the idea that Johnson and Aagard would be at the luncheon and that somehow their connection to Cliff had something to do with his death. It was hardly rational, but she felt she would gain some peace of mind by going—that she could obtain clarifying knowledge, and, most of all, help Cliff. Help Cliff? Cliff was dead. Help resolve her feelings for Cliff. Her father was looking at her again with that mix of paternal worry and bafflement. She nodded.

"Fine. We should get there early for the meet and greet."

"If you don't mind me asking, why aren't you taking Natalie?"

"Because she couldn't give a flying flamingo."

"A wh...? Never mind, Dad."

They arrived at the Beverly Hilton Hotel at around eleven. Inside, the lobby was a Hollywood dream of the fifties: all gleaming polished floors, towering stone-slab walls, and starburst chandeliers. The ballroom where the ceremony was taking place maintained a sinuous two-tiered design like that of a cruise ship, and was carpeted with some dreadful dark jewel-toned carpet that looked like it had been installed in 1970. At the front of the room stood a speaker's dais, a drape, and a projection screen. Tables set for ten stretched for seemingly as far as the eye could see, and the old guard of Hollywood was beginning to trickle in: a lot of white-haired men of surprisingly small stature, and a few—very few—older women in bugle-beaded suits who still believed in the power of Aqua-Net. A noxious hint of perfume came her way, orange blossoms and jasmine, and an underlying stench—it couldn't be, but she remembered distinctly a cat backing up against the garage at her father's on Crescent Drive and something spraying out of its behind.

Anne made straight for the ladies' lounge, which was vast and covered in pink marble. Staring at the gold-plated fixtures on the sink, she felt on the verge of hyperventilating. How had she gotten here? It wasn't exactly an existential question, but what precisely did she think she was doing? The floor seemed to be giving way, melting beneath her feet, and her stomach was lurching as if something had gone wrong with gravity. She was trembling. Looking up, she saw her face, drained of color, gazing back at her from the mirror. Next to her reflection was Shamari's. Anne was about to attempt some innocuous comment when Shamari took a cloth hand towel, soaked it under the cold tap, wrung it out, and placed it on the back of her neck. "You're going to be fine," she said quietly and distinctly, "everything's going to be all right."

"Thank you," said Anne.

"Just take a breath," said Shamari, dipping a hand into her Prada bag, her entire arm like a dowser's wand dragged toward a source of water. There appeared an expression of almost religious fervor as she found what she sought in its capacious depths. After a moment she withdrew her hand and produced, with a flourish, a shining tube of lipstick and proffered it; "This should look good on you. Here." Anne, more than a little perplexed, accepted the peculiar offering. Lipstick as panacea... She took the lipstick and applied a coat to her lips. Shamari watched Anne with an approving nod. "That's better." Shamari wore some designer outfit in black and stood with chin raised and shoulders back. She possessed an adamantine focus, not in the sense that her personality sparkled and gleamed but in that she was cold and hard and so sharp-edged she could slice through glass. Wary of Shamari's intense attention, Anne asked, "How do you get through these things?"

"Anything's better than being home right now. My two-year-old is like destruction on two tiny feet. My six-year-old just figured out how to make things explode in the microwave, and I had to take my thirteen-year-old, straight-A student son's cell phone away because he was using it to download porn."

"Oh."

"Sorry. You weren't talking about this luncheon, were you?"

Anne's head drooped, involuntarily and almost absurdly, like the wilt of a blossom caught by time-lapse photography.

"You meant Cliff."

Anne nodded.

"Hmm, I guess you try not to lose it or to end yourself and then, with time, you climb out of the abyss and keep on going. Nothing's going to make you feel better right now. You just keep on going. Like it or not, people are hardwired to cope—" She considered Anne's state and gentled her tone, "You'll be fine."

Anne pondered this. It sounded both bleak and practical. She could almost hear Uncle Manny saying, "Well, on the level, angel heart; I hear your little house party in the desert—the Nelsons' little party in the desert, I should say—was born out of a very…scandalous situation." Startled, she looked at their reflections in the mirror. Anne looked fragile, somehow hollow, while Shamari appeared as strong, solid, and impassive as steel. How did she maintain that façade? Did it come naturally? What was it like being married to a movie star? She had just read something in the *New York Times* about some farfetched proclamation James Johnson had made recently, something about being respectful of differing viewpoints, and a newfound appreciation of Clientology, and that even unambiguously evil creatures like Mussolini had a good side. She was having a hard time seeing Shamari and James together.

Shamari made a quick appraisal of her face in the mirror, a slight lift of the brow as if to say everything was in place, then said to Anne, "You know, the best thing you can do right now is focus. Keep your eyes on the prize."

"There's a prize?" Anne questioned. She glanced at Shamari again as she dabbed at her swollen eyes, waiting to see whether the irony and uncertainty in her question would register. Anne let her imagination go as Shamari's lips turned up in an expression meant to console. Sometimes a smile was genuine, signaling support, and sometimes it was the teeth-baring glint of a predator. Anne was having difficulty making the distinction.

Cliff had told Anne he was James Johnson's agent. He was called to Bill Aagard's set over a "scandalous situation" involving illegal substances, and Cliff knew James Johnson had plagiarized Anne's story for a movie and had conspired with Becky Nelson to try to *make it go away*. Anne wondered what else Cliff was aware of and if this had anything to do with him ingesting two prescription medications, neither of which, as far as Anne understood, he had any business taking, and then dying—must not, cannot forget the dying. The dying was all she could see.

"Anne," said Shamari, "I think you'll find getting along in Hollywood is about making concessions. Just don't make any where your family is concerned."

"I'm sorry," said Anne. "I'm probably just a little slow on the uptake right now, but I'm not really clear on what you're saying to me."

"What I'm saying is," Shamari set her bag on the marble sink again and crossed her arms in front of her chest. "What I'm saying is, what, exactly, did Cliff tell you about my husband?"

Anne was weighing why Shamari appeared so formidable, couldn't quite make it out, and replied without guile, "That he's up for an Academy Award."

Shamari considered Anne with an unwavering gaze then made a snap decision and told her something at which Cliff hadn't even hinted.

Chapter 7

AIN'T MISBEHAVIN'

Etta Johnson got her first pretty good indication of her son's sexuality in 1975, when she found the penis-shaped hash pipe hidden in a shoe box filled with contraband in James' closet. What she mulled over as she flushed the pot and other assorted mystery items down the toilet was whether she should tell her husband about her discovery—and what she would tell him, if she did.

James was the youngest of seven. His eldest brother had followed their father, Sam, into the Air Force and was now a test pilot; Mrs. Johnson's next son was a compliance officer with a multinational bank; the third son was an engineer, the fourth worked for the district attorney's office; while the two girls were, respectively, a teacher, and a homemaker. James was Etta and Sam's gift of middle age, now a senior in high school as they approached retirement. Mrs. Johnson, a pious woman, considered James a miracle, of sorts. In an hour she would leave the house in Baldwin Hills, near LAX, and make the long drive to Chatsworth to bring James home from the High School for the Performing Arts. She did coddle her baby, but that didn't extend to buying him a car.

After assessing what to do with the offending penis-shaped artifact she finally decided it would be best to simply slip it back into the box then return it to the shelf. The last time she'd considered consulting her husband before confronting James was when she had walked out of the kitchen to witness the dismaying sight of James sweeping up young David Jefferson into his arms, preparatory to carrying him up the stairs to his bedroom to indulge in the kind of practices Etta did not even like to *think* about. Or he would have if she hadn't appeared when she did. She had squelched her desire to call Sam immediately, and followed the boys upstairs. "David's helping me rehearse, Mom," James said disdainfully, before adding, "You'd better go home now, David, I've got to do calculus." She could see the younger boy quail; James had a habit of making people feel small. Etta walked David downstairs and patted his shoulder as she opened the door for him to go.

A specter of doubt haunted her mind. *Well*, she thought, *that homosexuality, who knows what white boys could tempt you to do? And this one, with his pink cheeks and dark hair, was nearly as pretty as a girl.* She took a deep breath. Personally, she didn't know a single black child that was gay—there, now she was calm.

That said, she had a greater concern. All her children were achievers; was her youngest a pothead? That wouldn't do. Immediately she regretted her husband's decision to leave Edwards and take a job with Hughes Aircraft. This damn city was too big, with too many wayward paths and empty promises, and now James had been accepted to Juilliard. *God, help me! What do I do?* she thought, edging toward meltdown. Needless to say, James disavowed any knowledge of the contents of the shoe box when questioned—perhaps a little too righteously—on the drive home from school. Unflappable, he maintained consistently that he was only holding onto the box for a friend. The idea hadn't ever even entered his loyal mind that he should peek inside. He had his standards, and Mrs. Johnson needed her faith in the infallibility of her children.

James Johnson loved Manhattan. He loved Juilliard. Most of all he loved shedding all the tiresome, uncool parental pressure, but not his monthly allowance, which he supplemented with a hefty income dealing pot and coke to his like-minded artistic classmates. His best customers tended to be kids enrolled in the music division, pianists particularly, their intensive practice sessions fueled by cocaine. When one of his regulars had a stroke while thundering through a particularly and peculiarly physical performance of Lizst, James had a rare attack of conscience. He gave up dealing (well, mostly), lied about his age, and got a job slinging drinks topless (okay, let's not forget the bowtie) at Studio 54.

The tips were phenomenal, but the sex—anonymous, plentiful, shameless, and always to an amazing pulsating bass beat—was better. The first time he was referred to as "beefcake" by a man tonguing him in the balcony of the disco, something resonated deep in his core and he, in his joy, ignited a smile that could light kindling. As it turns out, the man basking in the glow was a casting director, and a week later James had left college a semester shy of graduation and gotten a role as an eager young cop in what turned out to be the top-rated TV show of 1979.

Catapulting to fame was easy in L.A. However, dealing with his parents again was a problem for James. To celebrate his good fortune he took the folks to London over hiatus. Sam Johnson had been stationed at Alconbury for years and was especially fond of the British. So was his son. On returning to their suite at Claridge's at five a.m., lips swollen and clothes in disarray after a little adventure in the public convenience at Hyde Park, James was annoyed to find his father waiting up. Sam surveyed James' getup and the flushed, postcoital state of his features, and rumbled, "Boy, if you disappoint your mother, so help me God…"

Back in L.A. James dated for the first time in his life—a string of young ladies who attended his mother's church. It fed his ego, if not his libido, and his parents were elated. Finally, Mrs. Johnson introduced him to Shamari, a very tall, slim-hipped woman who owned a popular catering firm. Shamari Bess was a quick-witted good girl and adoring of her handsome beau. Six months later, as Mrs. Johnson led the choir at First African Baptist, they were married. Ten months later their first child was born.

One afternoon many years later, James made a rare family appearance to watch their eldest son play softball at his school. After the game Shamari noticed him congratulating a very handsome, very studly young coach and saw an expression in James' eyes that she had never conjured. Something illuminated within her, cast light on things that she had been vaguely aware of but had not wanted to see or understand: the commiserating looks and strange, oblique comments she received from people about James; the odd phone calls; the sense that there were compartments in his life that were closed to her; the times he came back from "a night out with the guys" or a location shoot with a charged intensity about him. All these things that she had willfully ignored stood revealed as pieces to a puzzle, and she now had the final one. She understood what had been hidden; the question was, what was she going to do about it?

That night, with the children put to bed, Shamari and James were watching TV. She turned to him and said, "James, I love our children, I love our family, I love our life. I have no desire to change that. Ever." James, only half-listening, patted her hand. "No, James, I need you to listen. I have no desire to change anything." She switched off the TV. He frowned and tapped his thumbs impatiently on his knees. "James, I saw you today, after the game, you wanted…" James became very still and his face emptied of expression. "I'm not an insensitive woman, but I need to do what's right by our family. Honestly, I have better things to do than dwell on your sex life, but if you do have a sex life apart from me, you had better tell me—" James rose from his chair as if to go. Shamari, board member of Children's Hospital, benefactor of their church, advocate of the homeless, said, "James, you sit your down-low devil's ass right back down and get on with it or you will live to regret it." He sat. And, after a few minutes of unconvincing denial, he got to the point. Shamari listened quietly, thought briefly, and said, "We will sleep in adjoining bedrooms, the children will know nothing of this, you will never come out of the closet. You do whatever you want, to whomever you want, but you keep it silent or you will deal with me." So things were very quiet, silent, just as Shamari wanted, or so she had thought, from that day on.

★★★

"I've never even told that to my mother," concluded Shamari. "Well, there it is. And I hope you've got enough sense not to let it go any further." They were alone. Shamari powdered the shine from her forehead, snapped her compact shut and gestured to the door. Anne let the story settle in her mind. Shamari had just outed her husband. Why to her? That just didn't make sense, unless the closet only existed for the moviegoing public. Shamari turned her steely gaze to Anne, softened her voice, and said, "There, much better. You look much better. Nobody should walk into this business blind like I did. You keep your eyes open; that's all I'm saying." Anne nodded and they walked back out into the ballroom.

Anne was placed at a table between her father and an old PR man who told her about rousting Marilyn Monroe from bed so she could appear at Grauman's and have her extremities impressed in concrete, about James Mason's unspayed, extremely reproductive cats, and about the fact that he was running in the L.A. Marathon at the age of eighty-three. Under normal circumstances Anne would have been rapt but she found her attention wandering.

Shamari Johnson, seated at another table, was in an animated conversation with an actress who had been in a few movies and then married a producer, adopted six children, and retired from the screen. She had taken her chair and literally turned it around so her back was to her husband. Every so often Shamari would catch Anne's eye only for their gazes to hurriedly deflect elsewhere; once, Anne's attention ping-ponged away to see Tessa Aagard sitting, elbows on another table, chin resting on her cupped hands, listening eagerly as George Clooney cracked up his tablemates and then tossed his head back with a big, toothy guffaw. Another glance-away and Sid Ganis stepped up to the dais to deliver a few helpful hints on acceptance speeches and then corralled the nominees into five rows to have their picture snapped. A talkative actress sitting center front of the portrait had to be shushed twice, "Sonia! Sonia! Are you with us, dear? Are you with us? Eyes front!"

Finally, Shamari turned in her seat and nodded to Anne as Bill Aagard and James Johnson stood tall in the back row and beamed for the camera. If Anne had attended the Nominees Luncheon in anticipation of some helpful, singular revelation, she was coming up snow-blind in a blizzard of information.

Chapter 8

U CAN'T TOUCH THIS

Four o'clock found her sitting in front of Phil Vasquez's borrowed desk at the Beverly Hills police station recounting the events of the previous weekend. Anne thought the detective was making a special effort to keep the tone conversational, "Do you know The Buccaneers, Ms. Brown?"

Anne, anxious to please, answered brightly, "That's a coincidence!"

Detective Vasquez's pencil was poised over a pad of paper. "Really? How so?"

"I just taught that fall quarter." He wasn't writing anything down. "Edith Wharton. 1938. She died in 1937 and it was published unfinished—but in '93 another edition was released with a new ending based on her notes."

Detective Vasquez appeared nonplussed. Anne wondered if she'd confused the dates. He set her on edge; she couldn't stop words from cascading out like a verbal waterfall. "Ah. It's the story of a group of naïve American heiresses who marry into the English aristocracy. The Americans get titles and the cash-strapped Brits... It's... It's a commentary on marrying for appearances rather than love." The detective set his pencil down and cocked his head. "But it's loosely based on fact. Consuelo Vanderbilt married into the Spencer family, later...

ah...well...made famous by Princess Diana, she...she was a Spencer. And, Winston Churchill, same family, the Spencers, his mother was Jennie Jerome, American, incredibly rich." Anne could see she was failing to connect.

"The Buccaneers, the one I'm talking about, Ms. Brown is an after-hours club in Palm Springs. Ever hear of it? The Buccaneers?"

Anne felt foolish; she hated getting things wrong; she shook her head. "I'm sorry, no."

"I hope you don't mind me asking you a personal question. But, did you find Mr. White, I don't know, effeminate, in any way?"

Anne bristled. "You mean, while we were fucking? Or just in general?"

The detective gave her a censorious glance and tapped his pencil on the desktop. "Ms. Brown, I'm just trying to get an overall picture, a blueprint if you will, of what went on in Palm Springs."

"Oh, you want to develop a *blueprint* of what happened. Sorry, for a moment there, I thought you were subtly asking if Cliff was *gay*."

Detective Vasquez said, "That is a valid question."

Hell. Just what she did not want to hear. If Cliff was gay why had they had that sexual soul-deep link, why had they felt such an immediate connection? Or was it just she who had felt it? There had been something very familiar about Cliff, familiar and, at present, indefinable. She could feel her heartbeat reverberating in her ears. "No, not in my experience."

"Viagra and kind of a prescription version of meth. That's what the P.M. showed in Mr. White, a pretty unusual cocktail. Did you observe anyone taking drugs? Did you witness any use of substances, by anybody, while you were at the Nelsons'?"

"Besides alcohol? No."

"No kind of—what you might term—jumpy or belligerent behavior?"

Anne remembered Keir's twitchy leg at the dinner table but discounted it as just a personal tic. She remembered Tessa's staccato speaking style and the authoritative dictates of Becky. She remembered Shamari's curt reply to her husband at breakfast. She remembered Ben Haber's uncontainable excitement over Cliff's Ferrari. "No."

"That took you a while."

"I was trying to remember, trying to be accurate."

Detective Vasquez leaned forward in his seat. "Yeah. That's usually a tell, like a body language thing; if you think before you answer it usually means you're telling the truth. Well, so far you seem to be doing a lot of thinking, and your story adds up."

"Have you talked to everybody who was at the Nelsons'?"

"Some, not all, but I'm getting the general drift."

"Did they know about The Buccaneers?"

"It's a sex club, Ms. Brown."

"You said it was an after-hours club."

"Good, you're paying attention." He made a pyramid of his hands, tapped his fingertips against his lips, thought for a moment, then pushed his chair back, from the desk, stood, and extended his hand toward Anne. "Thanks for coming in, Ms. Brown. And the book tip, I'll try to get my hands on a copy."

Anne rose and shook his hand. "A sex club?"

"You look worried, Ms. Brown. Anything else you'd like to tell me?"

Anne was focused on their hands. They were still clasped. Their palms together made a small humidity zone. He wasn't particularly squeezing her hand, but she felt pressed, like he was trying to wring something out of her. Was it about the nature of the house party? About some hearsay incident on a movie set? About a movie star and their sexual orientation? "I, I can't think of anything right now, detective." The conspiracy to cheat her of her books rights seemed an inconsequential detail compared to Cliff's death. What had their sudden alliance to do with him dying? Nothing. She was just a pesky chunk of rock flying through a universe riddled with gravity-sucking stars. If her earlier conversation with Shamari had pointed out anything, it was exactly that. He let go of her hand and reached into his pocket to give her another card. She felt like wiping her palm, but she didn't.

"Phil. You think of anything, you give me a call."

She stared at the card. Annoyingly, her need for him to address her suspicions became too much for her. "You—you don't think…" She glanced up from the card. "I don't understand the line of questioning, detective."

"You're not supposed to."

Paternalistic prick, thought Anne, but what she said was this: "Detective, was Cliff's death accidental or not?"

"At the moment, this is just a routine investigation. We'll be in touch, Ms. Brown."

Anne walked out into the police station's reception area and was heading for the door when she spied Becky Nelson bedecked in a Chanel suit, looking as out of place as a John Singer Sargent painting hung on a graffitied wall, shoving a smartphone at one underling and her purse at another. The harried-looking studio boss spotted Anne and raised a finger in a commanding "halt, please" gesture. Anne sputtered to a stop. Becky waved her over impatiently. "Did you see Detective Vasquez?" she asked, pushing back the cuff of her jacket with a perfectly manicured hand to look at her wristwatch. "Because, I have, like, three minutes I can give him." Anne heard this but her mind flashed to tales of the eighties told to her by her uncle and read about in a rash of "been there, snorted that" memoirs by some notable Hollywood has-beens—tales of years whited out by avalanches of cocaine. Uncle Manny said that Becky's crew had been coked to the gills. She wondered if Becky had, herself, snorted (or delicately smeared blow on her gums) or if she had merely supplied the stuff to others—not that she had any reason to believe that. But still.

"Well," said Anne sardonically. "You'd better get going."

Becky was surprised and disgruntled to be answered in that manner. She was used to being treated with heightened respect and didn't bother to conceal how taken aback she was. "Look, Anne, I know this has been…an unsettling…"

"Unsettling?" Anne repeated.

"An unsettling time for you, but no matter what you think, or what you've heard, I have, the studio has, and always will do right by you."

"Really, I'm not so much unsettled by you or the studio, but a lot more by the fact that one of your houseguests apparently died of a drug overdose while he was staying with you. That, that's really unsettling. Doesn't that bother you, Becky? It does me. It really, really does. I find it extremely…unsettling."

"Okay. Anne? I don't know where all this free-floating hostility is coming from." Becky's assistants tried to appear conspicuously busy. "But, I'll just make an observation. Sometimes when people die, or when somebody we love is very badly hurt, sometimes we get irrationally angry. And that anger is often misplaced."

"Thanks for the words of wisdom," Anne retorted.

"Oh, sit down for a second and shut up!" She dismissed her assistants with a wave of her hand and then proceeded to deliver, what sounded to Anne, like a highly refined movie pitch.

Chapter 9

A HARD DAY'S NIGHT

Imagine a time before you were born. Imagine a dowdy old university town on the East Coast somewhere in the nineteen-sixties. Imagine a boy and a girl living there. These two, let's call them Becky and Steve, spoon-fed each other fantasy. Their days were spent constructing an elaborate alternative reality full of sparkling waves and ribbons of highway and palm fronds billowing in the breeze. And so in constructing that fantasy they forged a bond that could last a lifetime. A bond that had existed long enough now to see dreams become solid, with Becky ensconced as head of a major movie studio and Steve decorating from Vail to Bahrain. They had one of the longest, and most photographed, marriages in Hollywood, and, as far as anyone knows, they never once fucked each other. You can take that any way you'd like.

Not that they didn't try. During a particularly agonizing stretch senior year in high school, when they each were anxious to shed their virginity before college, they had tried. It amounted to a drive around the lake, a lot of gossiping, and some hugging on Becky's front porch. When they tried to fit their bodies together they found it was lacking—like bumping up against a sibling—and, besides, the curves weren't in the right places; the muscles didn't correspond. It left them flat, limp, unaroused. No iris dilation, no heightened pulse. Becky thought it was like kissing a clam. Steve felt like he was holding an animated mass of raw pizza dough—all pillowy and yielding and soft. Profoundly embarrassed by this non-event, they didn't really speak again until a few years later—the only significant break in their relationship—after both had come to terms with their sexuality and come out, she while at Harvard Law, he while at Carnegie Mellon. They came out of the closet in college and reunited; then when they decided to face Hollywood together—in 1981—they promptly went right back in.

When Becky invited Steve to accompany her on the adventure, she put it like this, "Steve, I got a gig at a big firm out in California; you wanna come?" Steve, employed at the time drafting prefab cubicle-based office interior schemes in Pittsburgh, had responded with an explosively enthusiastic, "God, yes!" Not only was this a dream fulfilled. but also he was more than a little relieved to get out of town. He had recently acquired two Louis Comfort Tiffany lighting fixtures from a soon-to-be-demolished movie theater downtown and—wait, back it up: *acquired*, now that's a funny word; a more precise word would be *stole*; yes, he stole them. They were bewitchingly beautiful pendant fixtures, crafted in the teens, each was about the size of a toddler, their mottled glass luminously gold and cream and bronze. When he first saw the lamps in the ruins of the Rialto they tenderly hooked a portion of his heart. He had taken them home and draped them with a quilt on his bed. He slept in a careful arc with them at night. Steve loved them because of their artistry and because of the spark they struck within him. He wasn't quite sure if they would be crushed along with the rest of the building, or if somebody else was aware of their value. He just knew, as he waded through decades of dust and dirt in the derelict picture palace, he had to save them and now, no matter what; they were his.

Destiny presented egress when Becky, a week after the lights had been introduced to their new home, phoned and not only invited him to California but mentioned in passing that the local paper was heralding the arrival of an appraiser from Sotheby's to take a look-see in a soon-to-be razed theater. Steve suggested they leave immediately in his hand-me-down Volvo wagon. He insisted quietly, firmly, and repeatedly. Steve carefully packed their combined wardrobes around "the twins," and when Becky inquired as to the lamps' origin, he answered simply, "I liberated them." After which she let the matter drop, took the wheel, and steered a course down 81 toward Route 40 and points very far west.

Now, this is where it gets a little complicated, so just hold on for the ride. In the early twentieth century wealthy East Coast families such as the Rockefellers and the Astors would send their more-than-usually dissolute ne'er-do-well offspring various distant places out West. Places like Cody, Wyoming, which is, to this day, referred to as a town of remittance men, the remittance, or funds, to run huge ranches and keep their sons pickled in booze being transferred on a regular basis from thousands of miles away.

The rich folks of the West Coast liked to keep their black sheep closer to home. So the descendants of acting dynasties and railroad barons could often be found scattered around in places on the outskirts of Los Angeles. One such mildly insalubrious locale could be found in a canyon that wound down to the ocean. There, old country club outbuildings were furnished with family heirlooms and had electricity haphazardly supplied by hundreds of feet of orange extension cord, strung in dangerous loops and swirls, and pirated from municipal power lines. The pong of marijuana hung like a mist over the neighborhood, and toddlers ran naked from house to house. Of course, these infants often had European au pairs or nannies, the money for whom was provided by concerned grandparents, but once these young people began inhabiting the canyon things became—to put it mildly—very informal.

One denizen of this improvised habitat had been exiled in 1969 from San Marino by his oil-rich family for preferring cabana boys to suitable young ladies. He spent his days surfing and his nights toking. By the time the eighties rolled around he was thirty-two and ripped. He was physically gorgeous, and mentally—let's just say he had a Zenlike disposition derived from fumigating his brain. He was considered old by the other surfers, and inscrutable. His survival as one of the elders in the surfing community was based on his placid temperament and the fact that he kept his personal life closeted. However, as serene as he appeared, he was profoundly lonely.

In 1982 Steve and Becky Nelson were living in an apartment on Valleyheart Drive in Studio City. Becky worked twelve-hour days in the legal department at Warner Bros. Steve, equally driven, had recently been laid off from a design firm for sitting on a client's Pomeranian. After a week of self-castigation, Becky insisted he take a break. He spent his days trying to recoup at the beach. At ten in the morning he would load up the clatter trap Volvo with towels, books, and sandwiches and head out to Zuma.

At sunset an offshore wind stirred and with the water backlit, Steve spotted a dolphin riding, submerged, at the heart of a perfect azure wave. The moment struck him as magical—and even more so when the dolphin emerged from the wave on a board and stood to ride it to shore. What he thought was a completely different kind of mammal turned out to be a man. The man walked straight from the Pacific to Steve. In his early twenties, Steve Nelson always responded to a strong aesthetic impulse, and the cast-off oil scion in his early thirties, Alex G., always went where the sea delivered him.

Picture this: instant recognition. Who cares if their acknowledgement consisted of *hey* and *hi* and prolonged eye contact? No disrespect to Salinger or Robbie Burns, but their meeting was more of *Gin a body kiss a body—Need a body cry?* After a golden hour together in which they found an easy sensual bond, they linked arms and went back to the canyon of misfits. A week later Steve dug his Tiffany lamps out of a cheap storage facility shoved under the 101 freeway in Hollywood and installed them in what would be henceforth known as the Beach House.

Becky was fine with Steve and Alex's ardor. She, while still a relatively young woman, had come to find that her sexual desires didn't mix well with her highly developed sense of logic or her driving ambition. Whenever she thought of sticking her tongue in some comely woman's mouth, her judgment clouded, so she tried not to think about sex. As an adult, the ability to slip into fantasy—which had come so easily to her when she was young—seemed frivolous, a distraction; it was this focused, über-rational, all-business mindset that had served her well in the industry. Her partnership with Steve, she felt, was perfect. It coincided with her concept of a tidy, ironclad, long-term relationship, and she would never deny Steve a loving physical outlet. In the long run it seemed the most prudent course, but the future doesn't care for prudence or calculation; it comes no matter what.

When Steve and Alex weren't licking the sand off each other's bodies, they would drive into town and pick Becky up and spend their evenings together at grungy old theaters, like the Beverly, where their shoes stuck to the floor and the rotting seats smelled so bad they'd wrap scarves around their noses or breath into the back of their hands to filter out the stench. It was in such theaters that they would watch old movies, projected, as big as they were meant to be and without commercial interruption.

After sitting through two showings of *Taxi Driver*, the usually laconic Alex said, "I could do that."

"What? Go on a murderous rampage?" Becky teased.

"No. I could make a movie like that," said Alex.

"If you could make a movie like that," laughed Becky, "I'd produce it, and I'd find somebody to distribute it, and we'd all be rich and famous."

Steve looked warily from Alex to Becky and sensed—despite Becky's apparent playfulness and Zen Alex's vainglory—their personal dynamic was about to get very complex. Becky had gotten wind of something—it smelled like opportunity—and Steve was well aware she was a woman who liked to draw up lists, make plans, and exploit possibilities. Alex, with his elemental nature, merely existed in the here and now.

Alex said, "I am rich. I don't want to be famous. But making a movie would be cool."

"Done!" Becky exclaimed.

"Okay," Alex replied, only faintly excited.

As it turned out, Becky's instincts were dead-on. She helped birth the indie film movement of the eighties, her first movie made with a one-time-only burst of lightning effort from

Alex. Their debut project had been nightmarishly difficult and she—desperate to bring it to completion on time and on budget—had sourced the coke that fueled the crew's sixteen-hour days, and Alex's trustees supplied the one million dollars to make the film. Becky's enterprise was ceaseless; the movie did well and brought her to the attention of the Hollywood establishment, personified by one man: Robert Jerome "Bob" Brown.

Alex, coming off the "harsh" high of moviemaking, returned to his reclusive ways. Becky went from legal to low-end producer to studio brass. She sojourned frequently with the boss and the "old boys" at Musso's, where she ordered the same drinks as her peers (although she never touched a drop) and several bottles of Perrier for the table. Back home with Steve and Alex, however, she referred to that favored industry watering hole as "a cesspool of gin and tonic" and wondered, miffed, why she hadn't spent the time, instead, at The Grill on the Alley. By 1996 she was one step away from being a studio head and she had, by her own calculation, consumed some three hundred homemade chicken pot pies, probably the same Thursday-night special since the restaurant's inception in 1919.

Steve spent his time shuttling between the calm of Alex and the climbing of Becky. In the meantime he started his own firm—work was the only place he felt autonomous.

Twenty-five years into their threesome, Alex lost his short-term memory and he began to wander. Becky explained to the trustees of his fortune that Alex G. had been diagnosed with early onset Alzheimer's, and Steve bought a compound on acreage in Malibu. Alex's hippie hollow was rebuilt on the property; no detail was overlooked, not the orange extension cords, nor the Tiffany lamps, and Alex, as far as he could comprehend, was home.

★★★

Having finished her story, Becky sighed and shook her head; she looked glaringly out of place seated on the plastic chair anchored next to Anne's. "And so it goes. I don't have any more time for this right now, so I'll just get to it. If Cliff hadn't told you about your book rights, I would have. And you should fire your agent. I make a point of firing anyone with their head up their ass." Anne couldn't help thinking this was brusque, Becky Nelson endeavoring to be nice, attempting to create an alliance based on a carefully scripted intimacy. Unlike Shamari's bout of sharing that had begun with a barely veiled threat and then had poured out in something that resembled relief, Becky's story seemed specifically designed to garner sympathy. Anne quietly steamed for a minute. Anyway, why was everybody always telling her about their sex lives? Was it pertinent? Detective Vasquez walked into the lobby looking for his next appointment. "Fuck!" said Becky. Anne tried to see where Becky's new information fit in with her previous impressions. "You know what your father used to tell me?" Becky asked. "He used to say, 'Don't shit where you sleep.'"

"Sounds like Dad!"

"I would never screw you, or any member of your family. Remember that." She acknowledged the detective and then turned her attention back to Anne. "Let's do lunch."

Let's do lunch? Over my dead body was the phrase that vaulted to Anne's mind, her throat constricting with nausea at the thought. All she could see was Cliff's face, silver in the moonlight, eyes an impossibly deep blue, tapping at the window in Palm Springs—and she said out loud, knowing it would never happen, "Sure."

Chapter 10

I'LL BUILD A STAIRWAY TO PARADISE

Anne pulled up to her father's house on Crescent Drive, her mind teeming with thoughts of Becky who now seemed like a clone of him, or worse, his spiritual daughter, molded in his fierce potty-mouthed image and somehow capable of stirring up feelings of sibling rivalry never caused by her own sister. She was trying to calm herself when she noticed a Town Car idling at the curb. As she shut her car door behind her, the Samoan chauffeur she had seen standing by Cole Starkey at Cliff's funeral walked up the driveway. He was wearing the same black suit and seemed even more massive as he advanced toward her like an ambulatory wall. "Miss Brown?" He had the instinct that many large men do to keep his gestures small and his voice quiet.

"Hello."

"I'm Fal Loa. Mr. Starkey's driver."

"Nice to meet you, Mr. Loa."

"I have Mr. Starkey in the car, and he was wondering if you would accept an invitation to his home."

"He's here?"

"Yes," Fal Loa turned a little to the side so Anne could see past him. Through the car's back window she could see Starkey; he appeared to be nodding off.

Stoned or narcoleptic, thought Anne, reminded of her father's claim, "high as a kite at his own son's funeral." She raised her keys and pointed to the front door of the house. "Wouldn't you just like to come in?" She wondered how much Mr. Loa was paid to baby-sit Mr. Starkey.

"That's very kind, but Mr. Starkey doesn't like to impose."

This was all becoming a bit too *Sunset Boulevard* for Anne. "I see. When would Mr. Starkey like me to come over?"

"Now would be fine."

"Well, where?" She paused; she wanted more than anything to go inside, take a shower, sit at the kitchen table, and look out into the backyard, where the first spring flowers were blooming. She just wanted time to herself, time to reflect. "I guess I could follow you in my car." She was driving a car of her father's, a fifteen-year-old gas-guzzling Benz that she couldn't help associating with a particular kind of stodgy affluent conservative, for which reason she hated to be seen driving it. But whether she liked it or not, some of L.A.'s car culture was written into her genetic code.

"I'd be happy to drive you and bring you back. It's no trouble, Miss Brown."

She considered asking them to wait while she told her father where she was going, when Cole Starkey roused himself and leaned out the window. "Annie dear, it's just four blocks," he said, waving his hand in an indeterminate direction and jabbing the air with an unlit cigarette, "And, heaven knows,

I don't bite." It was the first time Anne had really heard him talk, beyond the primal wail at the funeral. She recognized the voice, it was Cliff's, but more ragged and with a very slight, decidedly not posh, English accent. Her response was purely visceral but she found his voice sad, soothing, and compelling. Perhaps it was this that caused her to climb into the back of the car next to him. Fal Loa put the car in gear and they cruised up the street.

Starkey was dressed in several layers, black T-shirt under a blue button-down cotton shirt, under a Savile Row tailored jacket, jeans, and high-top Converse sneakers. Even so, it failed to bulk out his long, angular frame, and he looked chilled to the bone. One of his elbows was clutched in tight to his body, and the hand brandishing the cigarette was thrust up in the air in a peculiar fashion like the forelimb of a T. rex. To Anne's surprise, his other hand appeared as if from nowhere and tipped her glasses so they cleared the bridge of her nose and bumped up against her eyebrows. This happened so quickly she didn't have time to register annoyance, or even feel any. "Vous êtes ravissante," he pronounced. He squinted at her critically and continued, "Why would a girl such as you insist on wearing those ridiculous things?"

"Contacts irritate my eyes."

"Hmph," he said in disbelief and added, "that's likely."

Anne caught Mr. Loa's eye in the rearview mirror. He shrugged minutely. "I just got back from the police station."

"I know y'did!" Starkey interrupted, rocking forward from the waist, eyes wide. "Exactly why I wanted to see you. Those fuckin' morons, those arses, say my boy was taking drugs. Ha!" He barked a laugh devoid of amusement and continued rocking.

"You don't believe it?"

Starkey lit his cigarette and pulled the smoke deep into his lungs, opened his window and exhaled into the twilight. "Believe it? Believe. I—fer fuck's sake—know that's the biggest bunch of bullshit since Nixon said he was not a crook!" Starkey was getting so agitated now that he seemed to be suffering some kind of minor seizure, unconsciously juddering his glowing cigarette up and down so much that Anne had to stop herself from flinching. "Clifford takin' drugs! CLIFF? Do you know what my self-righteous son of blessed memory, my self-righteous son, he of the completely unaltered states, did to me because of my indulgences?"

"No, sir," Anne replied.

"Don't call me sir!" he fumed. Anne said nothing. She didn't want to trigger another explosion. Starkey flicked the cigarette out the window then took Anne's small, graceful hands in his large, bony paws. He was long-fingered, with octave-spanning hands like his son; his skin was dry and papery, his grip light and almost fragile. "He had me committed! Twice! Thrown into the psych ward. Under lock and key for seventy-two hours with the white coats hemming and hawing about my destructive tendencies." He let go and leaned back into his seat with a tremor of spent energy.

"I'm sorry."

Starkey waved her apology away as if he were batting at an insect. "No, dear. No apologies needed. What I'm meaning to tell you, what I'm trying to tell you is my boy didn't favor the pills, or the needles, or the powders. He didn't. It's preposterous."

"Excuse me, s—"

"Don't say it!"

"I, I'm sorry. Are you saying the police, that the blood tests are incorrect?"

"Blood tests? I don't care about the bloody blood tests! What I'm saying, what I'm telling you is that I know my boy's habits," he paused briefly, "and taking meth and Viagra wasn't among them." The Town Car turned up a long drive and stopped in front of an overwrought half-timbered Tudor. He nodded toward the house. "Behold, my humble fucking abode. Come on."

"It was only four blocks."

"I've said so, didn't I?" He patted his hands against his jacket frantically, like he'd lost something. He removed a pack of cigarettes from his pocket with trembling hands, withdrew a cigarette, found a Dunhill lighter in his other pocket, and lit up. Starkey sucked in prodigiously as an ember fell from the cigarette's tip onto his lapel, where it began to smolder; he didn't notice. His expression, wreathed in a gray mist as he exhaled, indicated to Anne that he was somewhere else entirely.

"You set yourself on f—"

Starkey cringed, a look of pure astonishment on his face. "God fucking Christ! That's it! Set myself aflame. What next?" For all his histrionics, he was still smoldering. Anne slapped the ember out. "Bloody fucking marvelous… Fal, you may take the child locks off the doors now. At least one of us has retained their sensibilities." Starkey stared at his still-burning cigarette and dropped it, then ground it into the floor of the Town Car. Mr. Loa hefted himself out of the car and opened Anne's door for her while Mr. Starkey darted to the house as if avoiding being photographed. Anne, baffled and bemused, followed, and Fal Loa drove the car around to the garage.

Anne stepped under a carved stone lintel and into the home's soaring, groin-vaulted, churchlike entryway, where she continued to pursue this strange gentleman down three wide stairs to a cavern of a room with two fireplaces, three enormous if tattered Persian rugs, and four not insignificantly large couches scattered with throws and pillows, books and newspapers, vinyl albums in worn covers and CDs—some in plastic jewel cases, others loose—envelopes festooned with indecipherable scribbles and similarly inscribed paper napkins, and pack upon pack of cigarettes. She gingerly elbowed a pillow aside, revealing clustered cigarette burns in the couch's upholstery and a handful of vividly colored capsules and pills wedged in the seam between the back of the couch and the seat cushion. Starkey rummaged through the crumpled packs in hopeful search of an undamaged smoke. Having found one that wasn't crushed or snapped in two, he first offered the cigarette to Anne, and when she declined, he placed it between his lips and didn't apply a match. "Oral fixation, one of my lesser vices. At least the contentious bitch..." he noted Anne's puzzled expression... "The Contentious Bitch, alias my-soon-to-be ex-wife, at least she got me to stop lighting up. Well, she had until recent events, but I do try. Not that it's worth half my estate. Where were we?"

"You were talking about Cliff and drugs."

"Of course we were. That's right. Now, I've heard of mixing

Viagra and ecstasy —Sextasy—it's real popular, and I, for one, find much to recommend in it—but Viagra and Ritalin? *Ritalin*? A drug you give amped-up kids to calm the little bastards down? Nah. The drug of choice would be methamphetamine. Viagra and meth. Whatever, it's a club thing, and it's not Cliff.

Anne fixed on his last statement. "Not Cliff, the club thing? Or, not Cliff, the drug thing?"

"Take your pick, sweetheart. Take your pick." He jerked upright, suddenly possessed by an imperative urge, immediately Anne was reminded of his son. "Now. There's something you have to see. This way!" He led her down a coffered-ceilinged hallway to a library that instead of books shelved innumerable CDs and obscure LPs then through a door out onto an emerald expanse of lawn to a building with a six-car garage below and a chauffeur's apartment above. Fal Loa stood, sentry-like, outside his apartment's door at the top of a stairwell, as if this was his natural position.

"Fal, who has the keys to the Ferrari?" Fal Loa's face remained impassive but Anne detected the slightest ironic flicker in his expression as he started down the stairs and dug in his pocket retrieving a set of keys, which he then handed wordlessly to Starkey. Without any further comment Loa rolled open one of the coach-style garage doors. Once the garage was opened, Starkey stepped into the gloom and leaned—arms folded on his chest, cigarette dangling from his fingers—against the gleaming car within. "Police brought it back this morning." He tossed the keys in the air. "Look sharp!" Anne caught them. "It's yours now."

Anne stared. "I beg your pardon? I, we, we only—"

"A word of caution, love. It handles like a rocket. So be careful, right?"

Anne held the keys out at arm's length. "Sir, I can't accept this; it isn't mine and…"

He clamped his hands over his ears and made a face as if someone had sounded a car horn in the middle of an aria. "*Sir? Sir!*"

"Mr. Starkey, this is not my car. Your son, I, we just met, and—"

"Yes, you just met. And. Plenty of *and*. If you're concerned, I know he didn't die in it, *if* that's what you're worried about. I'm sure we'll have all kinds of things to sort out later; just take the car now."

Anne drew in a breath deeply and centered herself. "Mr. Starkey, I can't accept this car, and I would like—I need you to clarify what kind of things we have to sort out."

"You were with Cliff all weekend; he told me so, Annie. Was he taking drugs?"

"No."

"Well, that's something that needs sorting out, don't you think? I mean…You were there, you say Cliff wasn't on anything and yet…"

"Mr. Starkey…"

"Fuck me! If you aren't the most formal little thing?"

Anne winced.

"Now, don't shrink up like that. My son loved you. He told me so. Fit to light up the world, he was. So excited."

Anne's breath seared her throat and she felt a strange sensation in her chest, as if something was clutching her heart.

"So excited, so elated, and then... Hey, presto! He's dead. And you can be *abso-lute-ly* sure that one of those others who was there with you, out in that fucking desert, knows the whys and wherefores. You can bet on it!" This time the more agitated in speech he got, the more focused and still became his demeanor; his limbs had stopped their constant motion, his gaze locked on Anne. "Christ! I need a Xanax. Do you want one?"

"No, thank you." Anne was mortified to realize her cheeks were wet with tears and her jaw was trembling. "I'm sorry. I didn't mean to…" She shook her head and wiped her eyes.

Cole reared back like a falcon settling on its perch as he saw her distress. He paused. His head bobbed slightly from side to side, increasing the avian resemblance, then he swooped forward, enfolded her in his arms and cradled her head to his narrow breast with one huge yet kindly hand. "Shh. Shh. Baby girl. Don't cry, sweetheart, don't cry. There now, it's all right. There."

Anne squeezed her eyes shut until all she saw was black, all she smelled was French milled soap, burnt lapel, and a whiff of tobacco; all she heard was a consoling murmur so much like Cliff's; and abruptly she stopped crying, as swiftly as silence seems to fall in a forest after a single gunshot.

"Good girl," said Cole as he stepped away from Anne and opened the driver's-side door of the Ferrari. He urged her forward. "C'mon. Get in!" Too discombobulated to argue, Anne did as commanded. Cole circled round to the other side and stepped into the car. Anne nodded placidly, scanned the dash: lots of gauges and buttons and levers. Starkey took the key from her fist and put it in the ignition. "Now, this is a six-speed semiautomatic. When you're going around town it's just gas and brakes, yes?" Anne nodded. "When you want high performance, press the 'sport' button, here."

"Okay."

"The paddle shift is this, just above the steering wheel, see? Just a gentle tap and it's engaged. The Scaglietti goes zero to sixty in about four seconds and zero to two hundred in about ten."

Anne gripped the steering wheel; it gave her a much needed sense of control; she felt herself calming, stabilizing. "I'll never use the sport button."

Cole laughed. "Of course you will. Now, when you come back I'll teach you how to maneuver this thing the way you're meant to. I'm too tired now." He climbed out of the car, came round to Anne's side, and motioned for her to open her window by rotating his cigarette. "You don't mind, do you sweetheart? You have my number?" Anne shook her head. Starkey pulled a slim wallet from his pocket, opened it, and plucked out an old-fashioned calling card with a flourish. He was about to hand it to Anne when he paused and asked, "Do you have a pen?" Anne drew one from her purse and he used it to scribble his number on the back of the card, as the front was, for some reason, adorned with his name alone, before returning it to her, along with the card. "Go. Go on now," he

Chapter 11

GOOD GOLLY MISS MOLLY

After the initial tension, knee quaking as she put her foot to the accelerator, Anne found driving the Ferrari relaxing—particularly listening to the engine's hum and changing rhythm as she cruised the streets. Instead of heading back toward her father's house, she steered north on Coldwater Canyon to the cresting ridge of Mulholland Drive over to Laurel Canyon, until, finally, she wound down Kirkwood to Elusive Drive. The sun was dipping behind the horizon and amber streetlights began to illuminate the canyon. She stopped in front of a cedar shake bungalow, curbed her wheels on the incline, parked the car, shuffled through her bag for her phone, and called her sister. "Hey, Nat. It's Annie. I'm outside your house. Could you come to the door?"

"Why!"

"Could you please, just do it?" Anne responded.

Natalie stepped out onto the porch, phone jammed to her ear. She scanned the road, trying to catch sight of her sister. Anne half-stood in the door of the Ferrari and waved. Natalie's arm dropped from her ear, phone dangling from her hand. "Shit! What the… fuck…is that?" Anne told her. Natalie registered further astonishment and then motioned Anne to follow her into the house.

Inside, Natalie's house was a bit bigger than Anne's apartment: living room, kitchen, two bedrooms, one bath, 980 square feet in total. Finally, a scale Anne could relate to. It smelled like supper—sautéed onions, roast chicken, and something else slightly sweet and creamy. "Tomato soup," said Natalie ladling out two bowls and setting them on the kitchen table. Anne related the events of the past few hours. When she got to the point at which Cole Starkey gifted her his son's sports coupe, Natalie snorted, "He's pretty high-functioning for an addict!"

"Nat, what am I going to do?"

"Annie, doll, don't let yourself get violined."

Anne raised an eyebrow, "Violined?"

"As in: don't let yourself get played like one, or manipulated." She gave Anne a hard stare. "Expensive gifts given and secret histories shared? Please! They're trying to control you. Starkey is trying to manipulate you. So is Becky, and Shamari makes three."

Anne tasted her soup. "This is delicious."

"Are you listening to me? Him giving you the car is like Dad trying to give you the paintings. What is it with men that age?"

"I think there's about a twenty-year gap there, and I'm listening," Anne assured Natalie.

"He looks eighty," said Natalie.

"I guess that's the pills…you wouldn't believe what was lying around his house," Anne answered, remembering burn marks in the upholstery, glinting silver things embedded in the oriental rugs, and Cole's casual offer of Xanax.

"Whatever. However old he is, it's the same principle. And he isn't even Dad, but he's playing the same games. Do you think he…no…I can barely say it…Anne, do you think Mr. Starkey has designs on you?"

"That's disgusting, Natalie."

"Believe me, I know. "Natalie raked her hand back through her graying hair. "They're trying to engender a sense of obligation, every single fucking one of them. A very deep sense of obligation. It's fucking creepy, sister mine."

"His son is dead. Get your head out… What if Mr. Starkey's right? What if Cliff was—what if it wasn't an overdose; what if it was a homicide?"

"In that case he should talk to the police or the DA, or hire a private investigator. What can he possibly expect you to do about it? For God's sake Annie, don't get messed up in this. Hello! Have you been listening to me? Movie people have a long, ugly history of hushing up murder. I can think of three suspicious deaths—no four, four that never came to trial. Don't mess with these people. That is, if there's anything really to mess with. Could all be a chemically induced delusion."

"Mr. Starkey wasn't delusional. And, he's music, not movies."

"Even worse. And I'm talking about more than one person here. Anyway, you'd be surprised what grief can do to your head," Natalie asserted. Anne studied the contents of her bowl and then looked up. "I'm not talking about you. Who wants to think their son partied too hard and died?"

Anne wondered if she'd been the guest of honor at this particular party or not. "Nat?"

"What?"

"How do you think a sex club operates?" Anne inquired.

"I guess you probably pay some kind of fee and then you go have sex with like-minded people. Why? Is there something I should know?"

"That detective, Vasquez from Palm Springs, wanted to know if I knew about a club there, The Buccaneers."

"What? The *Buccaneers*?" Natalie had a wry expression on her face. "Don't tell me… It's where you go to have pirate sex? Like, with a parrot on your shoulder?"

"Natalie! You never take me seriously!"

"How about… Perverts of the Caribbean?" She rolled her eyes, "Buccaneer, oh pul-eeze! Who thinks of these things?" Suddenly she became indignant, "Why did Vasquez ask you that? Wait, Cliff didn't ask you to go there with him, did he?"

"No!" Anne tried not to let her mind slide down any distracting avenues. "I don't know why he asked me. Do you—do you think they hand out mood enhancers at clubs like that?"

"You mean like sex toys, or are you talking about Viagra?"

"Viagra. Drugs."

"I can't imagine they'd take on the liability. No. But I'm

sure your fellow club mates would have plenty on hand. Do you think that's why the detective wanted to know? That he thought Cliff went to The Buccaneers and—"

Anne, mentally quelling several of her own questions, felt a sudden need to change the subject, "Those deaths you mentioned—the four hushed-up Hollywood deaths—were they recent?"

"Define 'recent,' " replied Natalie.

"See! I thought so. You're talking about the thirties, or something," accused Anne, "I know, it's probably in your teaching syllabus: *Depravity and Death in Art Deco L.A.* What? Next you're going to tell me Uncle Manny dated Thelma Todd. People can't, people don't do things like that anymore!

"Don't be naïve, Annie."

"I'm not."

A cell phone let out a piercing, god-awful trill. "I think that's you, Annie."

Anne withdrew the phone from her purse, glanced at the screen, sighed, and answered. "Hi Dad."

"Your car's here. Where the hell are you?" Anne had already begun rubbing her eyes with the base of her palm even before Bob had spoken with his usual tact and delicacy. Natalie stood up, gave Anne a commiserating glance, shook her head, and cleared the soup plates away.

Anne arrived back at her father's house and parked the Ferrari, very carefully, in the garage. Walking inside, she found, with a twinge of guilt and a wave of relief that Bob was out at his weekly bridge game. While he was gone it seemed the perfect time to take a voyage on the Internet Sea, all in the name of "research." First up, she checked out the Ferrari. Unsurprisingly, it was an extravagance; it cost close to $400,000 and there were only around fifty of them in the continental United States.

What further mysteries would Google reveal? She typed in "Cole Starkey." The search took 0.32 seconds and the name spilled out 448,000 results: he had sold his record label in the mid-nineties and now was a man of even more considerable means and influence than before. Anne was boggled by the means. She knew her father was more than well-to-do, but the search results revealed that Starkey existed in an entirely different class; he didn't so much put Bob Brown in the shade as eclipse him. Anne's father was worth millions, Cliff's, billions. Cliff hadn't mentioned any siblings, and according to Wikipedia he was an only child. With Mr. Starkey's numerous wives, Anne concluded he must have knocked all the viability from his sperm with an excess of coke sometime in the mid-seventies. Coke again, it seemed to be on her mind.

Finally, she searched for "Buccaneers Palm Springs," and when the club's home site popped up she clicked on it. The copy was arch and peculiar, and the meaning wasn't exactly concealed, "For men who crave boundless adventure, an island of pleasure awaits you. Whatever your desire we'll fulfill it. Taste the lash, revel in forbidden sights, or relax in our anatomically correct spa." Anatomically correct spa? Was that a spa with a penis shaped waterspout? Anne didn't really find this appealing, but then she obviously wasn't part of the target clientele. So Detective Vasquez was implying that Cliff was somehow associated with what appeared to be a gay sex club? It didn't make sense to her, and she couldn't pretend to understand what the police were thinking, but she was determined to find out.

Anne put her laptop to sleep. A few minutes later, after a little hurried searching through her pockets followed by a semi-frenzied rifling through the contents of her purse dumped on the bed, she had the two calling cards she had collected earlier that day. She picked up the detective's card and gazed at the multiple phone numbers as if they could offer up answers. What was it about The Buccaneers? Had the police received a tip that linked Cliff to the club? Or was there a phone record; did that provide the link? Had he left his cell phone at the Nelsons'? If the Nelsons had turned the phone over to the police, wouldn't it have been returned to his next of kin, like the car? His father had insisted he hadn't died in the Ferrari. How could he know, anyway? Did he die at the club? Had Cliff tasted the lash or reveled in forbidden sights at The Buccaneers? These questions chittered, nattered, chattered at her like excited chimpanzees, but the loudest was the one she didn't want to think about; they had had sex several, blissful times and foremost in her mind was the last, with the split condom: he said he hadn't been in a relationship for six and a half months. What exactly did he mean?

There it was again, the now familiar surge of nausea. Moments later she was cooling her cheek against the tile floor of the bathroom having introduced her dinner to the toilet bowl. Eventually, the nausea subsiding and realizing the awkwardness of her position, she got up. After brushing her teeth, she took off her clothes and hopped into the shower. There she let the stream drench her skin, her feet turning pink against the porcelain, the insistent hot pelting of water left her drifting. Finding no shampoo, she lathered up a bar of soap and scrubbed at her scalp as if she were hoping to break through her skull and scour her brain clear of the unpleasant thoughts that assailed her. She stood so long under the spray that it turned cold, something of which she only became aware when she started shivering. Anne came to her senses, shut off the water and rigorously toweled herself dry. Feeling as if every cell in her body was crying for rest, she dragged herself to her bedroom, slipped on a fresh pair of pajamas, and crawled into bed. It was all of nine o'clock.

A couple of hours later, Anne woke to the sound of her father slamming his car door closed. She walked out into the hall landing and peered down the stairs in time to see him enter the house.

"Dad?"

"Hey, pumpkin! Your dad is on a winning streak. How's about I make you an ice cream sundae?" Bob Brown never tired of telling his daughter with pride how he had been a soda jerk as a fourteen-year-old in 1943, and while she was growing up he had made her egg creams, chocolate phosphates, black cows, banana splits, and milk shakes. "Eat your ice cream, it's full of protein!" he would urge. Anne had always assumed he'd been indulgent toward her because of the guilt of having been around so rarely. In reality, he always worried she didn't eat enough. "Honey, were you asleep?" Anne shook her head and came downstairs. She felt ravenous.

As always, Anne found watching her father make sundaes peaceful and lulling. It showed an aspect of his character usually hidden, one that Anne imagined only she was privy to. He put a cup of sugar and a dash of salt in a cast iron skillet with a quarter cup of water and cranked up the burner until the water and sugar formed boiling crackling syrup. Then, he turned the flame all the way down and added four ounces of bitter chocolate. Once the chocolate was melted he stirred

in a pat of butter and the chocolate sauce went silky. Anne
scooped out the vanilla ice cream and her father poured on
the chocolate. When it hit the frosty ice cream the sauce
stiffened into something like taffy. Nobody made a sundae
like her father. He handed her a spoon.

"You're still looking a little peaked to me. How you doing?"

"Fine," she forced herself to grin. She found herself wanting
to protect him from the knowledge that earlier that evening
she had boarded the Anxiety Express and was now hurtling
her way deep into her darkest and most neurotic imaginings.
She felt she had to guard him from her sudden almost-
certainty that Cliff was gay or bisexual or super-promiscuous
and drug-happy, that she'd been infected with an incurable
disease or was pregnant. Of course, most of all, she had to
prevent him from getting wind of her wretched judgment, of
her newfound ability to jump to any and all dismal or bizarre
conclusions that came to mind. So instead she just told him
the story of Mr. Starkey and her unexpected inheritance. Her
father was not pleased. She could see him working his jaw.
Any minute she expected an eruption of molten invective,
but he surprised her and tamped his temper down, way, way,
down.

Bob noted her perplexed expression. "Don't look so shocked,
kiddo. I'm going to tell you something my cardiologist told
me. Sometimes in this life all you can change is your attitude."

"I'm sorry, Dad. What?"

"Sometimes in this life all you can change is your attitude."
On first hearing, it sounded like a bromide, but…

Anne swirled some chocolate around the tip of her spoon and

thought about her overwhelming desire to return to New York. She let the ice cream sundae slip down her throat and thought of the multitude of things in life that were agitating her. It sounded trite, but on reflection, what the physician said felt right; it could apply to her too. She gathered up another spoonful. Her current attitude was urging her to get away; she was anxious about what lay ahead if she stayed in L.A.; she had to choose between fight or flight. She had three more days before she could take a pregnancy test, at least another week until she could be tested for HIV. Obviously, the development of the latter was unlikely, but that didn't make her feel any better. It didn't do much good knowing she was spinning out of control when her entire world was tilting off its axis. Suddenly her conversation with Cliff at Las Palmas del Rio after the condom broke seemed much more significant. "Dad? Do you think I could get in to see your doctor in the next couple of weeks?"

"Not a problem, Chipmunk."

Chapter 12

WORD UP

A week passed, then another, and Anne, as if seeking a state of stasis, remained cloistered in her father's house like a silent-film star recently introduced to sound. She resisted her sister's bold attempts to penetrate her psychological defenses (even if the strain of maintaining that resistance was wearying) and tried to accustom herself to her father's barely disguised watchfulness. The night of the Academy Awards broadcast he donned earphones to watch the three-hour ceremony to ensure Anne's presence. She sat beside him reading *The Places in Between,* an account of a walk across Afghanistan that was an ideal distraction from her current circumstances as it was so far from them. She was engrossed when a tap on her knee brought her back to the room. Bob gestured at the screen and Anne saw none other than James Johnson accepting the Oscar for Best Actor, a surprise, not just because of her acquaintance with him but also because he often struck her as having a performance range that ran from righteous to righteously indignant, i.e., he didn't so much transform for the camera as gaze heavenward, or glower. She returned her attention to the book but a few minutes later felt another tap, this time indicating the appearance of Bill Aagard graciously (or, at least, faux graciously) clapping in a reaction shot as another nominee beat him to Best Director.

Every day she wiped the Scaglietti down with a diaper and then locked the garage door. Every day she walked down to

Brighton Way or Canon Drive for a chocolate fix and then on to the library, where she would sit reading for hours. She liked glancing up to see purposeful old people with their armloads of books, teenagers traveling in pods and decked out in gadgetry. Then one day—it was a Friday—Anne agreed to meet Keir Bloomfield for tea at The Peninsula in Beverly Hills to discuss his "adaptation" of her novel. She had decided on a new course for handling stress while waiting for her medical appointment; that is, she would do her best to entirely ignore and avoid all thoughts pertaining to it. She was determined to keep them compartmentalized (i.e., locked away) and to stay busy. If someone had mentioned the word *denial* she would likely have looked shocked. A meeting with Keir Bloomfield about something that she should have cared very much about but that now barely sparked any interest in her seemed an appropriate diversion.

When Anne stepped into the hotel lobby she was directed to what was called the Living Room. The space was decorated in Hollywood Regency style: marble floors, Aubusson carpets, tall windows that let in golden shafts of light, ivory walls, fatly upholstered butter-yellow couches interspersed with black lacquered chairs around damask-draped coffee tables set with silver and porcelain.

Keir was notably absent, instead, Anne saw Toni Todd sipping from a champagne flute and Tessa Aagard studying a menu card. Despite an age difference of fifty years, both women's faces had a sculptural, impassive, shiny-skinned, plump-cheeked quality Anne found unnerving. Hollywood replicants. Botox, Rejuvaderm, facelifts, fat injections. She looked around; surfaces glinted with polish, bibelots and massive floral arrangements stood out in the refined clarity of smog-free winter sunshine. Tessa glanced up from her menu, "Oh, you're here!" She stood and embraced Anne as if she were her oldest friend; her clingy knit top revealed spindly arms, and her tight trousers emphasized her pelvic area. Anne estimated Tessa was about five-foot-eight and she was sure she wore a size two; Anne herself was significantly shorter and a size four. Toni rose, dressed in shades of cream, with a twining necklace of coral branches, mother-of-pearl, and diamonds sparkling around her neck. Anne was duly dazzled.

Toni was well used to this reaction. She touched her fingertips to the mix of seashells and jewels at her throat and tried to dispel the aura of glamour by explaining it away. "Something shiny to distract the eye. Do you know Duquette?"

Anne shook her head, "No."

"Tony Duquette, he did this," indicating the necklace. "At my age, wearing pale colors to bounce light up to the face has such a becoming effect." Toni took Anne by the hands. Anne wondered why relative strangers in California were so demonstrative. She couldn't decide whether it was entirely genuine or entirely artificial, either way she found it hard to get used to. "Keir sends his apologies. He could barely get out of bed this morning," she smiled sadly at Anne, a testament to her power to project, considering her brow couldn't move; her huge darkly dramatic eyes stood in sharp contrast to her powdered skin and ashy white hair.

Anne could feel the strength of sinew in Toni's hands. Keir wasn't here because he was sleeping? He was depressed? While she wondered about Keir's mental state she caught the scent of roses with some other cool, damp, sweet scent underlying it. Violets. Anne found herself idly pondering: if she had known her grandmothers, would they have smelled this way? Her mother's mother had died of cancer before she was born. Her father's mother, had she been alive, would be an inconceivable one hundred and seventeen. "Inconsolable. Simply inconsolable." Toni continued. "We're so sorry we didn't have a chance to speak to you at the funeral."

Anne remembered Keir and Toni at the funeral. Keir was weeping nonstop. Toni's hand, glinting with diamonds, never left his shoulder. What was their story? And why were Toni and Tessa in the tearoom and not Keir?

Tessa sat and patted the seat beside her on the sofa. "Me too, I really meant to talk to you at the funeral so I invited myself along. Sit."

As Anne planted herself next to Tessa, Tessa reached around and gave Anne another hug, the kind that twists your head ninety degrees and flattens your nose into someone else's knobby shoulder. Toni took her place on an ebonized chair and there were smiles all around. Anne was reminded of a window display at Bloomingdale's. She couldn't help suspect that these open displays of affection were about as sincere and heartfelt as a model's smile on the cover of a magazine or the over-the-top clinging and purring backstage at a secondary school play.

Tessa said bluntly, "We saw you talking to that detective."

"Detective Vasquez," Toni added.

"After the service," Tessa clarified, unnecessarily.

"I met him the other day at the police station," said Anne. "He asked me about drugs and nightclubs." She looked at one and then the other to see if their faces registered any reaction, though it was hard to see through all that cosmetic work.

Tessa nodded. Toni motioned to a waiter and, almost instantly, a full-on formal tea was delivered with strawberries and Chantilly cream in three long-stemmed crystal coups, scones, and finger sandwiches, and a three-tiered platter of petit fours and pastry. Tea with the ladies struck Anne as a surreal addition to an already bizarre situation. She found herself wondering when the Mad Hatter would arrive.

"I'm starved," said Tessa, scraping the cream from her strawberries and placing a single sandwich and a solitary tart on her plate. Toni glanced disapprovingly in Tessa's direction and then turned to Anne.

"Sometimes it's indecipherable, how events throw people together, don't you think?" asked Toni.

"I suppose so," countered Anne, noncommittally.

"We thought we could illuminate things," said Toni.

Tessa agreed, "Back story. Fill you in."

"An overview," Toni finished the thought.

"Thank you. I shouldn't be surprised, but everybody has been so, so pleasant to me, so eager to talk. Even Mr. Starkey," said Anne, filling her plate.

"What? You had a conversation with Cliff's father?" asked Tessa incredulously.

"At his house," Anne answered.

"That is, my poor child, very unusual," stated Toni, wearing an enigmatic expression on her taut face. She was quiet for a moment, casting her gaze upward as if trying to examine the inside of her skull for some vague notion, then she drawled, "Where to begin?" in a theatrical manner that would have made Bette Davis proud.

Before she had summoned the words, Tessa made a fluttering gesture with her hands and interjected, "Maybe I can explain?" Toni merely nodded, as if she had been expecting a prompt, or at least some additional dialogue. Once again Anne couldn't help but note the artificiality, and more than a note of studied performance. "Did you know Cliff represented James Johnson and Ben Haber?" asked Tessa.

"I knew he represented Johnson."

"And they both just worked with Bill, my husband," Tessa explained as Anne remembered something she'd read in a text on dramaturgy that insisted important points should be repeated in threes.

"Oh." Anne looked to Toni and continued, "Does he—did he represent Keir, too?"

Toni set her teacup down. "Just friends, old friends. I think Cliff told you about their rather juvenile supper club."

The motto suddenly popped into Anne's head, "*Entertainment or Death?*"

Toni could barely suppress her distaste. "Precisely. Keir tells me he coined the phrase. What did they call themselves?" This was clearly rhetorical so Anne allowed herself to look wide-eyed and curious before Toni supplied her own answer: "The Cannibal Club, that was it. One can only hope the name was metaphorical. Of course, that was…but still, bonds from your youth…" she picked up a finger sandwich and bit it crisply in two.

Anne remembered her dinner conversation that first night in Palm Springs, and Cliff's somewhat disrespectful tone when speaking to Keir. "I had no idea. The Cannibal Club—"

"It's true," said Toni. "From what I gather, Cliff was the alpha dog of that pack. They came from all over for the funeral. New York, London…"

"Van Nuys," Tessa chimed in, absurdly. Toni gave a little moue then raised an index finger to her lips to conceal a smile elicited by this inapt mention of a déclassé valley location. Toni cleared her throat, "There I go, off on a tangent. Tessa, dear, you may have the floor."

"Well, Anne, you might know this already because of your Dad, but anyway, when you work on a movie it kind of takes over your life: incredibly long hours, intense short relationships. You're with the same people ten to sixteen hours a day for six to twelve months. You kind of become like a family." Tessa had rearranged the position of the two items on her plate in the course of this short speech over and over again but she hadn't eaten a thing.

"A family," reiterated Toni, "a dysfunctional film family."

"That's my point," added Tessa. "Like all families, there are flare-ups."

"And reconciliations," said Toni.

"That's right," Tessa wrestled the conversation back with amusing ill grace. "Becky's studio made Bill's last film—it won't be released until next year—but there were a few bumps along the road during the shoot that the Nelsons were trying to smooth over because at some point, the film family has to come back together and do publicity."

"What kind of bumps along the road?" asked Anne, wondering if they were referring to the "scandalous situation" in which someone was "beyond hammered, beyond high."

"The first problem was pretty minor. Ben, Ben Haber worked for about three weeks. It was his first feature. He was kind of keyed up, anxious to get it right, really intense, but in all the wrong directions. He was doing a love scene, he was supposed to be doing a love scene with this incredibly cute actress, and we were rolling and I was sitting next to Bill and we were watching the take and Ben does this thing. I mean he knuckles this girl on the arm; he picks up his fist and he drags his knuckles down her arm, like a monkey, like a chimp, like some ape just smacking her to signal his attraction. I mean, he was mauling her: chemistry zero! I can't believe it. Bill has his hand over his mouth and I can see his face is turning red but he lets them finish the scene. And after he yells cut, he turns to me and smiles this huge fake smile, like a ventriloquist, and between his teeth he says to me, 'Oh, that was pretty!' And then he walks over to Ben and Sloan—I mean the poor girl—and he tells them he's very happy with them but he wants them to try it again. This time he wants them to imagine it's pitch black in the room and they can't see a thing; he wants them to close their eyes, and play it like they're out of their mind in love and they're discovering each other for the first time in the dark. You know, I thought it was brilliant direction…but they ended up doing sixty-four takes."

"And that's a lot?" asked Anne, all innocence.

Toni snorted. "That's sadistic."

Tessa blinked rapidly and swallowed up a heaping spoonful of cream.

"Thank God," said Toni, watching Tessa ingest 100 calories. "I know, you can say I'm a diva, but really…"

"Obviously Toni's right: it seems an insanely high number, real Kubrick territory, but there were reasons. It might appear, at first glance that Bill was being a crazy perfectionist. I mean… if you break down a shooting day into setups for each scene, then this one, which should have taken a couple of hours, took twelve and put them behind schedule, which in turn made everybody from the crew to the studio edgy because of the increased cost… Well, let's just say it doesn't look good for Bill. He's the director, point man for the people who actually make the movie… He's supposed to do everything as efficiently as he can so as not to excite the attention of the studio or its multitude of bean-counting minions. Naturally, a delay of that kind makes everyone antsy, but, as I said, there were reasons. One, in particular: it was very hard for Bill to get an actual, mm, *performance* out of Ben. I suppose you'd say he had no choice—he had to do take after take—because he couldn't fire him as he was a political hire."

"I thought I was following, but you just lost me," Anne said.

"Uh. Well. It's like this… Certain…stars…" began Tessa.

"Oh, come on, just spit it out dear," urged Toni. She gave Anne a portentous look.

"Okay. James Johnson was one of the," Tessa framed her next word with air quotes, "producers." She looked at Anne pointedly and then went on, "One of the producers on the movie. And he had certain demands that had to be met for him to take the role."

Toni butted in. "Anne, you seem like a very bright young lady. Are you familiar with the term 'chicken hawk'?"

Anne's eyes widened. "In what context?"

"As in when James Johnson forces casting choices because he likes sleeping with younger men," said Toni, seemingly oblivious that her husband was her junior by thirty-five years.

Anne immediately thought of Shamari, her fierce protection of her three children, her multimillion dollar home, and her designer clothes. Then Anne thought of Shamari's mixture of active charity, insightful pragmatism, and knowledgeable pessimism. "Is there a reason you're outing James Johnson to me?" she asked, carefully keeping her tone light and polite.

"Besides the fact your inamorata just died under somewhat suspicious circumstances?" *Inamorata*? From the Latin, or Italian, meaning ladylove, or girlfriend. Toni had a habit of using words for the way they sounded rather than what they meant. In general, people got the gist. Anne clenched her linen napkin in her hand and took her cue from Tessa, who plowed on determinedly.

"Thank you, Toni," said Tessa, meaning anything but. "So. We've got James: big star but a pious, churchgoing, family man. Right?"

"From what Toni has said so far, my guess is you're going to tell me that's not the case," said Anne, trying to keep the cynicism out of her voice.

"Yep. Well, no. That is, not exactly. Let me… Anyway, when a movie star finishes their work on a film it's customary for them to hand out gifts to the crew, like jackets, or baseball caps, bottles of champagne, stuff like that. Just kind of a nice memento for everybody who worked together, so, the day James wraps, his assistant starts handing out these cards, like the ones you get at Christmas when someone's given to charity in your name. On the outside of the envelope it says *from: James Johnson*, and on the inside there's your name in the middle of the card and it says in big bold letters you've given a hundred dollars to 'No to Drugs—Yes to Life.' Like, most people would prefer something tangible, but you can't argue with a charitable donation, right? It's all for the good."

"Right," said Anne.

"Well, it turns out when the assistant hands the card to Bill, the donation's made out for ten grand," she paused, then repeated it again for emphasis, "ten grand, ten thousand dollars… When he flips it over and reads the fine print on the back of the card it states this nonprofit, this 'No to Drugs—Yes to Life' campaign is run by The Church of Clientology. So this thing that appears innocuous and well-meaning is, in fact, loaded with bullshit associations he doesn't want any part of. And, Bill, he goes off. Collars the assistant, gets his first A.D. to call Johnson back to the set, but it turns out Johnson's already left, left for good, done with the movie. So he turns to me in the middle of the set—*in the middle of the set*—and starts yelling, which is totally out of character, because I'm telling you, this man—this man is all about the image. And he asks, well no, he's hollering. How would it go down if he—Bill— started handing out beaucoup bucks which were supposedly in aid of charity but actually, and I'm quoting here, *in creepy promotion of a fucking nutty pseudo-religion created by a fifth-rate science fiction hack writer*? Johnson must have really pressed Bill's berserk button because he mentioned J. Paul Stoddard by name and began ranting about Stoddard's history of mental illness and spousal abuse, then he frothed that Clientology was nothing more than a crock of shit get-rich-quick scheme invented to bilk the credulous, massage the egos of the narcissistic, and cheat the government. And all the time I was shriveling inside thinking "WHOA! Whoa there! Even if I agree with you, the last place you want broadcast your private views are in the middle of a film set, in front of the star's assistant, at the top of your lungs. It was the meltdown-to-end-all-meltdowns."

"Ben Haber's a Clientologist; Cliff told me," said Anne quietly, "second-generation, or something."

"And Shamari is a congregant at First African Baptist—do we sense a conflict?" Toni inquired primly.

Anne helped herself to another cup of tea and loaded up her plate for a second helping. She wondered if it was just the result of stress and anxiety, but all her senses seemed sharper, more acute. And what was this thing going on with the light? Surely it couldn't be that much more luminous in California than it was in New York? Los Angeles had southern latitude, but that wouldn't account for the way things glowed and glistened; the strawberries heaped in front of her, the sunlit leaves emerald and shimmering and swaying outside the windows, Toni's gem-blue eyes. Everything had a scent; sometimes it was good, and sometimes it was bad. Plus, the way she was eating: one minute compelled to satisfying a craving, the next struggling not to messily unswallow. She squeezed a wedge of lemon into her tea and watched it go from murky brown to translucent hazel. "Beautiful," she thought. She looked up to see Toni and Tessa regarding her questioningly.

"No. I get what you're saying," said Anne, adding a spoon of sugar to her cup. "At least part of it. I can't think of a single major African American movie star who's openly gay."

"Not one," agreed Tessa.

"Not one major American male star, period," Toni said, fluttering her famous eyelashes in a manner that could only be described as ironic.

"And I guess," Anne paused before continuing, "that accounts for the Clientology involvement, too."

Toni and Tessa nodded in unison.

"Assessing," said Toni.

"Or blackmail, depends on what you want to call it," said Tessa.

Toni stood up. "Well, my darlings, I must fly. Kisses!" She made her exit, regal, upright, her bearing the result of years of Pilates, calcium supplements, and predawn miles in the pool.

Tessa and Anne watched her progress across the room, and then she was gone. Tessa sat back down. Anne hesitated and then did the same. "Old school, all the way," said Tessa, referring to Toni. The room seemed somewhat diminished by the star's absence. "She and Lauren Bacall," Tessa went on, "Keir's top scribe, and Bacall's former pool boy is pulling in twenty mill a picture." Tessa settled back in her seat. Anne thought it was funny that people in Hollywood actually ended up sounding like the blurbs in *Variety*. "Fantastic talents, both of them, just don't get between them and what they hold dear." Tessa motioned to the waiter and asked for a Greyhound. On its arrival she gulped down the grapefruit juice and vodka like a breakfast drink and said, "God! I'd so much rather imbibe my calories than eat them! Want one?" Anne just shook her head and smiled. "You know all about Toni and Keir, don't you?" Tessa asked. Anne knew when to play dumb. She shook her head, offered up a curious sounding "No," with an unspoken *do tell* appended, leaned forward slightly, composed her features into their best attentive expression and listened intently.

Chapter 13

TWISTING BY THE POOL

Carrot-topped Keir Bloomfield smeared zinc oxide over the bridge of his freckled nose and jammed a beloved golf cap that even he had dubbed "dorky" down on the crown of his head. He was a sophomore in college (Dartmouth, in nowhere, New Hampshire) and he had returned home for the summer to the intense heat and sun of Southern California. He longed for gray skies and the stolid disposition of New Englanders. He was instead accompanying his landscape architect mom on a round through Beverly Hills. She had him scampering over flawless lawns, hauling and placing, then replacing, botanical specimens. Keir didn't like to sweat. For the record, he didn't really like being outdoors at all. He knew better than to complain. He was very familiar with indomitable single mom Zoe Bloomfield's stock answer to any and all filial dissent, "I'm putting you through college all by myself, and you don't want to help me out?" Then he got the incredulous look and the martyr's dismissive twist of the head. He had four more weeks before he could return to school. Keir drove to their last stop. Zoe reached to turn off the car radio. He swatted her hand away. "What is that noise?" she demanded.

"It's the Thompson Twins, and I'm driving."

"And that gives you license to make me insane?"

"Ma, we're almost there."

They arrived at a strange hybrid of Art Deco and Castilian Castle on Coldwater Canyon. The garden was English-style and troublesome to maintain. The owner was Toni Todd: legendary beauty; husband-collector; and, currently, Hollywood's comeback queen, as she had just recently maneuvered her way, at nearly sixty, into a leading role in a nighttime super-soap. In July, the show was still on hiatus so Toni was at home, often wandering the sprawling estate, making "improvements." Ms. Bloomfield had cautioned Keir to stay out of Toni's way, but to no avail; Keir was doing his best to conceal himself under a shade tree when Toni spotted his pallid white skin practically shining out against a dense background of blossoms and greens.

"Funny dumpling, come here!" she commanded. Keir obeyed. "You can help me hang some pictures. Think you can do that?"

"Yes, ma'am," Keir replied.

"And, then afterward if you're overheated you can take a dip in the pool."

"But my mom…"

Toni interrupted, "That's right, you're Amanda's boy. Keir made a funny little popping sound like a guppy. "Amanda!" she called out.

Ms. Bloomfield looked up from her sketchpad. She squinted in Toni's direction.

"Amanda! It's getting late. You go on home. I'm going to

require your boy's services, a little manpower. I promise I won't keep him more than an hour, then I'll drop him off at your place."

"Mrs. Todd, ma'am, Mom's name is Zoe."

She turned to Keir, with a slightly frightening smile on her face. "Of course it is. Don't worry. Don't fret. I'll ferry you home, or you can borrow one of the cars. Unless you don't want to," she said, pausing by a massive, intricately carved double front door. To Keir, who lived with his mother in a depressingly sunny window box of a house in Burbank, it looked like the gateway to some promised other world, a rich, dark, cool place, reminiscent, in some ways, of what he'd left behind at Dartmouth. Toni observed Keir surreptitiously, noting the hungriness in his eyes; she felt a kind of hunger too; she had some interesting notions about male vitality and the regenerative powers of sex, and this particular nineteen-year-old suited her perfectly.

At the end of summer, after Ms. Todd and Mr. Bloomfield had enjoyed several rigorous and restorative sessions, she made him a proposition; an entrée into the film industry in exchange for a suitable period of physical, if not matrimonial, devotion. When Keir replied earnestly that he usually preferred the company of men, Toni countered, "One must always cultivate friendship. I'm talking about marriage. When you get older you'll come to appreciate what I mean."

At twenty-one, after a love affair with a tan, domineering, lunkheaded lacrosse player went sour, a despondent Keir graduated from Dartmouth and took a job Toni had arranged for him as assistant to a British director. The opus was a comic book turned major motion picture. Keir listened dutifully as the director complained, with consummate skill, of being "nobbled by the malevolent FACKING studio" and then virtually leapt as he was sent to fetch his laundry, market for delicacies at Irvine Ranch Market and Chalet Gourmet, tend his brick-sized Motorola cell phone, and drive him from club to club on his evenings off. Then there was one notable three a.m. when he had to rush to the director's Santa Monica rental in the deep of the night to catch a blue jay that was systematically flying into every window in the house in an attempt to escape. The crystals of white powder clinging to his nostrils could perhaps explain why the director wasn't able to throw a towel over the bird himself and toss it outside; something that could also provide a clue to the frenzied stream of kibitzing he subjected Keir to while he chased the unfortunate animal down.

After the bird incident, the director found Keir indispensable. He relied on him for practically everything. He kept him by his side like a lithe good-luck charm. It was on one such occasion while Ian (the director) and Keir were in an unusually intimate situation (or, by that time, a not-so-unusually intimate situation) that Keir took an unmistakable step up the ladder of success. He was reading the day's new script pages out loud while Ian bemoaned his $100 million "filmic fiasco" and laid his perspiring forehead against the younger man's bare pelvis, when Keir chimed in with what seemed to Ian to be surprisingly good notes. Thus, his screenwriting career was born.

Delighted, Toni bought him a Lexus, then, a few years later on his twenty-fifth birthday, a condo on Wilshire in Westwood.

When he was twenty-seven, Keir nursed Toni through her second face-lift, a fairly primitive affair involving an early-model cosmetic laser that turned her skin to strawberry jelly, along with incisions under the chin, behind the ears, and in the eyes' orbit just below her brows. He served her chilled pineapple juice with a straw and a Vicodin chaser, plumped pillows, applied antibiotic salve, and on the hour placed ice packs around her swollen face. All the while, Toni's white Persian cat, Renee, sat on Toni's chest and stared up at her adoringly. The cat creeped Keir out, and, besides, all that fur couldn't be sanitary. But, every time he shooed Renee away, Toni patted the bed and the cat flounced back into place. A week later, after he'd driven her to the surgeon to have her sutures examined, the doctor puzzled over why the stitches above Toni's eyes had disappeared. Keir had no doubt the cat had licked them out but thought it better not to mention it to Toni, who was delighted at her rejuvenation. For his devotion during her transformation back to forty, he was secured representation at CAA, and finally, when he turned twenty-nine, she called in his debt and they were wed.

★★★

Tessa finished her second Greyhound. "I think the standard sentiment under these circumstances is, I've got your back. But maybe watch your back, yeah, watch your back, would be more apropos."

Chapter 14

COME FLY WITH ME

Back in her father's kitchen on Crescent Drive, indulging in a delayed freak-out, Anne began calling airlines trying to book a red-eye back to New York. The cost of a last-minute ticket was astronomically ridiculous… She was more than aware she was experiencing the wildest of wild mood swings. Anne was seriously considering abandoning L.A. and what had, not so long ago, seemed to be a very lucrative movie deal but now was confirmed to be mere illusion. However, she couldn't just grab the nettle and slam down another thousand on her credit card. She couldn't. There were things she needed to do there first.

Bob materialized in the doorway. "What's the matter now?" he asked. After she told him, he grunted and left the room only to return a moment later jangling his car keys. "Okay, I'm taking you to Van Nuys."

"What?" Anne couldn't imagine what the link could be between what she had told Bob and what he had just said. "Van Nuys?"

"It's an airport," he responded. "Joe Merlin's flying to Manhattan tonight and he'll bring you back Thursday. Okay with you, princess?"

Joseph Merlin was an independent producer notorious for

his temper and lauded for his impeccable taste. He joked he was too fat to fly commercial, but he had joined the Big Boys' Club when he sold his company and trademark to Universal and bought a Learjet. He had since parted ways with the studio, but he retained the services of a full-time flight crew and the privilege of traveling whenever he pleased.

On the ride over the hill Bob told Anne, "Okay, everybody pretty much hates Joe. He's loud. He's rude. Crass is a nice description. But he owes me, I trust him, which is more than I can say about a lot of people in this town, and he'll look out for you. If you get him going on movies, or movie history, he knows his stuff and he's good company. Ask him about silent movies and before you know it you'll be home. I'm worried about you, kiddo. You okay?"

"I'm fine, Dad. I just have a couple of things I have to do in New York."

Anne's father looked like he didn't believe her for a second. "You got your coat?"

"It's in the back seat."

"What about your doctor's appointment?" he asked.

"I'll call from New York and reschedule."

"Phfff!" Bob exhaled.

Anne boarded the plane shortly after six p.m. and was greeted by a tall, glossily blond-haired and singularly beautiful flight attendant. She saw two assistants in expensive suits sitting with open laptops balanced on their knees. At the front of the plane in the cockpit she glimpsed the pilot and copilot, both intent on the instruments and definitely ex–Air Force. However, Anne's attention was truly drawn to one person seated halfway down the plane. There he was, red-faced, sweating, tugging at his tie, and yelling into his phone: Joe Merlin. "Fucking shit!" he sputtered, spittle flying from the corners of his mouth. "You tell her it's not a fucking 'blatant' fuckwad advertisement! It's a fucking feature film! And product placement is something for which yours truly is eternally grateful. Tell her 'her character' would BLOW SATAN HIMSELF for a chance to drive a BMW. You got that? How the hell does she think I pay for these things, anyway? Goddamn motherfucking cocksucking bastard of all bitch-bastards! Goddamn it to hell! God damn HER to hell!" he said in enthusiastic farewell, then glanced up, to see Anne staring at him, frozen in place and blinking like a rabbit that was fervently hoping that the lights heading toward it were not at all dangerous. Strangely, as soon as he noticed her presence Anne unfroze and walked, albeit warily, to him. Merlin wiped his perspiring brow with a silk handkerchief, hefted his not inconsiderable bulk to his feet with some effort, and offered his hand to Anne to shake. Suddenly his voice was low and pleasingly well-modulated, "Hello, Anne. I'm Joe." Indicating a seat directly across from him he said, "Please." Anne sat. He patted her shoulder and she could feel her spine compress. Hand still on her shoulder, he leaned slightly forward and peered into her face. "Your dad's a lantzman, a mensch, you know these words?"

"I do."

The flight attendant made her way toward them. "Excuse me, Mr. Merlin, Ms. Brown, we're about to take off. Could I ask you to buckle up?" The engines began to rumble. The flight attendant turned and pushed a briefcase out of the way under a seat with the toe of her pump. Joe huffed and frowned and took the two sides of Anne's seat belt in his meaty hands and buckled her in and drew the belt tight. Anne rested her hand briefly on her stomach. Joe nodded and lowered himself into his seat. The jet taxied into position, paused, and then took off with exhilarating speed and an easy glide aloft accompanied by the white sound of the accelerating engines. During the ascent, Joe continued to study Anne, who, as she watched through the window as the city below turned from slate into a glittering sprawl of light, felt a surge of relief. Home was six hours away.

The plane leveled. Joe released his seat belt. "So, when are you due?"

Anne jerked in her seat as if she'd been goosed.

Joe wagged his finger, "In this I'm infallible, just like the pope," he chuckled.

"I'm sorry?" said Anne, still intent on denying the obvious.

"I'm never wrong about these things. I've got a sense. No sushi for you, no cheese, plenty of milk—organic only, plenty of protein," Joe announced. "And, don't forget 400 milligrams of folic acid a day. Eight to ten days after conception the blastocyst implants—that's when you gotta get goin'."

Joe Merlin's well-intentioned babbling forced Anne to realize the extent of her denial. Her present mental state could easily be accounted for, not just by what she had been through lately but also by this *what if* she hadn't wanted to face. Her body and psyche could very well both be awash with a witches' brew of hormones. She could no longer idiotically avoid thinking about the possibility.

What if he was *right*? What if she *was* pregnant? *Oh, God*, she thought, *I am pregnant*. She felt anchored, not unpleasantly, in her body. She let the feeling settle and looked to see Mr. Merlin regarding her with some concern. He reminded her of someone; now who was that? Oh, that's right, it was her father. Anne, though rapidly having to come to terms with carrying a child, suddenly, inexplicably, felt profoundly at ease and buoyed by the promise of a better future. She wouldn't go back to Los Angeles; she would return to her classroom. Becky's studio could do anything they wanted with her book. She felt herself relax into a fantasy of acquiescence. It really was so simple; her preliminary contract had said something about rights to the novel in perpetuity throughout the universe. It sounded florid and silly, but what it really meant was she was willing to relinquish control in return for a sizable check. She would contact her agent on Monday and sign the final draft of the contract as soon as she could. She didn't care anymore. It didn't matter. Becky could have the script for her most bankable star; to hell with it.

"By the way, I'm sorry for your loss," said Joe.

"Thank you. Did you know Cliff?" She still felt oddly serene. *That's it, chalk it up to hormones*, she thought, abdicating from all sense of self-determination.

"Sure. As a rule, agents..." In deference to Anne's condition, Merlin—an old-fashioned man in some ways—swiftly revised what he had been about to say and offered up something in a slightly less vulgar vein, "Sure I knew him. He was one of the rare good guys. A real straight shooter—unlike his fuck of a father," he added, sheepishly. "You'll pardon the expression."

"A straight shooter," Anne repeated.

"Your dad's kind of wondering why the quick trip to New York, what with your current obligations and whatnot. I take it he's not wise to…?" he nodded toward her belly.

"We haven't really discussed it. No."

"Far be it from me to interfere," said Merlin, looking as if he'd like nothing more than to do so.

"Joe? You seem to know a lot about pregnancies," said Anne, moving the conversation on. "I wouldn't be totally off the mark by saying you have children, would I?"

"No, you wouldn't. Twin girls. They're in college. I worry like a son of bitch all the time. Wish I had boys instead. Girls, like you, are a real pain in the a—no, a real worry."

"I'm going to ask you a weird question, but I think we qualify as friends now, and I'm asking you as a father."

"Go ahead," said Joe.

"Can you think of any reason Cliff would have gone to a gay sex club in Palm Springs the night he died?"

Joe looked at Anne with an amused expression. "Ah! I see," he said, folding his hands over his great mound of a stomach.

"Can you think of a reason?" Anne persisted.

"*I* would think Cliff went to a sex club to get one, or more, of his clients *out*."

"Oh!"

"This thought hadn't occurred to you?"

"Oh. My. God."

"Oh, Annie! The things you don't know about Hollywood,"
murmured Joe. What Joe had summarized in one sentence
was what Tessa and Toni had been talking about all afternoon.
Anne was beginning to suspect that pregnancy impaired
smooth cognitive function; either that, or there was something
in the air in L.A. she wasn't used to that made her less than
sharp-witted. "Look at you, Anne. You're going to keep the
baby?"

"If there is a baby I'm keeping it," she responded, surprising
even herself with her vehemence and resolve.

"Okay. Then trust me, you need to pay attention. Your *genial*
hosts that weekend, she who runs the studio and he who
makes with the upholstery. Not so genial. Hah!"

Anne's eyes dropped closed involuntarily. Suddenly she was
extremely tired. She considered telling Joe what Cliff had
told her about "she who runs the studio" and "one of his
clients" but suspected that information would find its way
immediately back to her father. She buttoned her lip.

Joe wasn't about to let up. "Everything the big studios
do in Hollywood is predicated on the sexual fantasies of
heterosexual fourteen-year-old boys. You understand what
I'm saying?"

"No."

"Leading men are straight. Period. On-screen and off. Cliff's
agency—Becky's studio—raise fortunes based on that fantasy.

Steve Nelson, he owns a house in the Hollywood Hills. There's always sevruga and Cristal stocked in the 'fridge, there's a discreet cleanup crew, and the key goes out on a regular basis to any movie star—straight, bi, gay, married, unmarried—who wants to blow off steam."

Anne looked down at her abdomen. "You're saying Cliff died because somebody's sexuality was about to be revealed? And he didn't take the drugs. Somebody slipped them to him knowing he would have a heart attack. Is that what you're saying?"

"Well, no, I'm not saying that—you are—but it sounds like a plausible theory. Just don't let *you* get stuck holding the bag."

"Me?"

"Let me repeat, billions of dollars are paid to support a fantasy. You know, the dream factory? I take it you saw the Academy Awards."

"I did," she said, failing to mention she read through almost the entire broadcast.

"And who won best actor?"

That, Anne remembered. "James Johnson."

"You know, it's not original of me, but the Oscars sometimes seem to be, to me, no disrespect to your father—God forbid—just a big party for a bunch of delusional narcissists who like to give each other awards every year for dress-up and make-believe." Anne bit her tongue. She knew, very well, that Joe Merlin had, in the past, collected two gold statuettes for Best Picture. Joe shook his head, "Doll, you're an open book. I'm talking about actors." He laid his hand on his heart. "And, I say it because I love, you understand? I say it because I love. The Academy, it's their one big shindig a year, their annual revenue comes from one goddamn—eh, who cares. Your dad would have my head if I knocked the Academy. I was talkin' about actors."

"What do you owe my father?"

"What?"

"He said you'd look out for me. Why is that?"

"Like I said, your dad's a mensch. He gave me my first job. Came to my wedding when I married my husband in Massachusetts."

Her eyes widened.

"Like I said. You'd make a lousy poker player. But you're cute as a bug, so I want you to listen to me," said Joe. "This so-called writer they've assigned—pfft! Talk about *by the numbers*!" Joe grunted in disapproval. "You want somebody who can pick a side, make it edgy, make it true, make a stand; none of which is gonna happen when you're dealing with Keir Bloomfield."

"I thought he had a great reputation?" Anne clocked that the mighty Joe Merlin hadn't a clue what Becky's studio had been up to.

"Sure, he grabs a story right by the balls and drags it straight for—the middle." Joe feigned a yawn.

He continued to talk. Mouth open, mouth closed. Something

about there being no real working producers left in Hollywood—with the possible exception of himself and Scott Rudin—whom he was describing as both a genius and a hothead. Pot. Kettle. Black. Anne glazed over. "You're practically gray with exhaustion," Joe admonished. "Go to sleep."

She drifted into sleep and, once there, into a deep swaddling dream, and deeper still until she felt Cliff—yes, Cliff—pressing her into bed, fastening her with his body. His arms around her, his cock inside her, his face to hers, their lips parted, the stubble of his beard, the salt on his skin, the taste and feel of him—profound, transcendent, climactic. She gasped, arched, and woke only after they had glided to a halt on the runway in New York when the gorgeous flight attendant gently shook her shoulder. The cabin of the plane was empty of the producer and his assistants. They had already disembarked.

Feeling strangely free from the laws of physics, Anne climbed down the stairs from the plane. She saw that dry feathery snow was falling from the sky and dusting the black pavement with white. It was both beautiful and eerie. Then the quiet of snowfall was broken by Joe Merlin bellowing into his cellular; somewhere, no doubt in an inappropriate time zone, someone was getting reamed. The assistants stood staring at the ground outside a limousine while Joe paced the tarmac, clothed only in his underclothes; a tentlike T-shirt, an enormous pair of baggy boxers, cashmere socks, and a pair of dress shoes. He barked an obscenity and scratched his pendulous stomach; it could have been he was scratching at his testicles, but she couldn't really make out the geography of his body, even though he was down to his skivvies. Anne approached the assistants and one of the suited young men opened the door of the limousine for her and the other took the bag from her shoulder and placed it in the trunk. She was about to ask a question when one of the assistants said, "Don't be alarmed, Ms. Brown; Mr. Merlin is a clothing-optional personality."

As if that explains anything, thought Anne, but she just smiled and accepted the lift back into town, the assistants seated across from her, Joe Merlin, half-naked, radiating heat, still on the phone, seated by her side.

Chapter 15

THAT CERTAIN FEELING

At last…sanctuary. Home. Arriving back long after midnight on Saturday, Anne slept until ten a.m. She woke, took a loaf of bread from the freezer, popped it in the oven, and put the kettle on the stove. She spent about an hour slathering slice after slice of bread with butter and downing them with successive cups of sugary tea. Propped on the table in front of her was a dog-eared copy of *Pride and Prejudice*. Anne stared at the page but she didn't read. She thought. What if the oracle of her future was a gutter-mouthed, temperamental, two-hundred-and-eighty-five pound moviemaker? Having never been pregnant she had no similar experience with which to compare it. The thought of having a child wasn't objectionable, but the prospect of raising one was confounding. She wondered whether if she begged the dean she could cancel her unpaid leave of absence for the following quarter. She thought some more. She slept. She ate. She didn't leave her apartment once. She didn't answer the phone. Her father called. Her sister called. Her mother called. Joe Merlin called—it was easy to guess who'd given him her number. She went to bed for a long sleep at eleven o'clock and was awake, refreshed, at seven.

On Sunday morning she took a stroll and picked up some things at the market. A few doors down she bought a pregnancy test at the pharmacy. No matter what the results were, she planned to call her gynecologist on Monday. Back in the lobby of her apartment building she unlocked her mailbox and pulled out a tranche of mail.

Back in her apartment she dutifully read the instructions to her test and then she peed on a stick. Lo and behold! Joe Merlin was right. She was pregnant.

Pregnant. Well, she could hardly say she was stunned. It all made sense. No, she wasn't stunned. Why, then, this peculiar feeling?

She wondered who'd written while she was gone—probably just the usual assortment of junk. Everyone she knew had long given up on the post office.

Baby? What baby?

Her fragmented thoughts continued to skitter and scatter through her mind even as she shuffled through the mail, so much so that she was barely concentrating on what she was doing, until she came upon a padded manila envelope that appeared to contain a disc. Then she saw the return address: Cliff W., 6014 Deronda Dr., Los Angeles, CA 90068. She felt a surge, like that moment of acceleration a split-second before liftoff—earthbound—and then, not. Cliff. Maybe if she hadn't been so hesitant about accepting his invitation, ("I don't want to spend any more nights away from you,") maybe he would… Maybe she would… She checked herself. "What ifs" were fine in fiction, but in real life they were often so much pointless crap. She strained to make out the postmark. It looked like Los Angeles. Los Angeles was ninety minutes from Palm Springs—if you weren't in a sports car. Had Cliff driven home the night he died and then back to the desert? Did he drop this packet in a mailbox early Sunday morning? By the time it had been picked up he would have been dead.

She couldn't breathe. She stared at the envelope. She opened the envelope. Inside was a CD marked with a Sharpie: "Angel Annie—me playing Tchaikovsky's Piano Concerto #1, graduate recital '95. Tchaikovsky, one orgasm after another, just like you. I love you, Annie. Should we make this arrangement permanent? Cliff."

It was a bona fide marriage proposal, from, as it turned out: the beyond. The universe swirled wide open and then shrank to the size of a pinhole. Anne's knees gave beneath her and darkness swarmed her vision. In what seemed like an eyeblink she was sprawled on the floor staring vacantly at the plush (almost waving) pile of a hooked rug. She looked around wildly, the only thought in her mind—not the fall, not her slightly altered perceptions—was a childish, panicked, *Oh no. Where's my CD? Where is it, where is it?*

She scrambled to her feet and spotted the CD under the coffee table. It appeared to have survived the quick trip to the floor. She inserted it into the stereo. The room was filled with the sound of a graduate recital with full orchestra. It sounded a lot better than any recital Anne had ever been to. Celestial? No, that wasn't it. It sounded to her untrained ear as if the piano was singing, intimate, a human voice; it was a thousand-pound instrument, yet to Anne it sounded distinctly human. A voice, emotive, gentle but strong, soaring above the other instruments, a voice ascending higher and higher. She closed her eyes. The piano-voice seemed to caress her. She knew. It was Cliff.

It was from that moment that she thought of the fetus growing inside her as a human being that could hear and would one day be able to accomplish wondrous things. For no rational reason she began to think about schools where concert pianists could be trained; she was aware of only two,

Julliard and USC. She had previously griped that new parents were all certain their children would grow up to be either brain surgeons or prima ballerinas—nobody foresaw a career in accounting or mail delivery—and here she was with a baby barely there and she was considering that she might be carrying a future prodigy. Just like its father.

The only trouble was she had a fear of prodigies. She remembered what Cliff had said about being a concert pianist, "Too much isolation," and then recalled what he had told her it had done to Glenn Gould. Hypochondria and a weird attachment to physical objects, like the chair from his parents' bridge set that he had dragged to concerts and recording sessions, a chair that as it got increasingly rickety and baled together with string and wire you could hear creaking, loudly, as he played. Then there was the great Van Cliburn, pulled into a messy palimony suit brought by his undertaker boyfriend. She had never been party to pianist gossip before Cliff.

While the music played she placed an arm protectively across her abdomen and began to chat unabashedly with the embryo about the normalcy of her background among skyscrapers versus its paternal background of palm trees and freeways, when there was a buzz at the door. It was her mother, in a temper and, unusually for her, without the buffering effect of alcohol betwixt her and the great wide world. Both the personal visit and the state of sobriety were uncommon. Jill Shayes, coat and huge shaggy hat made of faux fur, swept her daughter with a glance, "I have to hear from...Bob?!" she could barely force out the despised syllable, "That you're knocked up? You? *My* daughter, who I raised? And I have to hear it from *him*?"

"I just found out myself, and since when do you talk to my

father?"

"Since yesterday."

"Who called who?"

"Who do you think?"

"Daddy called you."

"Give the girl a prize," Jill said as she removed her hat and coat and crossed to the couch. "Do you have any coffee?"

"You want *coffee*?"

"Don't be a bitch, dear. Mommy's trying to set a good example." She dropped the hat and coat in an unceremonious heap on the couch. The glossy synthetic pelts looked just like a dead animal.

"Would that be the caffeine-and-cigarettes-daily diet?" Anne snapped.

"I'll get it myself," said her mother.

Perhaps, Anne thought, one of the points of attraction between her and Cliff had been the understanding of what it was like when a parent was an addictive personality, a pill popper or an alcoholic, or both. If her mother had really smoked and drank and chugged the coffee while she was pregnant, that would explain, among other things, Anne's size. All her nearest relatives were beanpoles. She had a vision of Jill Shayes, wearing an Yves Saint Laurent peasant blouse, frosted hair, frosted lipstick, puffing cigarette smoke over her nursing baby's downy little head. As she listened to her mother bang around in her closet-sized kitchen she thought about the fact that while her half-sister was collecting graduate degrees in the seventies, her mother, as far as she knew, had had covers on *Bazaar*, *Cosmo*, and *Vogue*. She, herself, must have been the most puzzling child imaginable born to a fashion model: scraped-kneed and scholarly. Her own child most likely would be (following the rule of skipped generations) a tall, trippy, clotheshorse, with musical aptitude.

Anne's mother emerged from the kitchen carrying two mismatched mugs. The one she handed to Anne was emblazoned with The Rolling Stones' lips and lolling tongue logo; it reminded Anne of her mother's infrequent drunken hints that she had once had a "thing" with one of the Stones back in the mists of time. So what Jill said next was surprising. "Friend of your father's," she said, nodding at the mug. "You owe him a very big thank you."

Anne looked puzzled. "How's that?"

"Back in the day he set what my attorney called *The Jagger Standard* for child support. Thirty grand a month, minimum, for the rich guy's babies," Jill was lost for a moment in perfectly posed reverie, head cocked slightly back, eyes cast to the side. "A big thank you." She continued to muse, and added acidly, "That's one man who believes in family values." Anne noted that when her mother wasn't a tedious, repetitive inebriate she was actually quite funny. Jill looked around Anne's apartment as if it were sorely lacking in civilized amenities, like appreciable square footage. "You know, Cole Starkey's a billionaire."

"Yeah. And, I'm not carrying that old lizard's child, so what?" Anne retorted.

"No, but you are carrying his only heir."

It suddenly became clear to Anne why her mom had sobered up.

Chapter 16

THERE WILL NEVER BE ANOTHER YOU

Anne's journey back to the coast was instigated by a call from her father. "That degenerate junkie dick, Starkey, wants to adopt you!"

"What, Dad?"

"Did you talk to him?"

"I, no!" said Anne.

"Goddamn it. I should have known," her father muttered.

"How'd he find out I was pregnant?"

"Believe me, he has his ways."

"But, this is… I'm not a kid anymore and I have a father. You!"

"That freaky fucker. I don't want you talking to him. I don't want you talking to his lawyers either. Do you even have an attorney?"

"No. My agency has attorneys."

"And, another thing," her father went on, "you remember

Dawn White?"

"I saw her at the funeral," said Anne. She remembered a sylph-like figure in pearls and her long, long, shining silver hair—she didn't seem to move, she was surrounded by a group of women, almost like a tableau, and she certainly didn't cry. Anne thought at the time that she must have been in shock.

"I didn't want to tell you this, but she's pressuring the D.A. to have the body exhumed."

Anne felt something like a splinter of ice sink into her chest. She moaned and found herself clutching for something that wasn't there.

"Okay. Okay, honey. Simmer down. Ms. White has made some kind of legal assertion stating that Cliff's, uh...body was never properly identified; she claims that fuck Starkey was tripping on LSD when he viewed—though how she knows that, I don't know—so he was incapable of making a positive ID of anything, or anybody"

Anne felt herself engulfed by a completely irrational thought. Aloud she asked, "Where's Cliff?"

"Pumpkin, hey. You gotta stay calm. She's not saying Cliff isn't dead—she just wants to make sure the man we saw buried is her son. She, I don't know, maybe she's hoping that somehow—as if by magic—it'll prove not to be. But, sad as it is, we know it was, right?"

"Was it a closed casket? I don't remember..."

"Yeah. Closed casket as per the instructions of his father. She says she was never allowed to see her boy. She just wants to see for herself," Bob was interrupted by a beep on the other line.

"Daddy, hold on a sec." It was Cole Starkey, calling from just four blocks from her father. "Cole, hold on a second." Anne got back to her father, "Daddy? I've gotta take this call but I'm coming home."

"Good. Joe Merlin's picking you up at five." Bob hung up and Anne, far past the point of being surprised, took the other call.

"Cole. That was my father on the other line. So, what's this about you adopting me?"

"Wh—a-adopting you? B-b-but, Annie, what an extraordinary notion!" Starkey sputtered, indignantly yet unconvincingly. "I've been overcome with joy since your mother called with the good news."

"Bada-bing," breathed Anne.

"What was that? Oh, it doesn't matter. The thing of it is, a man like me, a businessman, always needs to know what's what. I have—well—I've got more lawyers on retainer than I can count. I just happened to ask one of them—only a query, nothing sinister behind it—what kind of legal rights I had on a grandchild. I know, I know, it sounds monstrous. Now, don't be angry with me. Just listen. There's a good girl."

"Let me assure you, Mr. Starkey, I am not a girl."

"Of course not, of course not, sweetheart. I didn't mean to condescend," he said, while continuing to do exactly that. "How could I know they'd misconstrue? Especially in such a bloody stupid fashion. Please, Annie dear, hear me out."

"No, Mr. Starkey. You hear me out," Anne said, feeling a wave of irritation rise within her. "I can assure you that both you and Ms. White will have equal access to my child."

"Oh, Annie. Your tone alone speaks volumes and as for your words—are you saying neither of us are going to—"

"I repeat. Both you and Ms. White—"

"Dawn?" interrupting, Cole sounded horrified.

"Cliff's mother," Anne continued.

"Trouble is, Anne, you'll absolutely love her. And that's the danger. Before you know it she'll have snatched your soul, just as she did mine, won't she? I remember the day she left me, sunlight glinting in her hair, baby Cliff balanced on a cocked hip, smiling with all the wonder of Christmas morning. It's a gift you know: utter charm laced with pure poison. I never knew what hit me. One minute all I felt was the love in that smile, and the next minute she drove away and never came back. Still got the scars where she cracked my chest and clawed out my heart. But, let me tell you, she always comes off like a bloody big-eyed woodland creature. Voice like a songbird. Face like an angel. Honey just pouring from her lips. All I ever wanted to do was lick up the sweetness," Cole paused.

The outpouring from this older man caught Anne off-balance. Again, he reminded her of Cliff with his tendency to form—what she was beginning to see as—sudden, intemperate, unrestrained attachments, and to make emphatic bigger-than-life proclamations. Then she recalled that Cliff's mother never got to see his dead body. Cole Starkey might remind her of his late son, but he and Cliff's mother still seemed to be engaged in some war of attrition, a battle for control for their child even after his death. And here was Cole, this seemingly all-powerful man begging for Anne's favor; she couldn't help but wonder at an ulterior motive. When she made no response to him, he continued.

"Give her a fortune, your son, stand in a court of law and watch a judge grant her every desire, and still she's the one that's wronged; she's the self-sacrificing ruin. Above it all, she is, a veritable hermit now, up in the canyons. Never goes out. Won't speak to me, and then this, this, witch who won't see me, starts chatting up the authorities, dripping poison in their ears. Saying I was stoned, intoxicated, tripping or whatever nonsense, so much so that I was incapable of recognizing my own—"there was the sound of an unsteady inhalation of air, "incapable of recognizing my son. Can you imagine?"

"Were you?" Anne asked.

"Was I what?"

"Were you stoned?"

"Anne, I've been waltzing through the doors of perception for more years than you've been alive. I know what I know. I know when I'm—what would you say? Plastered? Blotto? Baked? Pissed? Spaced? This isn't about me being any of those things. This is about Dawn trying to cut away what's left of me and lock it in a mayonnaise jar under her fucking vegan kitchen sink."

"How many times have you been married?"

"Only once that mattered."

"Why'd you keep doing it?" she asked.

"It's an awfully big house to rattle around in on your own, don't you think?"

"You could get a cat," Anne suggested.

"Don't try to be clever."

"No, sir," said Anne.

"It's Cole. Remember?"

"I remember."

"And Dawn. Don't forget Dawn. She'll be gunning for you now, dear. Don't say you weren't warned."

"I can't wait to meet her."

"That'll happen sooner than you think, I imagine. Yeah, sooner than you think. I'd lay odds that at the sight of you those great shining eyes of hers will well with tears but nary a drop will they spill, duchess. After she's sure you've noticed how distrait she is, she'll start in with some wild invention, some marvelously facile excuse for why she didn't seek you out at the funeral. She'll spin it from purest silk straight from a worm's arse. She always could make any old nonsense sound like prophecy. Just like in her songs. It'll all be very fine, very cod-poetic. But remember what I've told you then. Remember."

There was something in the depths of her mind grappling its

way to the surface. All at once it broke through. "Cole, you said, when you gave me Cliff's car, that he didn't die in it. How did you know that?"

"They told me so. The police."

"How'd they know?"

"Not to be disgusting, Annie dear, but when a body dies... Well, it's messy, things get...released. The car was clean."

Always analytical, Anne asked, "Did you ask about his clothes?"

"What about his clothes?" puzzled Cole.

"If Cliff's clothes were clean he didn't die in them either."

Anne heard a distinct, abrupt cough like a sob, then a sniffle on the phone and then Cole cleared his throat. She recalled him at Cliff's graveside, arm clutched to his body, rocking and wailing uncontrollably. "Cole? Cole, I'm sorry. I'm coming back to L.A. tonight. Can I come see you soon?"

Cole, his voice strained, managed a reply containing an intimation of his usual vibrancy. "Of course, Annie love. Just give me a ring before you come over." And then he hung up.

On the flight to Los Angeles Joe Merlin was abnormally quiet and gently solicitous. The touchdown on the runway, this time in Santa Monica, was so smooth Anne couldn't distinguish flight from contact. Walking down the gangway in the cool March night she smelled the ocean, watched as ranks of palms rustled in the wind, and immediately spotted her father and sister. Her heart felt at ease. Only to lose that sense of comfort when Detective Vasquez cruised purposely into view, crossing in front of her family in order to greet her at the bottom of the steps. Anne saw that Natalie had a restraining hand on her father's arm. She could feel the protective bulk of Joe Merlin standing behind her.

"Just a minute of your time," Vasquez said, blocking Anne from taking the final step onto the pavement. "I'd take it as a personal favor, Ms. Brown, if I could persuade you to stay in town for a while," sounding like the living cliché of a fictional cop.

"Why's that, detective?" asked Anne.

"Don't have an answer for that right now, but I might in couple of days."

"Well, I'll be here."

"How long, Ms. Brown?"

"Indefinitely."

"Glad to hear it."

Joe Merlin loomed over Anne's shoulder, "Is Ms. Brown a person of interest, detective?"

"Everybody who spent the weekend of February 16th in Palm Springs is interesting to me, Mr. Merlin."

"Is she listed as a person of interest with your police department?" Joe insisted.

"No, sir."

"Thank you." Joe stepped forward, propelling Anne, forcing the detective to step aside. Joe paused in front of Detective Vasquez and leaned over so he was peering down directly into his face. "What kind of an investigation is this, anyway?"

Detective Vasquez smoothed back the lapel of his jacket, ever so slightly, and revealed the corner of his shoulder holster. "That's what I'm trying to find out, Mr. Merlin. That's what I'm trying to find out."

A Daimler pulled up on the airstrip. Fal Loa exited the car and opened the passenger door. Cole Starkey unfurled from the car, as if a ribbon were attached to the top of his head, and his tall, emaciated form waved, just barely, from side to side as if being buffeted by a light breeze. He surveyed the company. "Fuck me. The gang's all here. What?"

"That's it!" said Bob, his face reddening. He shook off Natalie, and gently but firmly pulled Anne into the car. Natalie followed and before Anne could speak they were heading north on Bundy.

Natalie, as they drove past the entrance to the 10, said, "Dad, don't you want to take the freeway?"

"No. Bundy to Sunset to home. So, pumpkin," he said, eyes on the road, but his chin ever-so-slightly canted in Anne's direction, "How you doin'?"

"I'm fine, Dad." Bob Brown was, not so discreetly, staring at her in the rearview mirror as if he had emotional X-ray vision.

More obviously, Natalie had twisted in her car seat and her face was peeking out from behind the back of the plush leather. She grinned and reached for her sister's hand and squeezed it tight. "You're so full of shit," she said affectionately and wouldn't let go.

Chapter 17

AU FOND DU TEMPLE SAINT

Uncle Manny arrived the morning after Anne returned from New York with a plan. It was a gray drizzling day in March. "Bob, do you want to see a property with me in Pasadena?"

"Are you buying something?" Bob inquired. "Because I gotta tell you, this market has only got one way to go: down."

"Yes, I know," Manny assured his financially astute brother while his niece looked at an assortment of eight generic-looking cereal boxes in the kitchen cupboard. They all contained inordinate amounts of flax, whole wheat, or oats. "Anne, do you want to see a Frank Lloyd Wright with me?"

Her father answered for her, "Sure, that's a good idea. I've got some things to do today. Pasadena? What's that one, Manny?"

"La Miniatura."

"Isn't it sitting—I heard it floods all the goddamn time. Is that right?"

"Yeah, but that might be the least of its problems. We'll see. Anne, you interested?"

"Sounds good, Uncle Manny."

"You drive, Annie, I'll navigate."

Thank god, thought Anne.

First they drove the freeway east for forty-five minutes and then through leafy streets past historically preserved houses and wound their way down into a dell of stately homes from the teens and twenties. Anne caught a glimpse of a stony, stacked, filigreed box surrounded by trees. They looped around the street, drove down a driveway that appeared to be meant for another house, and finally arrived at the back entrance of La Miniatura.

Electric blue tarps were lashed to the multileveled roof and over the corners of the façade. "Take a gander at the work of genius, Anne," Uncle Manny gestured aloft. "It leaks. And, wait until we get to the studio; it seems Mr. Wright forgot trees grow. Bye-bye load-bearing wall!" he was almost chuckling as he opened a large wooden gate and called inside. "Hello? We're here!" He turned to Anne, "My friend's trying to restore it. He might not be home but he left the house open for me."

Anne followed her uncle under a portico to the door. They entered through a narrow space that opened onto a living room with a twenty-foot ceiling, towering windows, and interior walls of the same pierce-patterned sandy concrete blocks that made up the exterior. In the gloom of the gray day it appeared that they had walked into a geological anomaly. "Wow," said Anne, "impressive and oppressive at the same time."

"Frank was about your size, sweetheart. So hallways, stairways, even you should watch your elbows."

"Why so cramped?"

"Because he wanted you to experience his buildings a certain way. Just the way he wanted you to. No variations. No pictures on the wall. The only furniture he allowed was designed specifically for the house—and there's the effect that he meant the design to have—one minute you're walking through a low hallway or portal, almost cocooned, the next, you emerge into a great open space like this living room, an *a-ha* moment. Lots of flash, but the guy's substance sucked— let me rephrase—his construction materials sucked."

Anne frowned. She knew this was another object lesson. Apparently, Uncle Manny had now taken it as his prerogative to teach.

"He got away with it, the leaks, the crumbling materials, the aesthetic control, because he had panache. Little guy, but he wore a cape and carried a cane, and when wealthy clients complained, he told them off, or hung up on them, or told them they were unworthy jackasses." He looked at Anne like he was trying to make a point.

"Uncle Manny, are you mad at me?" asked Anne.

"Never, Annie. I just want you to know the answers to all the questions you need answered are here, not in New York. They're right here. Did you ever think about who else was in Palm Springs the night Cliff died?"

"Pretty much everybody, except Tessa and Bill Aagard."

"And, what about that young actor?"

"I don't know. He just didn't make that big of an impression on me. Cute, kind of malleable, he really wanted to be liked. Sweet, but just kind of, not all there." She shrugged her shoulders.

"You've got to see the whole picture. The trees that grow, the concrete that you dumped too much sand in, the lay of the land, only then do you see an enduring pattern. So what about the people who did make an impression on you?"

"Uncle Manny. You want to tell me something about the Aagards?

"Me? What the hell do I know?" Uncle Manny took a handkerchief from his pocket and blew his nose. "Your sister wants me to hire a driver." Anne didn't know what to say about the sudden shift of topic. "Don't act so surprised. If Natalie had her way I'd be playing pinochle at Sunny Meadows with the colostomy club crowd. I'd rather croak."

"Did you really run over a newspaper kiosk?" asked Anne. Uncle Manny merely grunted in response. "What if you moved in with Dad?"

"What if you moved in with Dad?" he retorted.

"I kind of have," said Anne.

"I haven't lived in the same house with your father since I was seventeen and he was seven. Take it from me, he's only gotten worse."

"What kind of kid was he?"

"Cute. All kids are cute. Then they hit fourteen and all of a sudden they've got lantern jaws and Neanderthal brows. Boys, that is," he sighed. "Take it for what it's worth, Anne. But in the end everything boils down to control. Driving your car, running a studio, every relationship you will ever have or have had. It's all about control. Take your big sister, for instance, she's all in my business because her own father barely knows she's there. See what having a sympathetic ear gets you?"

Anne hugged her uncle. He smelled like bay leaves and, quite frankly, dust from an old cathedral. There were springy white patches of stubble near his ears where he'd missed shaving, and for the first time, in her arms, he felt insubstantial. "Uncle Manny, have you lost weight?"

"Don't you start," he shrugged her off and turned up the collar of his tweed jacket.

"You think if you bunch up your coat I won't see how thin you're getting?"

"No. With me everything's out in the open. Nothing up my sleeve, nothing hidden, unlike every person you met in Palm Springs." He was deflecting, but Anne kept listening.

"So, you're saying, what you're trying to tell me is, everybody at Becky and Steve's house in Palm Springs was hiding something? Everybody, including Cliff?"

"Including Cliff." He touched a damp-looking stain on the wall and tasted his fingertips. "Bees. Taste." Anne touched the tacky surface of the wall and tasted honey on her fingers. "Most people are hiding something. For instance, I think you're hiding something from me and your father; what you have to unravel is why that's important. Or if it's important."

"Can we see the rest of the house?"

"That's why we're here."

Anne, tucking her elbows into her sides followed her uncle as he stooped to negotiate a stairway down to a dining room that opened through a set of French doors onto an ornamental pond spilling over its banks. "This is why it leaks? The house—" she peered outside and surveyed the landscape, "is sitting in a gully?"

"He was trying to save money for his client by buying the cheapest piece of property in the neighborhood. In the long run, it's been an architectural nightmare."

"Okay, Uncle Manny, let me see if I can translate. Life has no shortcuts, address your problems head on, if you need answers start asking questions, and something about sweet things and hidden things. But, I'm, you're gonna have to give me a little while to figure that one out. Does that cover it?"

"That about covers it. Except for what you're not telling me and your father."

She kissed her uncle's cheek. "Let me find out whether or not it's important. Say, did we get sidetracked? Didn't you want to tell me something about the Aagards?"

"No. *You* wanted *me* to tell you something about the Aagards. Why was that?"

"Tessa Aagard told me to watch my back. I think it was something about Toni Todd. But, I'm not really sure."

Chapter 18

UNDER PRESSURE

Bill Aagard, a first-time film director, met Tessa Moynihan, a production coordinator, at a budget meeting for a film called *Double Down*; it had something to do with Vegas and the mob and a group of card cheats. Bill had started as a fashion photographer, he progressed to videos and ads, and because of his sensually textured imagery he was tapped to direct a low-budget if vaguely "high-concept" film for Fox Searchlight.

The problem, as usual, with making the movie came down to money—or the lack of it. Although Bill was quite a big, imposing man topping out at over six feet, he was surprisingly docile when confronted with cuts to his project. He didn't like discord. He was gentlemanly, his nature was to please, and coming from the world of promotions he had never had the occasion to quarrel over money. When the producer informed him that he'd have no camera crane, no access to extras for his teeming casino and, for that matter, only two walls of a set for a pivotal scene, he said, "We'll figure it out." He walked calmly down the hall to his office, closed the door behind him, and the rest was silence.

Unbeknownst to him he was being tailed. Tessa Moynihan had observed him as he had reacted stoically to the latest bad news and had sensed his inner distress. She paused outside the office door, wondering if this was the appropriate thing to do. Deciding it was, she raised her hand to knock, immediately reconsidered, and walked straight in. What she saw was unexpected. Bill Aagard was slumped on his desk with his head in his hands, his broad athlete's shoulders were trembling, and when he looked up, startled by her unannounced arrival, she saw his handsome face was red as a beet and marred with tears.

Tessa closed the door quickly behind her, surveyed the scene, and chirped merrily, "Mr. Aagard? Or may I call you Bill? She waited for a beat as if she was honestly waiting for an answer, "Okay, Bill it is! Bill, you have got to butch it up, honey!" Bill wiped the tears from his eyes with the back of his hand. He should have been embarrassed or angry but was so Novocain-numb he wasn't. Curiously, at the same time, something about this woman made embarrassment unnecessary. He had been giving serious consideration to comfort gorging on something—preferably cake—but now, even in his numbness, was focused on whatever this unexpected, amazing creature was going to say next. "May I give you a little advice, Bill?"

"I thought you just did," he responded.

"No. Really. These people expect you to bite back."

"Interesting. Won't you sit down?" Manners always trumped tears with Bill.

Tessa plunked herself down on his desktop. "Listen. It's a game—if you don't play—they don't respect you. It's all about pecking order. Assistants like me, or like I used to be last week, we get cold coffee and glitchy BlackBerrys tossed at our heads, and we catch, we deal, and we make the coffee hot and roll the calls. But you're a pitcher—"

"Oh, God! Baseball metaphors. I hate baseball," Bill moaned.

163

"Okay. No baseball. What you've got to do is barge back down into the conference room," she insisted before Bill interrupted.

"I don't barge. I've never barged."

"No! No! Like this!" Tessa jumped off the desk, scowled, adjusted her crotch, cocked her shoulders, and then slammed her fist down on the desk. "Now, you do it."

Bill laughed, he thought bird-boned Tessa doing John Wayne was extremely funny. "Okay."

"No! Do it!" she exclaimed.

Bill stood, shifted his weight awkwardly, and hitched up his belt. He looked much more Danny Kaye than Robert Mitchum. Tessa pulled a face, shook her head, and stamped her foot. "Not like that. Do you want to make this movie, or what? Get your hand right down in your pocket and make like you're shoving your equipment over to the other side— like it's the biggest thing in the room—then take your other hand and—BAM!" She smacked her small fist into the desk again, "Right on the table. HARD! Like it's a substitute for You-Know-What."

"Ah, Ms. Moynihan? Are you trying to teach me how to be a dick?"

"I'm just illustrating how the sharks swim," Tessa replied.

"Why?"

Bill's question halted Tessa's flood of stream-of-consciousness chatter. For Tessa, self-examination while in full flow was almost unknown, she usually just allowed herself to be swept along by the compulsion to get the next word out; she would think about what she had said and what she meant later—well, sometimes—okay granted, very infrequently. "Why? Why not? Right?"

"Okay by me, Svengali," Bill agreed.

"Who?"

They continued in this vein throughout the making of the film. With Tessa coaching, Bill "butched it up." He got his crane. He started smoking Cuban cigars and alternately ranted at and stroked the producer. He got his extras. You can see where this is going. They made a very successful team. *Double Down* cost fifteen million dollars but grossed over a hundred million in domestic release.

Tessa bought Bill a fishing vest, which he received with an uncertain, "Thank you," followed by an inquiry as to its sartorial appeal and the usefulness of its many pockets. Tessa explained the macho attire of his predecessors: John Ford, John Huston, Victor Flemming, William Wellman, and William Wyler, and suggested he fill the pockets with cigars and viewfinders. Bill adopted this look, so eccentrically old-fashioned as to be new again, and soon filled his cedar-lined work closet with multiple identical vests, jeans, and Egyptian cotton shirts, hung one after the other on padded satin hangers.

His next film, *Quark*, was budgeted at eighty-five million and Tessa was listed as a producer in the credits. When it broke box-office records over the Fourth of July weekend, they decided on a mutually beneficial partnership, and Tessa Moynihan became Tessa Aagard. They announced they were

Chapter 19

EVERY BREATH YOU TAKE

Anne expected The Buccaneers to be some gimcrack, seedy
nightmare, covered on the outside with weathered wooden
panels while within would be a world of piratical tack with
swags and ropes and men in velvet doublets—minus pants.
However, when she pulled up in Cliff's Ferrari outside the
club the morning after her trip with her uncle, she saw that,
on the exterior, at least, it was a rambling white resort with
a tailored garden of ocotillo, barrel, and saguaro cacti planted
in beds of crushed granite. It looked bright and inviting.
She walked up the immaculate pathway and pressed the
bell at the front door. A deeply tanned man, chunky with
muscle, answered the bell almost immediately. He was in his
late fifties, early sixties, wearing a white tank top and black
spandex bicycle pants.

"Hello," she said extending her hand, "I'm Anne Brown."

Smiling in welcome, the muscled man shook her hand
vigorously and announced, with cordial enthusiasm, "I am Jan
Prins." He paused for a minute, looking at the car past her
shoulder, and added, "Come in!"

The floors were polished white marble. It was absolutely
quiet, as if it's only occupant was, and was forever, the man
who answered the door. There were mirrors clustered on
every wall. Zebra pelts were in abundance, as were orchids,

African antlers, and Brancusi-like metallic, phallic, sculptures. It smelled like vanilla inside and it was completely spotless. Not at all what Anne had expected.

Jan Prins was looking at her inquiringly, "I do not often see people like you here."

"Women?"

He laughed, a little too uproariously and clapped her on the shoulder. Jan packed a wallop. Anne canted precariously and with quick reflexes he caught her by the other shoulder. "Oops!"

She was trying to figure out his accent when he said, "I forgot since I left the ballet how little women are."

"The ballet?"

"Principal dancer with the Royal Danish Ballet until I fell off a, hmm, I think you say, catwalk, and broke my back. They said I would never walk. Look at me!" He stood even more erect and expanded his chest.

"Amazing." Anne smiled, quelling the thought that he looked like a cross between a pigeon and a bodybuilder.

"No. It was a hundred percent me. I heal myself and I work and I work until I am as you see. Walking, dancing, living."

"And in this beautiful place," Anne regained her composure.

"Ach. The desert is good for my bones. Therapeutic. I love heat. But I have sold this beautiful place." He looked around regretfully. "Please." He led her by the slightest touch to the elbow, as if she were made of gossamer, to a reception room and a long angular couch upholstered in raw silk. "Sit."

"You're leaving the desert?"

Jan seated himself next to Anne. "I cannot refuse such a price. So much money," he said thoughtfully.

Anne found him refreshingly forthright; she couldn't help but ask, "Are you always so open with people?"

"Hah! There is no such thing as this American idea. Privacy! No such thing. You want to know anything about me? I post it on the Internet. No such thing. No secrets. No problems. No privacy."

"Wow." Anne was thunderstruck.

Jan shrugged. "It is I."

"Do you mind if I ask who you sold to?"

"I sell to the Clarity Foundation. They want to make a rehab facility," he wrinkled his brow as he remembered the words exactly, "For chemical dependency. It is good. Healthy. This is always a healthy place. Now it will stay healthy."

"The Buccaneers."

"Fun! It is healthy! It is good for you!" Jan said heartily.

"Of course." Anne nodded in agreement. "Jan? Could I see the anatomically correct spa?"

He beamed with pride, "You hear of my spa! Yes. Follow me."

The spa sprung huge, an ancient, Italianate fountain at the head of an Olympic-sized pool. Like the metallic sculpture in the living room, while anatomically correct, it proved to be more decorative than functional. It hardly looked real. Anne walked up to inspect the aged stone. It couldn't have been as old as it appeared, unless some eighteenth-century duke had been openly and unabashedly gay. It was decorated, not with sporting porpoises and mythical beasts, but with men clambering out of and over rocky outcroppings and carvings of several particularly louche figures exposing themselves to the water, fully aroused.

The fountain may have been primarily decorative, but there was a lot of fully functional apparatus arranged poolside, sitting in the baking sun. There were saddles, tables, swings, and unidentifiable—to Anne's eyes—things. Some of them with moving parts, others with manacles. Jan picked up a wrench and tapped the top of a throne-like aluminum chair with a very obviously placed protuberance.

"Yes. I do not think I sell these on Craigslist. But when the club is open everything is au fait, absolutely correct. At night we play. In the morning everything goes outside. We scrub. The sun shines. Everything is clean. And now," he sighed, "It goes into a crate."

"Will you open another club?"

Jan stuck out his lower lip. "I do not know. Maybe something new... Maybe I will go to San Francisco. Only it is cold and damp and reminds me of home. No. Something new. Someplace warm."

"Vegas?"

Jan dismissed the idea. "No. It is not pretty. I must have beauty too. Maybe a bed-and-breakfast."

Anne nodded in understanding. "Jan, I think some friends of mine used to come to your club."

"I have a very large clientele. Who can remember them all?" His savvy eyes narrowed. "This is what I told that policeman the other day. I have no register like a hotel. I take only the best people in membership."

"So it is private?" She knew at once she had made a serious misstep.

"Now I think you are from the Department of Health? Everything is au fait. Like I said. Condoms. Hand sanitizers. Clean. Have I not shown you? *I* am completely open. But for my patrons I am *discreet*. I have told this to the policeman, I have said, bring me a warrant if there is something wrong here. And there is never anything wrong here."

Apologetic, Anne blurted, "Oh no. No. I'm not a health inspector."

"Then what?"

"I write books."

"What kind?"

"Fiction."

Jan softened. "Ah, that is good. Fantasy I like. Fiction. But why are you here?" he said, turning to go inside.

Anne followed. "I wanted to see—it's kind of like research."

"When I saw you drive up in this car I thought maybe you had come to ask me to let your friend back in the club," Jan said cannily, "but I have sold it. I have told you."

Anne received a spark of spontaneous insight. She saw it all, Ben, the young actor, panting in the driveway over Cliff's Ferrari. She remembered Tessa and Toni divulging that James Johnson was sleeping with Ben Haber; she remembered Cliff represented them both. She heard Joe Merlin practically chastising her, "*I* would think Cliff went to a sex club to get one, or more, of his clients *out.*"

And she said vaguely, not knowing whom to name, "You know, when you're in the spotlight like that, things can get out of hand."

"Naughty, naughty! Naughty actor! I do not care who you are! Not welcome in my club anymore! No poppers, no drugs, no meth! I am strict!"

Holy shit! thought Anne: unfortunately, due to Jan's strange, slippery hold on syntax—no contractions, flipping tenses, sometimes dropping the plural, sometimes not—she couldn't figure out if he was talking about one actor, two actors, all actors, or, in this circumstance, she could probably narrow it down to two. Out loud she said, "I know. You have to be strict. And this clinic you sold to?"

"The Clarity Foundation for Rehabilitation," Jan answered.

"I think I've heard of them. 'No to Drugs—Yes to Life'?"

"I approve of such things," Jan nodded. "Very good."

As Anne drove away in the telltale car, she mulled and considered. In her mind Ben and/or James Johnson were implicated in the death of their agent, and beyond that… beyond that it seemed the church James so generously endowed was in the know and had bought the scene of the crime. *Crime*, she thought. *Was it something involving class D drugs, felony possession, or was it something worse?* What she hadn't established was Cliff's location. He had dropped a CD in the mail addressed to her the night he died from a Los Angeles mailbox. *Wait, was his Ferrari at the club or in Beachwood Canyon? Who was driving?* Hers were jumbled thoughts about what had truly happened to Cliff on the night of his death, and what she could possibly do next to uncover that truth, when she saw the driver in her rearview mirror slap a flashing light atop his vehicle, an action followed by the howl of a siren. She pulled over to the curb around the corner of the ex-Buccaneers club on Belardo Road.

Phil Vasquez parked behind her and walked up to her window. "When I said *in town* I meant L.A., Ms. Brown."

"Detective Vasquez! Were you following me?"

He merely frowned and looked at her as if she were an idiot.

Anne jumped out of the car. "Did you know that The Buccaneers belongs to the Church of Clientology?!"

Vasquez folded his arms across his chest, "A front group. And they haven't closed escrow yet. I was aware. And I might warn you, it's safer, for you, if you let the police conduct their own business."

Keyed up beyond belief, Anne breathlessly added, "But did you know James Johnson or maybe Ben Haber or maybe both were kicked out for doing drugs?! Kicked out of the Buccaneers! Kicked out on what could only be the Saturday, no, the Sunday Cliff died because that car was there! Jan Prins recognized my car!"

Detective Vasquez was quiet as he digested this new information. He squinted at Anne as if seeing her for the first time. "It's a hard car to miss. Ms. Brown. If it's not inconvenient, would you follow me to the station?"

Back at his office in the Palm Springs Police Station, Detective Vasquez talked. He talked about how interesting it was that somebody like Anne was easily confided in, as opposed to himself, someone who carried a gun and scrutinized all, reflexively, for a plausible motive. He talked about Clientology, "Not Clientology, per se, but I suspect every organization that charges half a million, large, for spiritual enlightenment. Movie stars make the perfect mark. Rich and insecure and looking for answers where there aren't any." He talked about fame. He talked about influence. He asked Anne, specifically, to watch herself and to stop asking questions.

Anne agreed affably to everything he said, adding salient points about sanitizing sex toys she had learned from Mr. Prins and relationship points she had gleaned from just about everybody she'd come in contact with in the past month. Then she inquired when Cliff's body would be dug up.

Detective Vasquez said, "You, Ms. Brown, are one of those people. I don't know if it's naiveté or blind luck, but one of these days you either have to grow up or open your eyes. I'd have thought, with your boyfriend dying, you probably would have done both."

Anne clamped her mouth shut and thought about the detective's most recent comment.

"Now, I'm not trying to offend you," said Vasquez. "I didn't know about," he consulted his notepad, "James Johnson and Ben Haber's activities. And that's helpful. But—" he let the sentence dangle.

"You just said I was being helpful. What if I continued being helpful?" asked Anne. She wanted to leave and get something to eat (something she was doing now in about thirty-minute intervals throughout the day). She craved a big glass of milk and some biscotti, but only one kind of biscotti, the biscotti from Zabar's that was made in a bakery upstate. The only problem was she was three thousand miles away. Her stomach was going to start snarling at any second, she could feel the hunger growing, but she needed more facts, more answers, some kind of sensible resolution.

"No," the detective said bluntly.

"No?"

Growing impatient, the detective folded his hands together. Anne could see a three-inch scar across his knuckles, a jagged seam of white against his tanned skin. She glanced at his face. Crow's feet around the eyes and a pronounced frown that made him look almost like a marionette—but he wasn't as old as his weathered skin would indicate. She placed him at around forty.

He returned the gaze. What he saw was a young woman radiating something he couldn't immediately define. He never thought anyone wholesome, but she came as close as he'd ever seen. He knew she was in her early thirties but she looked only old enough to baby-sit his kids. No, that wasn't it. It was something about her expression: intelligent but guileless. He thought about what he knew: she'd had a one-night stand with a Hollywood player now deceased; she taught at some college back in New York; her father, retired, once ran a studio; and she obviously hadn't exploited her connections. She was exploiting something else; she was talking about stars using drugs at a bondage bar and unearthing a cadaver and making it sound as sunny as a picnic on the beach. Was it her big eyes? Was it the way she tilted her head and listened? What was it about her that made people protective; what about her made people talk? He wanted to bottle it. Instead he said, "No. That's not how these investigations work."

There was a sharp rap on the detective's doorjamb. Anne swiveled in her chair. Vasquez looked up calmly at the police officer offering a thin file. The police officer said, "Snowbird from Winnipeg went missing the weekend of the sixteenth."

"I don't do missing persons," said Detective Vasquez.

"Richard thought you'd want to see this," countered the officer.

Vasquez took the file and flipped it open, took a glance and then closed it and placed it on his desk. "Thank you, Ms. Brown, for coming in," he said, cueing her departure.

Anne stood up. "Cliff died the weekend of the sixteenth."

Vasquez stood and buttoned his jacket and then offered his hand, "Once again, Ms. Brown, you think of anything else give me a call."

Chapter 20

CAN'T STAND ME NOW

Anne headed back to Los Angeles. Fifteen minutes out from the basin she slipped her earpiece in and called her uncle, who complained when he answered the phone that it sounded as if she were addressing him from the bottom of the ocean. Anne kept her eyes on the rearview mirror. Every time she changed lanes since passing some nowhere town, Banning or Hemet or one of those, a hulking SUV with custom rims and a leering grille that looked like a polished nickel maw loomed up behind her, like some kind of twenty-first-century version of the truck from *Duel*. "Uncle Manny, I might be being paranoid but I think someone's following me."

"Where are you?"

"Ah, I think the 210," she looked to her right. The freeway branched off up into the hills. The Escalade SUV was still right there, hanging on her rear bumper. I just went past the 2 North."

"You're in Glendale," said Uncle Manny.

"Where?" Anne felt a trickle of sweat run down the side of her ribcage.

"What? I can't hear you! Sweetheart, speak up."

Instead, Anne only got more hushed. "I don't know where I am."

A hospital complex sprawled on the hill just above the freeway. "No, I'm on the 134. Uncle Manny—" She was going eighty in the second lane from the right. She moved a lane over as the freeway made a wide curve, and the Escalade followed. The drivers around her Ferrari and the pursuing Escalade started to thin and drop back—so cautiously—oh so unusual in Los Angeles—as a steady stream of drivers attempted to evade this disturbance in the traffic flow.

"Anne! Get off the freeway."

Anne accelerated into the fast lane. The Escalade followed right along behind, dangerously close. The freeway straightened out. She stopped talking. She could feel her heart sprinting and felt quick searing heat spread throughout her chest as her breath became ragged with stress. The sound of the car's engine and a strange rushing filled her ears, or was that her pulse reverberating? She saw a sign for the Brand exit. A truck labored and ground its gears, trying to get up to sixty ahead of Anne and in the next lane over. The Escalade was doing a funny shimmy, drifting to the side behind the Ferrari and back again, just to emphasize its presence. Anne's mood switched abruptly from near-terror to anger; she felt fury at the Escalade's driver and deliberately pressed the "Sport" button on the dash, tapped the paddle shift on the steering column, yanked the wheel to the right, and as the engine engaged the Ferrari rocketed from eighty-seven mph to two hundred miles per hour in seconds, but it felt like a little eternity. She came within inches of the rear of a truck and hurtled across the other two lanes, head swiveling, eyes darting, internally screaming, on a sharp trajectory for the Brand exit. The Escalade had nowhere to go but into the side

of the truck or straight-ahead. So it was with some relief that
Anne found herself driving off the exit without her menacing
traveling companion and down a boulevard of glass-and-steel
office towers.

Suddenly, hands tight on the steering wheel, as she struggled
to return her heartbeat and breathing to normal she heard a
weird squabble of echoing, aqueous sounds, her uncle's voice
bubbling and popping to the surface, "Annie! Anne! What's
going on?!"

"You told me to get off the freeway. I—I had a little trouble—
but..." Anne looked around at completely unrecognized
territory. "But I don't know how to get home. Where am I?"

"You're in Glendale." They discussed, briefly, the route home
through Hollywood. Anne was trembling and concerned her
uncle would detect the quaver in her voice. "Now, Anne. You
call me the minute you get to your father's." Uncle Manny
signed off with the unwelcome information that his aged
bladder and enlarged prostate dictated the length of his phone
calls—but Anne quickly realized she'd nearly scared the piss
out of him as well, and she herself felt barely confined to her
skin. She desperately needed to shake the sense she was still
traveling at high velocity. As she drove she spotted an ersatz
town square marked by a sign reading "The Americana"
and another for "Valet Parking"; she pulled in, got out, and
handed over the keys to a waiting valet.

Her destination turned out to be a mixed-use condominium
complex and shopping mall. A kind of Disneyland devoted
to high-density living and consumerism. It was meant to
look like Charleston, but the multistory dwellings above the
bedecked store windows had vinyl mullions and vestigial
wrought-iron balconies. There was a tiny trolley that ran over

179

rails set into wooden slats, which was stuffed with exhausted
parents and shrilling children, and above it all Frank Sinatra
was crooning on a continuous loop. Scared and suddenly
depressed, Anne walked to a waiting bench. She looked to
the center of the spanking-new complex. Set in a green lawn
was a spouting fountain jetting water into the air; at its center
was a gold statue of man tilting in space that, the longer
she contemplated it, reminded her of an extremely chintzy
version of the statue in Rockefeller Center. It occurred to
her that an old movie starring Joan Crawford called *Mildred
Pierce* had been set in Glendale. The storyline involved social
climbing, adultery, murder, and a waffle house on Brand
Boulevard.

Thinking she would kill for a waffle, she remained static on
the bench. Her sense of time was getting gummy. She looked
over her shoulder in jumpy trepidation as if the indefatigable
machine from the freeway was about to roar into life behind
her, but all that was there was a carefully staged, and blatantly
contrived street scene. Anne thought about the man behind
the wheel, the driver of the Escalade; she strained to think
who it could be. Wondering if the Escalade's driver was after
her or if they had recognized the Ferrari. She remembered
the expression on Jan Prins' face as he looked past her when
she stood at The Buccaneers door, and puzzled over how he
knew the car, and if he knew Cliff, and if Cliff knew about
James and Ben. Of course, he must have known; he was their
agent. Anne had a good ear for dialogue and she remembered
Cliff's exact words, "As somebody said this morning, it's one
of my defining characteristics. I'm an agent. Figuring out
what's in your best interest is what I do." Exactly *whose* best
interest was yet to be determined.

She called her sister. Natalie answered and immediately
began telling Anne that Uncle Manny had called their father,

who had pulled Natalie out of a classroom lecture, and now Natalie was alternately fuming and worrying and insisting Anne sit tight; she should come home immediately; no, better yet, Natalie would be at The Americana in forty-five minutes and pick her up. "No," said Anne repeatedly. "I'm fine. Tell Dad and Uncle Manny I'm fine. I'll be home for supper."

Anne wondered if things could get any weirder. Minutes later she was traveling west on surface streets through Hollywood according to her uncle's directions, checking her rearview mirror compulsively as she went.

Chapter 21

ALL I DO IS DREAM OF YOU

Anne arrived at the base of Beachwood Canyon. She drove on and passed a pair of stone gates erected about the same time as the Hollywood sign, saw a grocery store to her left, a behemoth of a walled Spanish house directly in front of her and to the right a couple of houses with steeply pitched roofs, sort of like the witch's cottage in *Hansel and Gretel*. Deronda Drive was further north. She drove up the canyon and then followed a series of winding streets until she came to 6014. Cliff's house had a red tile roof and white stucco walls. The door gaped open. She parked the car, stood at the curb and looked through the doorway. She took in a steadying breath. Off the entry she saw west-facing wood casement windows that looked out over a canopy of trees and houses perched along the steep canyon walls. A figure stepped into silhouette in front of the windows. It was a woman. The figure left the window-frame, and within a moment appeared in the doorway. It was Dawn White. Dawn emerged into the day's light and extended both her hands in greeting. She had that intense, slightly whacked-out look Anne associated with addicts or religious zealots. Was there not one single normal person in all of L.A.?

It was all Anne could do to not look over her shoulder to see if she was welcoming somebody else, or if the Escalade had suddenly pulled up behind her. Cole Starkey may have deemed it charismatic but Anne thought Dawn's demeanor over the top. She forced herself to smile and say hello when all she wanted to do was run.

Dawn, hands still outstretched like a lovely version of the *Bride of Frankenstein*, said, "I knew you'd come." She looked into Anne's eyes intently, searching, clearly plaintive.

Anne let the tractor beam of Dawn's personality draw her inside. Down a few stairs was the living room. In front of a picture window was a Steinway—since this was another view facing the wooded canopy—it looked like the gleaming black nine foot long massively heavy piano was somehow suspended in the treetops.

"You can feel him in this room," said Dawn. Now she was really beginning to creep Anne out. "I can see him in this room," she continued. Anne looked around, hardwood floors, nice monochromatic furniture, framed black and white pictures of Yosemite—Jesus! Could they be Ansel Adams'? Anne saw a beautifully appointed room dominated by an enormous piano. The only two people standing, however, were she and Dawn White. Anne's hand grazed her midsection. There was one more presence in the room you couldn't see, but this one happened to be alive.

Dawn sat down on the tufted black leather piano bench. She played a few descending chords and a glissade. The sound coming from the keys was ringing; it traveled straight inside Anne's body and gave her a shiver of recognition. "Cliff gets his musical gene from me. His father is just a promoter. Did you ever hear him play?"

"I did," answered Anne.

"I don't feel it," said Dawn very quietly.

"I beg your pardon?"

"The lack of him."

Anne lowered herself onto the couch, after all this was Cliff's mother, and asked her, "You don't miss Cliff?" Anne was still surging with adrenaline and somehow it gave her the sensation she had in the Peninsula tearoom. It was that sticky attenuated passage of time, not in nice linear order, but distorted and peppered with moments of déjà vu. People and objects had luminous sharp visual edges. She could smell a citrus-scented floor wax. She could almost hear the words before Dawn said them.

"No. I miss him. I never saw his body. His father saw to that. Did you?"

"No."

"I'll tell you what I do know," said Dawn. "Whoever we buried in that coffin I have a right to see. Especially if he's my son."

"Have you contacted the police?" Anne thought of the conditional *if* in Dawn's last sentence. It suggested a state of unreality. Here was the prophecy Cole was talking about, but nothing about it was loveable, it was kind of warped and territorial.

"No. What are a mother's needs compared to a billionaire's? Why exhume his body? I'm JUST his mother, after all."

"I think what they look for, in general, in a case like this, is probable cause," commented Anne.

"That's why I contacted the D.A.," said Dawn.

Well, that settled it. Anne thought she'd better leave. She didn't find Cliff's mother poetic, she found her insane, and a little spooky. What she'd hoped for as she drove up the canyon was a glimpse of where Cliff had lived and maybe a sense where he'd come from, and a reason why somebody was chasing after him—or his car. She hadn't expected to see Dawn White (though she recalled Cole's warning). Now she realized that Dawn and Cole were exactly where Cliff came from, and it disturbed her. She expected the house to be quiet, maybe a place she could stop and think and reassess. She had thought for one brief, silly, moment while talking to her father two days before that someone had found Cliff, alive. But, now she quickly realized how impossible that would be, not only was he dead, but someone seemed very interested in hunting her (or whoever was driving his car) down too. Was someone trying to kill her? Or, was there some other explanation that her riotous hormones and the recent strange occurrences were obscuring?

"Look at me, Anne," demanded Dawn, leaning forward on the piano bench. Anne did so. It was the polite thing to do. Not to mention she had a momentary vision of Dawn launching herself at her, talons outstretched, if she refused. "I need to tell you something…" Anne listened carefully and Dawn's words flowed into the on-rushing narrative that made up her recent life, a river that contained not just the waters of her own story but also those whose tales she had absorbed—a story grown turbulent and dark with panic and a near-fatality on the road. However, she would have to think of that later. For the moment she was simply content to be alive and to be able to sink into yet another story and soak up whatever sense and information she could.

Chapter 22

I ONLY WANT TO BE WITH YOU

Dawn White turned seventeen in August of 1966. It was
a propitious year. Instead of driving her VW Bug from
Kitchener, Ontario, Canada to Montreal and matriculating at
McGill University, as she ought, she continued to drive until
she crossed the border at Michigan, and she kept on driving
straight SW until she reached Los Angeles.

She wanted to sing. She had aptitude. She had ambition. She
had studied piano and voice since she was eight. When she
was fourteen she picked up the guitar. A few years later Dusty
Springfield and Judy Collins had become her idols.

Dawn crashed at her aunt's on Primrose Avenue in
Hollywood and from the guest room she could see Capitol
Records. Of course, her aunt immediately called her parents
to alert them that their runaway daughter had been located.
Threats and scenes and the arrival of her baffled mother did
nothing to dissuade Dawn from pursuing her dream. Her
mother returned to Canada after extracting promises from
Aunt Patty that entailed curfews and immediate enrollment
at a junior college on Vermont. No promises were kept.
Dawn lied about her age and sweet-talked her way into the
Whiskey, and just about every other club on the Sunset Strip,
and habitually stayed until the wee hours of the morning. She
only visited the college campus on Vermont to buy pot.

Eventually, Dawn got her first break; she performed at an open mike night to a buzzing, very likely buzzed, industry packed audience, they were mesmerized by the clarity and roundness of her tone, her three-octave range, and—not least—her beauty. She was soon hired as a backing vocalist at Atlantic and Capitol and A&M and Nonesuch. She congratulated herself; she had gone from schoolgirl to the epicenter of a *happening* in the span of six weeks.

The artists she backed were at a pinnacle that she never expected to achieve. She watched, revered, and assimilated. Studio engineers and record producers were all men, all on the make, and to her young eyes—all of them closely resembled trolls. All had the same avaricious expression; all had the same unkempt, hunched air. She evaded them as much as possible.

One afternoon, while laying down a background track with three other girls for a bluesy folk singer, Dawn caught sight of a singularly different kind of man in the booth. He was heart-poundingly handsome, looked around twenty-three, twenty-four, and was over six feet tall. He stood straight-backed and sophisticated. His eyes were a clear, deep blue, and his hair was tousled and golden blonde. He was smiling, beautifully. Smiling at her. He put on a headset and spoke. He was a record producer. He was British and the deep timbre of his voice brought just the tiniest smile to her lips and a warm glow that traveled from her toes to the top of her head.

After the session they shared a joint in the parking lot and drove together to the grocery store where they admired the heaping ruby, emerald, topaz, and amethyst displays of California produce unknown in their native countries. After their goggle-eyed admiration of fruits and vegetables, they discovered they were hungry and went back to Cole's apartment five hundred feet above Sunset and grilled steaks and tossed an enormous salad. It was the most succulent meal they'd ever consumed. Whatever Dawn eventually came to think of casual drug use, she had to admit marijuana did marvelous things for the appetite.

Cole was reduced to a fit of giggles by Dawn insinuating herself into his lap while singing a sweet whisper of a song and then cooing suggestively in his ear like a sexy dove. It was at that moment, with a silken cascade of Breck-scented hair tumbling against his chest and her feather-soft lips fluttering against his skin, he realized with eruptive, mind-altering clarity that he wanted two things— he'd only ever wanted— *needed*—two things. He wanted to fuck, to make love to Dawn, and he wanted to bring her voice to the world. He discovered her, he possessed her, and Dawn, still a teenager, thought that was just super.

She began headlining at clubs where previously she had to beg the bouncers to let her in. Within twelve months of meeting Cole she had recorded her first solo album. She went on tour; Cole went with her; he hadn't left her side since the day they met. Her family worried about visas. Cole worried about how to invest the money she made and decided to start their own label. But first, he decided they should marry.

On a bluff in Malibu, each crowned with daisies they exchanged vows. Her parents heaved sighs of relief. Their daughter was married to a naturalized citizen and many in their generation had married equally young. Besides, Cole seemed a solid sort and had bought, for their first home, what her father called, "a banker's Tudor" in the wealthy suburb of Beverly Hills.

Dawn's career went supernova and Cole started buying other

record labels and folded them into his—their—own. By the time she was twenty-five Dawn was tired and recalcitrant. She refused to tour. She wouldn't record. She insisted on a break. Dawn wanted to sit in Cole's lap, as she did when they first met; she wanted to lean back against his chest in bed and listen to him read to her. She loved how his baritone rumbled through her skin. Cole obliged and within two weeks she was pregnant.

Unfortunately, Cole Starkey had some cute European ideas about the sanctity of his child's mother and the time during which Dawn had expected their romance to grow even deeper never materialized. Instead, after the pregnancy was established, Cole satisfied his sexual cravings with Playboy Bunnies and strippers. A friend of Dawn's told of his many peccadilloes while sponging her head at the hospital when Cole failed to appear in the delivery room. Dawn, who had been breathing rhythmically and had insisted on a "natural" childbirth, started screaming for a spinal block.

After Cliff was born Dawn confronted Cole. "You're fucking Bunnies? Idiots! And strippers? They're not even HOT enough to be Bunnies!"

Cole responded, "What's not hot after a fifth of Jagermeister and six lap dances?"

Suddenly, all that had been adorable about Cole, his quick wit, his sexual flair, his cocky attitude, his secret tenderness, his unflagging devotion to her career, became abhorrent. Dawn walked into the nursery, scooped up her baby and drove away, never to return.

★★★

"I never wanted him to go into business like his father. He could have been another Rubenstein. Oh, I could sing—but Cliff was a prodigy. My teacher's teacher studied with Franz Liszt. By the time he was twelve I had him studying with one of—did you know Rachmaninoff lived in L.A.? Oh. I guess that's not important anymore. What's important is that we, no, what's important is that you don't give up. Don't give up on my son."

"I'm sorry, Dawn, I never had a chance to give up on your son. He's dead."

"That's not what I meant."

Anne decided on another tack, "If you're successful with the D.A. and Cliff's body is exhumed?"

"I'll see."

"Okay. I think that's a good idea," said Anne in the most soothing manner she could. She had a sudden urge to tell Dawn what had just happened on the freeway, but stopped herself. After all, they were involved in first impressions now, and although Cliff's mother had been more than confiding, Anne didn't want to seem like an alarmist or a whiner. She did a mental check. Yes, she was still fine. She wrapped her arms around her middle. Would she insist on seeing her baby if it was stillborn? Probably so.

"All right, dear. I don't know where you're staying but I thought you should have the keys." Dawn stretched forward to the couch, pulled open Anne's arms and dropped a set of keys in Anne's hand.

Anne's hand was splayed open. Both Cole and Dawn seemed

to employ the same strategy. Anne felt each was trying to suborn her to their own cause— although the causes differed. Cole wanted primacy with his grandchild. Dawn wanted a sense of closure supplied by her son's corpse, a much more difficult proposition, if not impossible. One would be produced in a matter of months; the other was preserved in formaldehyde and lying in a box six feet underground. Possibility of closure: variable. "Ah, Ms. White. I don't think that's such a good idea. Na-ah. I mean Cliff's estate won't be settled now until, oh, at least until your issues are resolved, and—"

Dawn laughed. "It's not a bribe, *like that car out there.* I just thought you might like someplace to stay."

What was it about *that car out there* that was attracting so much attention? Anne thought, but when Cliff's mother laughed the peculiar urgency in her eyes cleared. Anne started to revise her immediate impression. Who wouldn't be over the top, fervid, if they'd been denied a last glimpse of their son when the rest of the world had buried him?

"At least don't you want to look around?" asked Dawn.

That seemed like a very good idea. Finding Cliff's door open was an unexpected bonus. Anne's fingers curled around the keys.

"Now, I should be going," said Dawn.

"Thank you."

"There are things here you probably need to see, and I don't. Take your time. Lock up when you go. If you go," Dawn said.

Anne was surprised by the sudden acceptance of this fractured family with its wildly different agendas. "But how do I get these keys back to you?"

"Don't worry about it. I wrote my number on the chalkboard in the kitchen and I only live up around the corner on Mulholland. You could practically yell out the window and I'd hear you." Dawn turned back to the piano, closed the fallboard, and stood up. She turned, the fingers of one hand still resting on the piano. She did have amazing poise. "There's some food in the 'fridge and, oh, you'll see." Dawn bent and brushed her lips across Anne's forehead; the gesture reminded Anne of Cliff at their last dinner, and then she left, closing the door carefully behind her. Anne hadn't moved from the couch. She sat for a minute and listened. Just the quiet of an old house and the ambient hum of the city below...

Chapter 23

I HEARD IT THROUGH THE GRAPEVINE

Anne remained seated on the couch. All of a sudden she experienced the awful vertigo-like rushing feeling she'd felt as she had sped off the freeway escaping the marauding Escalade, this was followed by the recall of a harrowing memory; it was of a recurring nightmare that had tortured her as a child. Her mother was explaining to her for the umpteenth time that she and her father were divorced. But in the dream Anne knew he was dead. He was dead and she'd never see him again. Bereft. Alone. Anne surfaced from the memory, as she used to wake from the nightmare. Gasping with tears stinging her eyes, feeling seasick and lost. She swallowed hard, shook her head, and said, to the empty room, "I can't do this now. Not a good idea."

Anne stood and hurried out of the house, pausing only to lock the door behind her. Driving home, she somehow contrived to get lost, snaking over to the canyon east of Bronson. Perhaps the fact that she was trying desperately to stave off hyperventilation had something to do with it. It was a few blocks in the wrong direction. She headed down the canyon. Waiting at the light on the corner of Franklin she spotted the Eminence Towers, an extraordinary piece of architecture skirted by a stone wall and an iron gate. She took a right on Franklin, realizing as she did so that she hadn't eaten since that morning and it was now late afternoon, a realization prompted by her stomach gurgling. A car darted out from in front of her and she lucked into a parking space directly in front of what looked to be a corner coffee shop.

Inside there was a scattering of people. Most were on their laptops or staring at their cell phones. A very few were actually conversing with each other. Although there were floor-to-ceiling windows, the place was dark. The walls were painted with a matte, dim, light-absorbing shade of eggplant. The furniture was of the yard sale variety, but most of the denizens were dressed in $300 jeans and distressed tees.

Anne approached the counter and surveyed a case of baked goods that looked like they should have been sold yesterday. "What'll you have?" The barista had a tattoo of a Greek key circling her wrist. She had white, poreless skin; bright pink cheeks; and jet-black hair an inch long. She wore a little black dress and a pair of scuffed Doc Martens.

Anne requested a cup of steamed milk, and the barista shoved a plate of carrot cake forward, "This is actually not disgusting."

Anne laughed and it felt good. "And a piece of carrot cake."

"Excellent choice." The barista turned to the massive espresso machine and asked "Whole, two percent, or nonfat?"

"Whole, please."

"You got it." She busied herself preparing the drink. Her motions were quick, decisive, and a little abrupt.

"You know that big building on the corner?" inquired Anne.

The barista turned around, "You a Clientologist?"

"No."

She turned back to the espresso machine. "I went in there once. They had an open house. I thought it would be good for business. Yeah, the word of God, and it sounded a lot like a motivational speech for used car salesmen. Boring! God! So boring! A little narrative drive and I would have stayed more than two minutes. Then when I tried to leave they were all over me with z-meters and training. I said to them, Hey, shitheads, *if* I wanted training I'd go down to Children's Hospital and train so I could hold sick babies and do something fucking worthwhile instead of wallowing in a lot of craptacular, self-indulgent, navel-gazing." Having finished the cup of milk she set it in front of Anne on the counter. "Didn't go over so well. They never come in here now. And I'm an SP," she said with emphasis, "and a squirrel. Imagine that, a SQUIRREL and a SUPPRESSIVE. They're not allowed to swear. It means I'm a nutcase dick-wad that doesn't believe in their total bullshit." The barista pushed the cake and cup toward Anne.

"How much do I owe you?"

"Pfft. It's on the house. Come back sometime and listen to me pitch another fit. I'm full of 'em. Tomorrow I think," she said casting her eyes around the room and speaking in a tone that invited a brawl, "tomorrow I'll be all worked up about people who can only communicate with little eensy-weensy electronic devices and how they all have teeny-tiny penises!"

Anne couldn't stop laughing. Then the door to the coffee shop opened and in walked Keir Bloomfield, either deep in conversation with an imaginary friend or speaking into his earpiece. "Jesus, Mary, and Joseph," the barista exclaimed. "Another one!"

Anne quickly turned to look over her shoulder; she recognized the screenwriter immediately, but he was looking off into space with a glazed expression and didn't spot her. Anne turned back to the barista and said, "I know him. But I can't attest to his penis size."

The barista barked a laugh that made heads turn and Keir waddled forward saying, "Anne? Anne Brown?" He squeezed her arm and ordered a piece of chocolate cake and a café macchiato. "Small world! I was just talking about you!"

"I'll bring your order over when it's up. That's nine dollars and forty cents," said the barista to Keir. He paid and put some money in the tip jar and hustled Anne away from the counter and they sat at a tipsy table. Keir pulled a face and then stuffed a wad of napkins under a table leg. He sat back up a little short of breath. "You're pregnant!"

Anne nodded her head. She wanted to gulp her milk and go hide. Keir continued, "This must be hell for you." Was this empathy? Who had he been talking to? Maybe she'd stay.

"I'm okay," Anne said.

"Really? I'm not," confided Keir. "God, it's so tatty in here." His lower lip began to tremble. It couldn't be because the decoration offended him.

Anne cocked her head and reached to pat his hand, but she hesitated before she touched him and let her palm drop on the table instead. Whenever anyone was consoling it usually triggered her waterworks. She didn't want to elicit the same response in Keir. Besides, listening to other people's worries was always better than focusing on her own. She asked, "What's the matter?"

"I don't know. I came out here to march into that Clientology building—Ben Haber practically grew up there—and you probably haven't heard, but there's been a real showdown between the Johnsons, after he won Best Actor." Anne remembered sitting next to her dad on the couch when his name was announced at the Oscars. "James and Shamari, some kind of blowout, and James put the little ones in day care here, at the Eminence Towers and, I don't know, I lost my nerve." He flicked a tear from the corner of his eye.

"Keir, why would you want to march into the Clientology building?"

"Because I miss Cliff and I—I..." He bit his lip so hard Anne thought it would bleed. It actually did start to bleed a little. Keir blotted up the dot of blood with his finger. The pain distracted him and the urge to burst into tears dissipated. "We were friends forever. I met him right when he came out of graduate school."

"Where'd he go to school?" Anne asked.

"Juilliard. He was going to debut with the L.A. Phil—I think his mom helped set it up, even though it was, you know, classical, not her scene. And at the last minute he decided he didn't want to. He used to joke about it; that's when we all met him, when he stopped practicing."

"The Cannibal Club?"

"Cliff told you?" asked Keir.

"Toni," Anne answered. "Cliff told me your motto: *Entertainment or Death*."

Keir slapped his hand over his mouth, "God, it sounds so horrible now!"

"It sounds like you were kids," said Anne.

"I was twenty-seven. Cliff was twenty-one. He was, he was..."

Like a confirmation, it just jumped from Anne's mouth, "Beautiful."

Keir nodded sadly. "I was going to say so funny, so glib; he just had this constant patter going like he was trying to make up for all the time he sat practicing. Cliff said that's all he ever did; his parents were such a nightmare. His mom, whoa! And his dad, bouncing from wife to wife, and you know how Louis XVI fixed clocks? His dad collected guns and then he started building them somewhere in that pile he lived in. Just disappear for hours."

"He was a gunsmith and a drug addict?" asked Anne, remembering something Shamari had mentioned about Cliff's father brandishing weapons and trying to balance that with her growing affection for Cole Starkey. Dawn hadn't mentioned anything about guns. Perhaps that particular interest developed after her departure.

"Yep, drug addict and he made guns," answered Keir.

"Okay..."

"I know, poor Cliff. He used to say that before he turned twenty-one it was just him and the Steinway, and the only one that had a voice was the piano. But after that it was like his tongue was unlocked; all he wanted to do was talk. I was a groupie, a fan, and all he had to do was go off on one of his stories. Now, Anne, I'm completely devoted to Toni. Everything I am I owe to her, and she's so understanding. But, but I always fall for the guy that's unattainable."

Anne raised an eyebrow, "Cliff was unattainable?"

He gestured toward her stomach. "Cliff was completely straight!"

"I get it."

"Anne. Anne, the night Cliff died I couldn't sleep. Toni always wakes up early. Earlier than me. But I couldn't. I couldn't sleep. Something was so wrong. I just felt it. So I sat out by the pool." He took a ragged breath. "It must have been about five in the morning. The sky was just beginning to pale, and I heard a car come up, real slow, real stealthy, in the driveway. So I hid. And look at me!" Keir looked down at his belly. "For me? Not so easy. I hid down by that wall back there. You know the one I'm talking about?" Anne nodded. "I heard a couple, kind of shuffling together, and talking real low, and I thought it might be you and Cliff, so, real careful, I peek up and over the wall, and it turns out that it's not you; it's Ben Haber and James Johnson all cozied up together. It looked like Ben had just come in; he's all rumpled and his shirt is buttoned crooked and James is rebuttoning Ben's shirt and tugging at him to come inside and Ben keeps talking about wanting a drink. And then James backhands him, right across the face. I can barely breathe and then I hear someone else breathing and I look up and there's Steve Nelson, standing right next to me in a white terrycloth robe, shaking his head, looking really irritated. He looks at me and says something like he's never played host to so many night owls in his life—but I can tell he's angry. Then he gives me a hand out of the shrub. By then Ben and James have gone into the house.

I don't think they ever saw me. But they had to see Steve. I didn't think anything of it at the time, thought it was a tiff, but now I wish I had."

"Did Steve report that to the police?"

Keir continued chewing on his lip. "I don't know. Maybe. You'd have to ask him."

"Did you tell the police?"

"I should have. Toni told me to. I meant to. But I got—I just got scared," whimpered Keir.

"Why are you scared, Keir?"

Keir cringed in his seat and wiped away some more tears. "I grew up here. When J. Paul Stoddard was alive they used to kidnap people and brainwash them and beat the living shit out of them. Clientologists. They're so secretive. You can't talk about anything you do there, all their levels, OT this and OT that. Now they've got a prettier face, all social responsibility with their own schools and drug rehab and a police force." He was beginning to ramble, the fear was discombobulating, throwing him off-balance, "And they give it a weird fake-sounding name like something out of an old science fiction movie, like Criminex, and Narcannot, and they plant fields of flowers for movie stars they want to recruit—but I think they still beat the living shit out of people." Anne wondered if Clientologists chased people down in giant SUVs.

The barista came by the table and set down a steaming macchiato and a huge slab of chocolate cake. "I brewed you another cup—I didn't want to interrupt—and I brought you a double slice of chocolate so you could share." She didn't hesitate for a second; she patted Keir on the back. "Eat, you'll feel better."

"Thank you," said Keir and Anne in unison.

"Forget about it. The Monastery of the Angels," she waved her hand in a northwesterly direction. Anne, looking up at the barista, noticed it had grown dark outside and that she had promised to be home in time for dinner. The barista followed her glance out the window and said, "Up the street, The Monastery of Angels, they're fucking cloistered, silent, Dominican nuns and they've got a website that tells you everything about them, balls-out on the record, exactly what they believe. They've got a little website and it tells you more in that single page than you'll ever know about Clientology. I'm just saying."

Chapter 24

SO ALIVE

In 1996 Keir Bloomfield got his first sole screen credit as a writer. Granted, it was on a low-budget, a very low-budget, movie that the producers guaranteed would be seen on oil platforms and tuna boats the world over. But it was a credit and it was his. Toni Todd, the film legend, had nothing to do with it; contrary to the advice of her facialist, she crinkled her nose at the whole project as if it had an offensive odor. Keir's illustrious agent at CAA secured the deal and took a whopping $2,500 fee for his troubles. However, the agent declined his celebratory invitation to drink martinis at Musso's, and instead he walked into the restaurant on his own and requested a seat at the bar.

The bar that night was packed, and so was every table. One booth in the corner, in particular, was loaded with Hollywood royalty. The man in charge was sixty-nine and still running a studio. His name was Bob Brown. There were agency heads and stars all at the same table, all male except for Brown's head of production, his trusty lieutenant, Becky Nelson. Aside from her presence, the place was awash with testosterone—and Keir loved it. He endeavored to find an opening at the bar to order but it was three-deep and people were doing their best to ignore him; that is, until a dazzlingly handsome young man with intense blue eyes, two elbows balanced on the bar, and a drink cradled in his hands turned to Keir and said, "I'm buying! What'll you have?"

"Dirty martini, two olives. What's the occasion?" Keir inquired.

"I just turned down Esa-Pekka Salonen!" blue eyes exclaimed happily. He set down his drink. He slapped Keir on the back and shook his hand vigorously, "I'm Cliff White." Keir nearly fainted. Those eyes. Those shoulders. He had no idea who Esa-Pekka Salonen was, but he was very glad his new acquaintance had turned him down.

Later, Keir gleaned over a succession of drinks that Cliff was referring to the Los Angeles Philharmonic. Cliff had given up his career and he was plotting to embark on another. He wanted to work at something new where he would be around people constantly. Having just come from an industrious hive of people persons, Keir suggested Cliff look into working at an agency. "Yeah," slurred Cliff. "My dad's kinda in talent management. Yeah. He'll know!" As the night wore on, they got drunker and drunker. Even the addition of two solid slabs of T-bone steak to their systems did nothing to the absorption of alcohol, and they ended outside the restaurant—from which they had been ejected with extreme prejudice—an hour shy of midnight, patting each other on the back while they took turns retching over the curb into the street.

When their stomachs were empty and their heads were still spinning Cliff stood up as straight as he could and said, "Whoa. Man, we need some fresh air." He headed off, up toward the hills, and Keir obediently followed. When they hit Beachwood Canyon, Cliff began walking on people's immaculate lawns, helping himself to cool draughts of water from garden hoses and coaxing Keir to do the same. Then they started their ascent into steeper territory and Keir queried their destination. "We're gonna climb the Hollywood sign, man," was Cliff's answer.

Heart pounding, suddenly not drunk at all, Keir did, in fact, climb the "H" on a series of narrow metal ladders. With every step the city spread wider and lights grew even twinklier at his feet. At the pinnacle he let out a whoop of ecstasy, the perfect expression of being alive and male and young, to the delight and echo of his companion, and the annoyance of several canyon neighbors, frequently awakened and beleaguered by similarly happy youths.

On the way back down from the sign they passed a red-tile-roofed house nestling in the trees on Deronda Drive. Here Cliff paused. "I like that house," he announced, in all seriousness. "One day I'm gonna live there." In this manner their friendship was established, brimful of high expectation, bravado, and excess. In Keir's eyes, Cliff was the master of adventure. In Cliff's eyes, Keir was the devoted foil.

When Cliff decided that, for their betterment or to "open doors" or some other such nonsense, they had to infiltrate what he termed—sounding as if he had been on some pretty wild drugs when he said it—"the inner sanctum of the secret societies within secret societies of the men in *power*" so they could enhance their (nonexistent) standing; Keir was all for it. Even if he didn't know what it meant. They paid visits to lodges scattered over the basin: Elks, Masons, Shriners, even The Rotary Club, and found them peopled, to their dismay with dull, middle-aged, civically minded men.

Cliff decided they'd fare better with the Clientologists, and although the church wasn't necessarily masculine, it was secret. Keir had severe misgivings, but he always deferred to Cliff's (not necessarily) better judgment. On their first and last encounter with the church, Keir gave a false name to a female assessor with an oddly thick neck. Cliff told a series of outrageous lies to a doe-eyed adolescent, just barely legal, who nervously replaced two metal rods in Cliff's hands every time Cliff set the metering apparatus down to illustrate each more fabulous point of his interview. Somehow they wriggled their way out of the building on Hollywood Boulevard at roughly the same point in the process and ran away laughing to get a drink at the nearest bar.

★★★

At that point, Keir's narrative petered out into incoherent gibberish and he finally dropped his great ruddy head into his pudgy hands and sobbed. Anne looked at the barista; the barista looked at Anne and nodded her head toward the despairing figure between them. Anne scooted her chair around so she was right next to Keir. She wrapped her arms as far as she could around his stout body and whispered repeatedly in his ear, as much for his benefit as her own, "It's gonna be okay. It's gonna be okay."

Chapter 25

One for My Baby (And One More for the Road)

Anne found her comfort zone in her pajamas, sitting in her
father's kitchen watching him make dinner, which on this
evening was chopped grapefruit and oranges and mango,
pancakes, and sausage. Breakfast, nothing could be more
perfect, plus another glass of milk. She couldn't get enough.
Anne knew she was in a regressive state, but after the day
she'd had, what she was beginning to think of as a near-death
experience, and long conversations with the following: a
former ballet dancer that ran a fastidious sex club, a tight-
lipped detective, a mother in deep denial, and a weepy
unrequited screenwriter, she felt in need of a little coddling.
Or the kind of coddling her father was capable of: he didn't
interpret or question events; he dealt with them, often with
an acerbic tongue, but in the meantime his was a business-
as-usual approach. As Bob Brown flipped pancakes, she went
to the refrigerator and got out a bottle of maple syrup and a
stick of butter, then she set the table and made her father a
pot of decaf.

Her father plated the food and they sat. Neither had said a
word in a very long time.

"Hey, champ. Why so quiet?" asked Bob.

"Daddy? What do you think of Steve Nelson?"

"He's an agreeable guy. Interior designer or something."

"Do you think he's gay?"

"That, I wouldn't know."

"Uncle Manny thinks he's gay."

"Honey, Uncle Manny thinks everybody's gay. You know? And what goes on in other people's bedrooms has never been any of my business. It's simply not my business. Lemme heat up the syrup." Bob stood up and popped open the microwave.

Anne pondered this statement while studying her father's back. He was wearing a navy sweater vest over a tan cotton shirt. Who wore sweater vests besides her father?

"Daddy?"

"Yes, Anne."

"If Steve Nelson knew something incriminating about somebody, do you think he'd tell the police?"

"Jesus H. Christ," groused her father as he poured syrup over both their plates. "I don't know, kiddo. Did you talk to the police today? Oh, that's right. You did, and then I did," he glowered.

"I'm sorry, Dad. Did you talk to Detective Vasquez?"

"Don't 'sorry' me, young lady. I talked to somebody I know here in Beverly Hills. You're knee-deep in this shit already. Could you dial it back a little?"

Anne was about to insist that being chased down by a madman had nothing to do with her dialing anybody, when her train of thought was derailed by the chiming of bells, in the style of a miniature Big Ben. Her father continued to bluster, "What the hell!" He slammed the syrup down on the table. The hell was, in fact, the front doorbell and Beverly Hills was not a neighborhood where people dropped by. He made his way, grumbling, to the front door with Anne trailing behind. Bob Brown's low-tech surveillance system consisted of a small hatch behind an iron grille through which he could peer at his visitors. Opening the hatch, he muttered so Anne could barely make it out, "Goddamn cocksucking bastard," then opened the door with a grand smile, "Cole!"

Cole Starkey stood at the threshold, a bottle of Oban Scotch thrust out before him. "Hello, Bob. This is for you. I was wondering if..." Anne stepped into view. "Oh, there you are!"

Bob took the bottle from Cole and said grudgingly, "Yes. Here she is. Come in."

Cole stepped inside and glanced around. Pop Art hanging from the walls, shining hardwood mahogany at his feet, he commented, "I always coveted your Warhol; didn't it used to be..."

"In my study. Yup. We were just having supper. Why don't you come into the kitchen?"

Cole noticed Anne's bare feet and striped flannel pajamas. "I'm sorry, I didn't realize it was so late."

"It's not late," said Bob. "You like pancakes?" He asked almost accusingly then without waiting for a reply, stated, "Well. That's what we're having." He turned and walked into the kitchen. Cole and Anne followed.

At the table, Anne ate a cold stack of pancakes then refilled her plate with a fresh stack that was warming in the oven. Carbohydrates made her feel friendly and relaxed. Cole declined breakfast-for-dinner but Bob poured a generous splash of scotch for them both. Cole warmed his tumbler between his hands. Anne chewed. Bob eyed Cole over the rim of his tumbler as he sipped the smoky beverage and let it warm his throat.

Cole raised his tumbler to them both. "Yes. Well. Cheers!" Anne clinked her glass of milk against his and then her father's.

"Didn't see your car in the driveway, Cole," said Bob. "You walk?"

"I did, in fact, yes."

"Wise choice."

"Whatever can you mean, Bob?"

"You're always getting lonesome-loaded. Thought you had a driver since you wrapped that bathtub Porsche around a tree last year."

"I have a driver for my convenience. Funny thing is, I often find it more convenient just to drive myself. For instance, when I picked up this scotch over at that new Pavilions on Santa Monica, it was so much easier to slip in and out without that great, hulking fellah dogging my every step. And who do you suppose was in front of me at the checkout but Ben Haber and another shockingly pretty-boy actor...

can't remember his name. Such serendipity." At the mention of Ben, Anne set down her fork. She tried to visualize the driver of the Escalade. He was big, in shirtsleeves, not a trendy young actor just out of puberty. "And they had the oddest assortment of things, not in a cart, but in one of those little red handbaskets: wine coolers, a pack of disposable razors, and two white tapers, you know, candles, two white candles. Doesn't leave much to the imagination, does it?"

Bob took another swallow of scotch. "Your convenience or court order?" he asked gruffly.

Cole smiled indulgently. "Sorry, what? I didn't catch that, Bobbo; all these years catching too many decibels played havoc with the old lugholes. Never mind, it doesn't matter. Don't you worry about *me*, Mr. Bob. You and I are about to become grandfathers," he raised his glass again. "To Anne and our first grandchild."

Not exactly fighting words. But before Anne and Cole had a chance to react, Bob Brown was up like lightning, knocking his chair back, flipping it onto the floor with a resounding *crack*! With one hand he took Cole's tumbler of scotch and hurled it across the room, where it exploded against the black-and-white tiles in a shower of liquid gold and glinting glass; with the other he grabbed Cole by the scruff of his neck (something Anne had never seen happen to a human being, as opposed to, say, a cat) and slammed his head with a thud, cheek first, against the kitchen table, and pinned him there.

Cole stared up at Bob with one baleful eye and said out of the corner of his mouth with as much aplomb as a squashed face could allow, "Don't tell me you don't feel *old* enough to be a grandfather."

Bob leaned in close and replied so quietly Anne had to strain to hear. "My daughter. Always, my daughter. If I see one lawyer, receive one writ of inquiry, get one phone call implying anything to the contrary, my happy shining face will be the last you ever see. We clear on that? *Are we clear?*"

"Perfectly," replied Cole.

"And furthermore—if you ever want to see this baby without serious supervision—you'll be going cold turkey. I've known you for the better part of forty years and for at least twenty you've been in an addlepated, drugged-out haze, and I'm not havin' it. You understand? *I. Will. Not. Have. It.* Not around my daughter. Not around my grandchild."

"But I…" responded Cole.

Bob tightened his grip on Cole's neck. "I'm gonna let you in on something eighty years of experience have taught me. For the better part, whatever the circumstances were that led you here in this life, whatever the past was, and whatever excuses you can come up with—this is it. This is a philosophy you can live by: *Nobody cares*, you have to *get over it*, and *grow a pair*." With that, Bob released his hold. Cole sat up rubbing his jaw. Anne looked from one to the other and realized why one had lost a recording empire and the other had exerted his authority for more years than she'd been alive. Again, Anne's mind was swirling. *We are such stuff as dreams…* She made a slight course correction—*we are such stuff as studio heads are made on.*

She pondered applying her father's philosophy to her own life and found it doable—except growing a pair—and decided not to sweat it. Furthermore, her inclination, should somebody have smacked her head against a table, would have been physical and retaliatory. Did Cole carry guns, or did he just tinker with them? Were Shamari and Keir's stories based on fact or were they just Hollywood rumors? Recording tycoon rebuilds Berettas to mend broken heart? Cole seemed completely nonchalant. He must have had more residual medication calming his nervous system than even she would ever have thought possible. Bob righted his chair and sat down. Cole, seemingly unflustered, observed, "Ah, family night at the Brown's."

"Get used to it," snapped Bob.

"I intend to," answered Cole. "Coffee?"

"Help yourself," Bob said.

Anne watched Cole walk to the coffeepot. He reminded her of an egret, tall and thin and showy and a little wobbly. She wasn't fazed by her father's anger; it was something she'd witnessed her entire life, never directed at her—always lambasting someone else, usually a colleague, one of his vice presidents, or a troublesome director. "That boy is a wart on the rear end of progress," was a description she particularly enjoyed, or this summation of the efforts of an unloved screenwriter: "A million chimpanzees typing for a thousand years couldn't come up with anything as putrid and shitty as this—unless they were typing with their asses." She did wonder how Cole managed to be so indifferent to Bob's volcanic temper. Maybe they had related to each other in this fashion for as long as they'd known each other. Her assumption was they'd once been friends; they had that familiarity, although they were obviously estranged. She'd have to ask. For the moment she filed it away and instead the question directed to Cole was, "Cole. Do you know Steve Nelson?"

He swiveled round, gesturing with the coffeepot, "Stupid prat! No. I don't. But I certainly think he's a person one should get to know. Bob, surely you have some idea?"

"About what?"

"About your protégé's husband," said Cole.

"Like whether or not he killed your son?"

Cole poured himself a cup of coffee. "Don't be an ass. No. Like whether or not he *knows* anything about *who* killed my son?"

"He OD'ed. I read it in the paper."

Cole turned to Anne. "Perhaps you'd explain."

Anne spoke very simply, "Cole does drugs. Cliff never did."

"Precisely," said Cole.

"Anne, you wanna talk to Steve Nelson?" asked her father.

"That would be good, Dad."

"Why all of the sudden, do you...?"

She thought of Keir in the bushes seeing James and Ben coming back from The Buccaneers, and Steve clucking and calling them night owls and wanted to know more. "I just think it would be a good idea," she answered.

"Okay." Bob drummed his fingertips repetitively against the tabletop. "Okay." He was thinking that this town was entirely known to him, it was *his*, and as long as he had control over Anne's access to those he'd put in power, then everything would, indeed, continue to be okay.

Chapter 26

A WELL-RESPECTED MAN

In the morning Natalie arrived before seven–thirty. Bob Brown was stooping to pick up the newspaper when she pulled into the drive. He straightened up as she got out of her car. "Don't kill your old man," he said. She kissed him on the cheek and he grunted and patted her on the back. Natalie found Anne once again in her pajamas, and back in the kitchen chopping apples and pecans before burying them in yogurt.

"Hey!" said Natalie. "You want to go shopping?"

"For what?" Anne replied, lifting her spoon to her mouth.

"For clothes."

"I hate shopping for clothes."

"Yep, and pretty soon you're going to go from stuffing a cute little cantaloupe into your jeans to trying to jam in a watermelon, and you're going to wish you had. Hey, and when's the last time we went shopping together?"

"Never." Anne looked down, "I'm not even showing yet—"

"So? We need a little quality time," Natalie said.

Their father had sat down at the kitchen table and was

reading the paper. "She's right," he commented without looking up.

"There!" said Natalie. "Dad, you want to come with?"

Bob Brown peered at his daughters over the top of his bifocals and they had their answer.

First they stopped at a maternity store on Beverly Drive, which Anne described as "a depressing collection of pup tents and leggings," followed by a "pick-me-up tour" (Natalie's words) on Wilshire: Neiman Marcus, Saks, and finally Barneys.

Anne was wondering how a little cotton knit onesie could cost so much when she noticed that the salespeople were all astir and moving en masse toward a large display for toddlers, as if they had just received a signal from the mother ship. "What gives?" she asked Natalie.

Natalie craned her neck and then pronounced, "I swear! I see that guy everywhere!" "That guy" was an actor three times married. All three unions had resulted in a set of children, and each successive wife was younger than the last. He was forty-eight and his youngest was a year old. "I was at the orthodontist and—"

"Why were you at the orthodontist?" Anne interrupted.

"Apparently, I grind my teeth in my sleep."

"Really?"

"So I got this biteplate, but I was waiting, you know, in the waiting room, reading some old copy of *National Geographic*, and Mr. Smoothy walks in with a couple of his kids. He, as you may have observed, is outrageously handsome and when he smiles you can probably see his shiny white teeth from the moon. But his kids, not so much... His son is at that adolescent point where he's growing so fast his features haven't caught up, and his daughter, well, I couldn't actually see her face because her spine had turned into Jell-O and she was flopped forward over her cell phone texting, no doubt, all her girlfriends." Anne laughed. "And, I'm the only other person in the waiting room. So they check in with the receptionist and then he turns to me and smiles that big smile, *BOOM*, and says, 'You have made an excellent choice! This orthodontist! This is the only orthodontist in L.A. who can fulfill your genetic potential!' And I'm thinking aren't orthodontists in the business of correcting what your genes screwed up? But I just smiled and thanked him and told him he had beautiful kids and went back to my magazine." Natalie continued to gaze in the actor's direction. "Boy, is he feelin' the love."

"Don't you think that's why he's an actor?" asked Anne.

"I think it's more complicated than that," replied Natalie thoughtfully. "Ask Dad about him. He produced one of his films about twenty years ago. I think he'd had his spleen out after a motorcycle accident. Dad liked him. Said he was a hard worker. Star quality, good actor, really hard worker, dumb as a box of rocks." Anne laughed and averted her eyes from the actor and the adoring salespeople. "No, you know, he must have had the accident while they were shooting, because he comes back to work and he's had some kind of religious conversion, and he's telling Dad all about it, smiling that big teeth-baring smile, and he says, *'Bob! Until you've hit your head on the pavement, signed the billion-year contract, been to the other side, you don't know what the heck I'm talking about!'* "

"Wow."

"Yep," replied Natalie.

A voice behind them said, "A billion-year contract? That's not poetry, ladies!" They turned to see Shamari Johnson with a two-year-old asleep in a stroller. "He's a Clientologist and a billion-year contract is what you sign when you're..." She *tsk-tsk*ed the spectacle. "Thinks he's Christ himself. Do *not* get me started." She scowled across the room then turned her attention to Anne. "You're not even showing yet, are you?"

Anne ran her hand down her front. "Not even a bump—but, you know…"

Shamari cooed and bent over the snoozing child in the stroller. "I do know! Now look at this big bump of a boy, and where's your daddy? Daddy's taken his nasty ass off to France." She tucked a floppy toy securely by the toddler's side. "And, Mommy's got herself a forensic accountant, isn't that right? I'm going to find all sorts of places where Daddy's trying to hide his treasure. But Momma won't let that happen—no sir—that treasure belongs to you, James Junior." She straightened and addressed the sisters while shaking her head. "Actors! Take my advice, girls—never marry one." She smiled confidently and, pushing the stroller, moved toward the elevator.

Natalie turned to Anne. "You know, I know you're trying to figure some things out, but I think you should forget about asking all these questions yourself and let the police handle it."

"Figure what things out?"

"Anne, don't be irritating," scolded her sister. "Believe me, I've never, in my life, been involved in a car chase, or—"

"Or what?"

"He's dead. He died of an overdose. You keep asking all these questions and you don't see any connection to what happened to you yesterday?"

"Obviously I see a connection," said Anne.

Natalie grabbed Anne by the elbow and pulled her over to a window near the dressing rooms that looked out behind the store. "See that building there? That belongs to our father. He's kept an office there since before you were born."

"He keeps an office there? What for?"

"I have no idea! But I do know if you need to find out about anybody in the industry, you could start by asking him."

Anne nodded toward the window, "Is that where Dad goes every morning on his walk?"

"Every morning."

"But what would Dad know about some teen heartthrob? I don't even think he knows who Beyoncé is."

"He knows who Beyoncé is because she's box office. Arguably. Anyway, like who?" Natalie countered.

"Like Ben Haber."

"For God's sake, Anne, even I know about Ben Haber."

"And who told you?"

Natalie was exasperated. "Dad! Dad told me!"

Chapter 27

MY HEART BELONGS TO DADDY

Once upon a time, a gifted comedienne, Marion Davies, fell hard for a married man, William Randolph Hearst. Mrs. Hearst, a former chorus girl, received, in a lucrative arrangement, dominion of the East Coast, the children, and the right to retain the status of wife to one of America's wealthiest men. Marion and W.R. got to reign on the West Coast and enjoy the company of Marion's theatrical friends. They liked to entertain. He liked to build things. One of the things he built was Hearst Castle in San Simeon. Another was a huge Beaux-Arts edifice on the corner of Franklin and Bronson in Hollywood. Originally, the building was intended for Marion Davies—decades and certainly a few eras later, it was sold to The Church of Clientology. While it no longer housed Marion's friends, its ghosts would have been gratified to know it was redubbed Eminence Towers. Across the street was a deli, rumored to be owned by John Gotti's little brother, a dry cleaner, a pharmacy, a video store, and a Chinese takeout.

In 1987 the Eminence Towers was a faded beauty. It housed a cadre of sweet-natured, evangelically inclined young people who worked round-the-clock, struggling to become OT Clear. They drank a phenomenal amount of coffee. When they did retire for the evening, it was to once glamorous apartments now furnished with peeling wallpaper and bare mattresses. The place stank of boiled peas and ham (the church provided a free lunch) and played host, that year, to a low-budget horror flick starring Bill Hickey and some homicidal puppets and a day care center. It was also the year Ben Haber was born to a pair of live-in assessors, Crystal and Henry Haber, originally of Ames, Iowa. They had come to California to find fame and fortune, but while eating pizza by the slice on Hollywood Boulevard they were approached by a pair of young men in somewhat nautical attire who offered a free stress test on a z-meter and they found religion instead.

Baby Ben was a charmer. To garner a smile he'd mimic, sing, dance—an adroit coping mechanism when faced with the hurly-burly of living in something akin to a commune. At the age of three he had headshots and appeared in two TV commercials. By the age of five he had steady work on Nickelodeon, and as he grew and moved on to become a regular on the Disney Channel his parents bought the family a McMansion in the Valley, studio adjacent.

At the age of eighteen he was playing sixteen, in the breakthrough role that made him the heartthrob of every twelve-year-old girl in America. He was Jimmy Bissell, eldest son of globe-trotting AP reporters Luke and Amy, who often left him to care for their brood of five younger children, despite him having only just become old enough to gain a driver's license. We'll ignore the problems with the premise and note only that Ben found the guy who played his father, Adam Baker, irresistible. Mr. Baker was thirty-six and hot. He drove a Harley to work. He didn't live with his parents. He kept all his income to himself. He had no religious affiliations. He partied, and often invited Ben. For the first time in his life Ben felt giddy, uninhibited; for the first time in his life, of his own volition, he was having FUN.

Ben had been raised in a showbiz bubble, tutored on set, coached by pros, managed by his parents—he had a vague idea that about fifty percent of his income went to "handlers": publicists, lawyers, The Church of Clientology, and he took it as a matter of course. When Adam suggested, after their amazing premiere season, that Ben buy a $1.5 million starter home next door to his own in the streets above the Sunset Strip, Ben's parents called the network and the head of their church, Dominic Semyon.

In a meeting in a high-rise in Century City, just a network exec and young Ben, the executive was exceedingly blunt. He said, "Unlike your parents and your Clientology friends, I don't give a damn where you put your dick, but I *do* care deeply about my franchise. While you work for me you will date women. You will be photographed with women. There will be blogs and articles and news items speculating about your clearly hetero love life. There will be no hints to the contrary. Prepubescent girls will pine for you." The executive adapted an expression that conveyed he was speaking to a very stupid, very valuable show pony. Ben was thinking about his love life, or more precisely his sex life, and was too busy to notice. "Do you understand what I'm telling you?"

Ben was made to understand, in the gentlest way, the implied threat to his (and several others') livelihood. And after several sessions of personal counseling administered by the head of Clientology, he complied. He bought the house next door to Adam and then he asked a friend of his from the Disney years, Penny Scott, to be his beard. He and Penny had bonded over a shared love of cats, chocolate chip cookies, and screaming pitch-black rides on Space Mountain on the company dime. There was a period when they would call each other on their cell phones and simply leave them on while they went about their business, just to feel connected. Later, when texting became the "thing," they did so without cease.

Penny was affable; she even joined Ben's church, and after they became a regular item in the tabloids her career began to pick up. Into their third season, Ben's show was going strong and his salary was bumped to a nice plump six figures an episode. His machine made sure he was perceived by the media as a young man with the qualities of integrity, responsibility, and steady devotion. Eventually, he and Penny came to share the house on Thrasher Way, but he slept, every night he could, next door at Adam's.

Chapter 28

GOT THAT VIBE

A few days later, Anne, wearing an updated swing coat her sister insisted she buy, walked into a showroom on Robertson. It held three pieces: an ancient roman marble tub; a sixteenth-century French tapestry of a forest in burgundy, green, and gold; and a perfect art deco mirrored vanity that looked like it was plucked fresh off the set of a Fred Astaire and Ginger Rogers musical. Anne thought bathing in such a place would be as cozy as washing up in the middle of the Smithsonian. A smartly dressed young woman seated behind a desk painted the exact Dresden blue of the wall looked up and inquired, "Anne Brown?" Anne nodded. "I'll let Mr. Nelson know you're here." A moment later an invisible door opened in the wall and Anne was invited to step through. On the other side of the door was a north-facing studio set up with drafting tables. Steve Nelson was standing at the shoulder of a draftsman indicating something on the drawing with a mechanical pencil. He smiled at Anne.

"How we used to work before all those CAD programs. Me, I prefer to do it by hand," said Steve. He pointed, this time to a visible door. "Let's go into my office."

The office was sunlit. It was furnished like a living room with a comfortable clutter, samples were everywhere: cloth, stone, hardware, glass, and carpet. Steve Nelson guided Anne to a slipper chair, like he was placing her in the most advantageous spot to suit the overall decorating scheme. As she sat, he looked at her with satisfaction. "I like your coat," he said. Anne noticed Steve had dropped weight since she'd last seen him. He had lost his tan and had circles under his eyes. He looked a good ten years older, and suddenly Anne wondered if he was ill.

"I hope I haven't come at a bad time, really, feel free to kick me out whenever you want," said Anne.

"No. I was meaning to call." He shook his head. Anne could see trouble in his eyes but what he said was evasive. "I always tell the kids who work for me that the only way to really know a city is to walk its streets, explore its every neighborhood, or at least those in which you aren't likely to get shot. If you traverse the streets of this city, you see that L.A. is a thousand cities in one. Trouble is, everyone here drives." Anne listened closely. "There's no mental geography," he looked haunted. "Everyone needs a sense of place, you know?"

"I think so," Anne said.

"I work for people who have so much money, they think— well, they think just about whatever they want but that doesn't make it true," he said displaying an open envelope. He tapped his finger against the return address. Anne saw a logo that looked like a "C" entwined with some triangles. She recognized the logo from the sign on the Eminence Towers, then she read a man's name, Dominic Semyon, the name her sister had first mentioned in the children's section of Barneys, and under that an address in Hemet, California. She could feel a weird tingling at the base of her skull.

"Where's Hemet?" she asked, remembering seeing the signs on the freeway as she drove away from Palm Springs and seeing the car following her not long after.

"Not far from Palm Springs," he continued. "It's an enormous commission, an enormous commission that I think I have to turn down; or maybe it would be better for you if I didn't." He pivoted on the balls of his feet to face her. There was a wild, lost look in his eyes. "I always think best at the beach. Do you want to come to the beach with me?"

For a man who felt that overreliance on driving was dislocating and alienating, Steve was able to comment on their whereabouts the whole way as he drove and drove to an uncertain destination. They sped through canyons. "The Bel Air Country Club used to own these giant tracts from here to the sea. Kept their horses up this canyon here in the thirties, later the studio moguls kept starlets there, in the stables, well, which was the euphemism for prostitutes. Starlets. Sometime in the sixties it all shifted. The place converted into a kind of hippie hollow and the stables became houses. Then the country club gave the land to the state—and everybody had to go."

A large black SUV changed lanes behind them. Anne caught her breath. Steve looked at her with concern. "Do you want me to slow down? Are you getting car sick?" The SUV disappeared into traffic.

"No. Thank you. I'm fine. This is just what I needed." Anne was forming another attachment, this time to Mr. Nelson.

He drove over rolling green hills dotted with shimmering pepper trees. Then they parked on a bluff above the Pacific. Steve exited the car and started down the bluff. Anne followed behind, digging her feet into the sand to keep from falling, yet ended up slipping and sliding down to the beach, just barely retaining her designation as a biped.

"Come!" Steve walked to the edge of the ocean with Anne practically jogging to keep up. He stopped just short of the surf. "The film industry, more than any business I know, is about cultivating relationships." He brushed some sand off her shoulder then said, "Turn around," which she did. "I'm not being fresh," he said, brushing down her back and butt and tugging at the hem of her coat. "You're covered with sand. There. What was I saying? Oh. Yes. This beach. This is where I got my first sense of place in L.A. It's a hard place to call home."

Anne replied. "I know exactly what you mean."

Steve looked directly at her. "I bet you do," he sighed. "I don't know what to tell you, Anne. I don't really do bumper sticker platitudes. I mean how helpful is a statement like: *Keep calm and carry on*, or *I've got nothing left to lose?*"

"I'm sorry."

"Thank you." Steve kneaded his forehead. "Stuff just happens. It's nobody's... Becky wanted me to... Uh... Listen, I've got pretty good instincts and this commission from Clientology screams hush money to me. Headquarters all over the world, why? I'm not close to any of their poster children—I just happened to host a party."

Anne's head was whirling with all sorts of blurry associations and half-understood events, and nothing was, as yet, clear.

"So I'm going to give you some advice." He handed her the envelope imprinted with the logo. "Go to Hemet. I don't exactly know how, but we'll figure that out later."

Anne folded the envelope and put it in her pocket. They stood for a minute watching the waves break and dissipate on the shore. Steve thought of Alex—at least he still knew who he was. Anne thought, "he who makes with the upholstery" had really come through, when he said, "You know, when we found out Cliff had died, I…do you remember how Ben said we should all be silent?"

"I left right after breakfast," Anne reminded him she hadn't been there when the police arrived.

"That's right. Well, Ben," he faltered. "I thought it was touching, that silence, but then, later, Bill was furious. He told me it was some crazy Clientology flimflam. He said when a Clientologist experienced trauma or injury they were supposed to be absolutely quiet so that *healing energy* could make its way through the ether to them—or something like that. On his last movie, the one he did with James Johnson, Bill said a stunt guy was hurt and he started yelling to clear the set and get the medic in and James, who was right there, went, 'Shh! Be quiet' and stood there, all sanctimonious and hovering. And Bill was all, *what the fuck?* Only for James to read him the riot act and berate him for *blocking his healing rays.* To which Bill replied, 'Oh yeah, no doubt your glorious and immortal founder implemented the cone of silence when he got sick of his wives screaming when he hit them.' They no longer get along, to put it mildly."

"Bill and James?"

Steve turned and looked directly into Anne's eyes. "Cliff was a good kid."

Anne slipped her hand into Steve's. "Thank you."

Steve shook his head. "I should have told the police. I'll tell them now. And you shouldn't go to Hemet. I don't know what I was thinking. We should. Or the police should. Yes, the police should." He squeezed her hand and walked with her back to the bluff.

"Do you think Mr. Aagard might have a minute to talk to me?" asked Anne when they had made it back to the car.

Steve took his phone from his pocket, leaned against the BMW, and while entering a number, said, "I don't see why not." He nodded as the call was picked up. "Bill? I've got Anne Brown here."

Chapter 29

I WAS MEANT FOR THE STAGE

When Anne mentioned Teuscher's, one of the places she frequented near her father's house, Bill offered to meet her there. She walked in to find him seemingly enchanted by a display case of candy—an unlit cigar in one hand, the other pressed in anticipation against the glass. For such a tall man, it was almost a childlike posture. They ordered cocoas and sat at a table he dwarfed in silly little curvilinear chairs.

"Are you comfortable?" Anne inquired, arranging the folds of her coat across her lap.

"Any place where there's chocolate like this I'm comfortable." He took a long contented drink of cocoa and eyed the two truffles on a saucer over the rim of his cup that sat on the table between him and Anne. He smiled at Anne. Anne smiled back. He looked so outsized, out of place, and outright enjoying the attention. "You know what I do as a director?" he asked.

"Enormous action adventure movies?" responded Anne.

"Nope. I'm a mirror. The most important thing I do is reflect my actors. I see everything they do in front of the camera. I'm a mirror. I see everything they do. They've got to be able to trust in the mirror."

Anne found this statement somewhat cryptic. "Ah. You know

Tessa, and Steve Nelson just now, right before he called, they both said you had some troubles with James Johnson and Ben Haber."

"James used to be a friend of mine."

"And Ben?"

One side of Bill's mouth went to the side and he shrugged.

"You don't like Ben." It was statement, not a question, but still Bill felt compelled to reply.

"People like Ben are transparent."

"Transparent?"

He took one of the truffles and put the entire thing in his mouth. "Transparent, like a vampire's reflection. As in, they don't cast one."

Anne tried to work her way through Bill's tortured metaphor to see what he was driving at. "Like he's a personality vacuum?"

"Kind of. But more like bait. Man candy. Man candy without a soul. He just sucks you in. Forgive the obvious allusion."

"Pretty harsh," While she considered this, Anne gestured at one of the truffles. "Please, help yourself." Bill scooped up the other for himself. "So. You think Ben is soulless man candy?" Bill shrug-nodded in agreement.

Anne found herself flummoxed and frustrated by their odd, imprecise back-and-forth. Bill's dubious assertion about Ben

Haber hadn't exactly been helpful. She was struggling to summon up a cogent question when Bill resumed talking.

"There's a hierarchy here. Movie stars are at the top. TV actors are kind of considered journeymen. Everyone wants to be on top. Ben wants to be on top. So he meets James at some fund-raiser and starts doing this puppy dog act. Phony adoration, and *oh, teach me Obi-Wan Kenobi.* I could puke. Then he gets him going to Clientology, and the church starts doing all the same seductive shit."

"Seductive?" interrupted Anne.

"Like, you're so special, we, and only we can really see how special you are; if you were one of us you could change the world with your specialness. We'll show you how; oh, and by the way, your new little soul mate? Ben? And all that stuff you do below the waist? He told us during an *assessment*. That's not validation of your bond; that's an aberration, an *incident,* an impediment in your *time track* and we wouldn't want that to destroy your career, because you have so much to give the world; you better come in for special training. Pretty soon, James believes all the same shit his boy toy's been inculcated with. Which is more than ironic considering what he's been inculcated with forbids everything that's not heterosexual, and everything James and Ben have together is definitely not heterosexual. And in a way, they really are soul mates because they're both so emotionally fucked."

"Do you even talk to James anymore?" Anne asked.

"Why bother?" he grunted. "He wouldn't listen to me. Love is a drug, and so can belief be, even when it's in something totally bogus."

"But you must have been talking to him for a while because—"

Bill interrupted. "Oh yeah! He wouldn't shut the fuck up. And the more he talked, the more he backed himself up in a corner. Church. His and hers. Equally homophobic. Mother of his children versus boy toy."

"Are they still seeing each other?" asked Anne, remembering Cole Starkey had seen Ben at the grocery buying wine coolers. She wondered if he was accompanying James to France.

"I wouldn't know. He's not talking to any of his old friends. I kind of doubt it. I think they both got what they wanted." He was looking at the display case. "Do you want anything?"

"Thank you, no," said Anne. "Who got what?"

"Ben got a movie role and James got laid by an awesome-looking twenty-year-old mimbo."

"I heard something about Cliff being called onto the set. On your last movie, with James and Ben, was somebody high?" Bill groaned and covered his eyes. "I'm sorry to ask. I just, sometimes when people tell me things about Cliff—Steve Nelson told me he was a good kid, and Joe Merlin said he was one of the good ones, and—I, I just want to know why."

"Who told you about that?"

"About Cliff being on set? Or?" asked Anne.

"On set. About trouble on my set."

Anne scanned her memory and remembered clearly, "My Uncle Manny." She could see he didn't recognize the reference. "Old-time production designer, Emmanuel Brown?"

"Oh, right! Wow. He must be..."

"He's ninety," said Anne.

"Wow. Wow, when I was at NYU he came and talked to my class. I'm sorry. I didn't realize the connection. Well, what did he say?" Bill inquired.

"I think he said something about somebody being beyond stoned on set."

Bill sighed. "Those people who told you Cliff was a good man. They were right." Anne could feel her eyes sting and her throat tighten like she was about to cry but she smiled instead and took a slug of cocoa. "I don't know how to put this," he cleared his throat. "I try not to be one of those asshole directors who screams all day, but," he paused, "but one day I'm on set, we're just coming back from lunch and, and we shot the morning with Ben and he doesn't play in the afternoon but James does and I see the P.A. knocking at James' trailer to tell him he's needed in ten and his assistant comes to the door and points toward Ben's trailer. So this kid, who's about Ben's age and a real go-getter but sweet as can be and really naïve, goes up and knocks on Ben's door. Ben opens the door a crack and then closes it. About twenty seconds later—too long, the pacing's all wrong, something's obviously up—the door swings open and out stumbles James right into the P.A., and then they both kinda bounce down the steps. Okay, by that point, I admit, I'm getting pretty steamed. It's obvious that James is drunk or stoned out of his mind so I wait for him to walk onto set, which he does kind of draped over the P.A., who's got a cut on his chin. And I'm thinking, I can't fire him, James. He's my friend. I've never seen him like this before, and besides, his doctor will just tell the studio he's suffering from exhaustion and they'll can *me* instead. So we've already set up the shot and we take our places and it turns out he's got his lines down pat, but he literally can't stand up. He keeps tipping over, or his knees buckle and then he pops back up shouting, 'I got this!' Well, he didn't have it, and I decide I'm going to fire him, him and that little pill-dispensing man-whore, and Tessa, who's been watching all this from video village, walks over and hands me her phone and says, 'Call Cliff instead.' "

"Oh," said Anne.

"Yeah. So Cliff gets to set in about ten minutes and the A.D. is trying to get me to reblock the scene, but as far as I'm concerned if he's doing it, he's doing it standing up. And I'm about to walk off set and Cliff comes up to me and he says, 'Bill, he can do it. I promise.' I tell him unless we tie James to a pole there's no way he can stay upright, but he convinces me, says it'll be better for everybody if we just get through this, and so we get everyone camera-ready and Cliff is standing next to me at the monitor. He sees how I've got the shot framed and when the A.C. goes in to mark it with the slate he, Cliff, crawls down out of the shot, and he's there, flat out on the concrete floor and he's, granted, out of the frame, holding James up by his knees. And James is standing, saying his lines perfectly every time, with Cliff sweating to keep him steady and stay away from the lens. Saved my ass, saved James', and indirectly saved that worthless little piece of shit. For an agent he, he just went to the wall for everyone he knew. He was okay—he was much more than okay—he was honorable."

Bill stared off into space for a minute and then he met the eyes of Anne, who had been thinking, *Honorable or world-class enabler?* But she kept a muzzle on it.

"Bill?"

"Yeah."

"Do you know where Cliff was the night he died?"

"I thought he was in his car."

"He was. He was found in his car. But, from what I can figure, he was put there."

"Put there, like after he died?"

"Yes."

"Why would somebody put him there after he died?"

"I think that depends on where he was the night he, he—"

"Died. Anne, do you know what a Dead Agent Attack is?"

"A what?"

"It's something Clientologists say. It's when the church goes after one of their critics to destroy their credibility. It could be as innocuous as an actress saying somebody is ignorant or it could be serious litigation. You just never know."

Chapter 30

BE LIKE THE BIRDIES AND SING

As Anne was about to embark on the short drive home from the Little Santa Monica Boulevard parking lot, she noticed, for the first time, the odometer of the Ferrari: it read 4,972. With that kind of mileage it was more ornament than car. For a second she considered filling the gas tank and heading back out to the desert—to Hemet—but a call to Detective Vasquez probably would be the more prudent course.

It was ten after six and the freeways would be a nightmare. By instinct it seemed she turned the car east. She drove Mulholland until the 101 above the Hollywood Bowl broke it and she dropped down into Studio City and crossed an old bridge that looked like a WPA project over the freeway and headed up the back way to Beachwood Canyon. The car glided into the driveway of Cliff's house. The porch light was on, so were lights inside. They must have been on timers. Anne let herself in the front door with the key Dawn had given her. The house was exceedingly clean. It smelled like orange peel. There were fresh flowers in a vase in the entry but the place felt completely empty. Anne stepped into the living room. It was still dominated by the piano.

She turned around and walked past the dining room and the kitchen, then on down the hallway, poking her head through doorways, finding first an office and after that, a bathroom. Something about the bathroom struck her as interesting, and she didn't think it was her innate curiosity or nosiness. She stood at the bathroom sink and opened the medicine cabinet. There were a lot of Kiehl's products, a packet of antihistamines, some dental floss, an Ace bandage, aspirin, and not a single bottle of prescribed medication. That was odd. Everyone had something, antibiotics, or just an ancient tube of acne ointment. Especially if their purported cause of death was an overdose. Anne wondered if Cole had cleaned out Cliff's stash.

She left the bathroom and moved on to the bedroom. Inside, she noted a large closet, a rather small double bed (which suggested a paucity of overnight guests), a chest of drawers, and a desk with a dark laptop plugged into the wall. Anne opened the closet and looked at dress shirts and suits and an assortment of ties. There was a parka hanging at one end that could have been used on a polar expedition and a black wool overcoat that was probably only worn when Cliff had traveled to the East Coast. She opened the chest of drawers. Everything was arranged so neatly: socks were wrapped in balls and ranked in rows, boxers had their own drawer, jeans were next, long sleeve tees and then short sleeve tees, and in the drawer under those, sweaters. Anne lifted a blue cashmere sweater to her nose and breathed in. She took off her voluminous jacket and laid it on the bed and pulled the sweater on over her head. The feeling that his hands were running down her body overwhelmed her, that touch, the scent of him—soap and sweat and warm skin—the darkness as her eyes closed, the softness all around her—dizzying. She opened her eyes with a start. She felt the silken wool under her fingertips, and shook her head to scatter the sensation that Cliff was present, like that starlit night in desert. She passed her palm over her face and then she went under the piles of clothes in each drawer and ran her hands underneath, into every corner, and found—nothing.

Next, she sat down at the computer and turned it on. Cliff was logged out. She sat with idle fingers on the keyboard, thinking about his password, wanting access, a way back in, when she heard the front door open and heavy footfall in the tiled entry. Either there was a giant woman who had access to the house, or a man had just walked in. Had she left the front door open? Suddenly, her only thought was, "How do I get out of here?" She stood, lamely entertaining the thought of scooting under the bed when she heard a familiar voice.

"Ms. Brown? I saw your car in the driveway."

"Detective Vasquez?" Anne's hand was clutched at the neck of Cliff's sweater.

The detective stood in the doorway of the bedroom. "What're you doing here, Ms. Brown?"

Anne, who had momentarily lost the power of speech, took Cliff's keys out of her pocket, meaning to show them to the detective, but instead she dislodged Steve's envelope and dropped it on the floor where she crouched and jammed it back in her pocket. Flustered, she could only stutter.

"Hmm. I, however," he pulled a sheaf of folded paper out of his suit coat, "have a search warrant."

"Why?"

"You may not have noticed, but this is an ongoing investigation, Ms. Brown."

"No. No! Why are you here?" insisted Anne.

"You are being obstinate. I ask the questions. Like, that

sweater's big on you—is it yours?"

Anne gestured, in chagrin, to the bureau.

"I see the computer is on. That you?"

Anne nodded.

"And have you been, I don't know, looking around? Touching everything?"

Anne's voice went small. "I have been. Yes."

The detective passed Anne and picked her coat up off the bed and handed it to her. "Ms. Brown, I'm going to have to ask you to leave." She started to pull the sweater off. "Just take the sweater with you." They walked down the hallway to the front door.

Anne paused. She saw two nondescript sedans, presumably unmarked police cars, blocking the Ferrari Scaglietti in the driveway, and two large white vans out on the street in front of the house. There were a few men and one or two women in each of the vehicles. Her hand went to Vasquez's arm and she said very quietly, "Those are mobile labs."

"Yes, Ms. Brown. Those are mobile labs." Anne turned her head to the detective. "Why?" was written all over her face. Phil Vasquez cleared his throat and said, "Can I offer you a lift home?"

"Why can't I take my car?" asked Anne.

"We'd like to take it into headquarters and examine it again, is that all right with you, Ms. Brown?"

"And the labs?"

"Are for the house," concluded the detective.

"I've never seen a house so clean," said Anne, but it ended up sounding more like a question.

Phil Vasquez replied, "So was The Buccaneers. You told me all about it. You can dip a thing in Clorox and it's still going to register something under infrared."

Anne couldn't seem to move her feet. She was rooted in the entryway. "What're you looking for?" Her guess was he hadn't heard about her incident with the Ferrari on the 134.

Detective Vasquez put his hand to the small of Anne's back and gave her a slight shove. "Let's talk about it on the drive to Beverly Hills. Shall we?"

On the twenty-minute drive back to her father's house, Detective Vasquez's jaw was clamped as tight as his hands on the steering wheel. The car had a computer screen mounted on the dash, as in a patrol car, but the detective had switched it off and turned it as far away from the passenger seat as it would go. The only noises Anne made were little enraged puffs as she exhaled through flared nostrils. Theirs was a conversation of sorts, but it didn't involve words. Detective Vasquez pulled into the circular drive off Crescent and shifted the car into park in front of Bob Brown's house. As soon as the car was stationary, she flung her weight at the car door and was up and out of the car rigid with anger. The detective spoke. "Ms. Brown…"

Anne turned on her heel and stared in at the detective through the open passenger door, "If you call me that one more time!" she dug into her pocket and threw Steve Nelson's envelope into the car.

Vasquez fumbled his catch, but he did make a successful grab for the envelope. "What the..." He scanned the address and the return address. "What the hell is this supposed to be?"

"You're the detective! You're the detective! You tell me!" shouted Anne before she slammed the car door shut.

Phil Vasquez quickly exited the car. "Please. You can't just..." he said to Anne's back as she walked to the front door. He hurried to catch up with her.

"I'm hungry!" Anne snapped. "I'm going inside."

"I'm sorry," he said.

Anne halted. "What?"

"I'm sorry," he repeated. "Can I get you something to eat?"

He really did look sorry, enormously sorry. Anne wondered why. "Like what?" she asked.

"Do you like burgers? Milkshakes? Fries?"

"All of the above."

"Okay."

They ate at an In-N-Out Burger on Pico. Phil—Anne thought of him that way now—inquired about the meaning of an envelope addressed to Steve Nelson from Dominic Semyon at a Clientology office located in Hemet. Anne told him everything she knew, including Bill's version of James Johnson and Ben Haber's relationship. When she had finished her recitation Phil frowned, "I just, Dead Agent Attack? Do I have to put you in protective custody? Ms. Br... Anne? Do I?" He looked around the fast food joint as if one of the other customers there could answer his question.

Anne drained her milkshake. "I think I tell you a lot more than you tell me," she said as she patted her mouth with a napkin.

"That's generally how these things go." He started doing that business with his hands again, making the apex of a triangle with his fingertips.

Anne concentrated on his hands to keep from crying and said, "I think there's a lot more that *you know* that I don't. Isn't there?" But, instead of saying it, it sounded more (to her own ears) like the quavering of a tree frog. Apparently the detective noticed the quavering too, but he got the message.

He felt his insides become liquid even as his face stiffened into a mask. Anne's eyes had gone all wide and glossy. Unlike anyone else, she made him want to ignore protocol. Perfectly aware he was thinking with his dick and not his brain (well, maybe a more accurate description was he was thinking with his brain flooded with dopamine and norepinephrine), he tapped his clasped hands against the laminated tabletop and then relented. Somehow he wanted to make things better, better for *her*, specifically. "Ms. Brown, I do have certain information that you cannot share with anyone, not a single soul, or it could jeopardize the entire investigation. Do you understand?"

"I understand," said a voice that Anne recognized, though she was only faintly aware that is was she who had spoken.

"Nobody. You can tell nobody."

Anne nodded her consent.

"Aw f…" He made a minute gesture, straightening his shoulders. "Okay. As per Dawn White's request, and consistent with the directives of the district attorney for Los Angeles County, and pursuant to certain evidence I, I cannot specify," his face colored, "the body interred at Holy Cross Cemetery, otherwise known as Clifford White, was exhumed and determined to be that of one Ryan Simms, white, thirty-four, six-foot-two, blond, blue-eyed, resident of Winnipeg, citizen of Canada."

He stopped. How could he have been so stupid? How was this information going to make things better for Anne Brown? He had just taken her from the certainty of death to the unresolved emotional wilderness of missing persons, or worse. And in his experience, people who had gone missing for over a month never came back. They were just dead and nobody who had cared for them knew where they were, but that didn't stop them from wishing they did. Under the table he clenched his fist and drove his fingernails into the fleshy part of his palm until it hurt. "What I meant to say was, I, do you understand now why you can't go around talking to everybody? You've got to stop that."

Anne stared directly into Phil's eyes. Her lungs felt like they were going to explode. All she could do was keep breathing. If she stopped breathing there wouldn't be any oxygen for the baby. Ryan Simms?

"You've got to stop talking to everybody," repeated the detective.

Anne stood up. She wanted to be outside where it didn't smell like grease and meat. She walked out of the restaurant. It was raining. The streets were shining. If she were in New York it would be snowing and the air would freeze the membranes of her nose and all she'd smell would be ice. Sharp and cold enough to make her skin crack and her nose bleed. Here, it was just wet and soft. Phil was taking her arm and bustling her to the car. Why were people always encouraging her to sit down? She didn't want to sit. She pulled her arm away. "How's that going to work, detective?" I mean—Cliff's house is a crime scene. Right? So when his mom comes by there'll be tape and she won't be able to get in and what's she supposed to think? Because, officially, the, the dead person we buried is still Cliff White. She told you it was a mother's right to take the last look. And now it's not even Cliff. Now? Now what?"

Rain was dripping from her eyelashes, running into her eyes and down her cheeks. The rain was coming down in big fat globs—warm conditions over the ocean—collecting in the clouds and dumping down on L.A. when it hit the cold mass over the mountains. Rain, how could something so fine creep into your bones and make you shudder? Phil put his arm around her shoulders and oddly, tenderly, placed her in the car. "I'm taking you home."

Inside the detective's car Anne asked, "Do you know where Cliff is?"

"At this moment, I don't know."

"At this moment," Anne repeated. "Do you think he's alive?"

"I, I don't know." Phil had forgotten to turn on the windshield wipers and the view out the window was a giant runny slick. He turned the wipers on.

"You're lying. I asked you what you think. Do you *think* he's alive—that's an opinion."

"Opinions don't get you anywhere."

Detective Vasquez parked the car in front of Bob Brown's front door. "Can I come in? I want to talk to your father." Anne looked at Phil or, rather, through him as if a movie were being projected behind his head. He turned to see what she was watching and quickly realized it was inside her head. Anne was collating every major impression she'd had since she stepped off the plane in Palm Springs four days after her birthday in February. She realized her behavior conformed to a basic premise: that people were generally good and motivated to do good for others. This idea, sitting in the car, struck her as amazingly deluded. People were generally interested in themselves and would do anything to protect that interest.

"Can I have that envelope back?"

"That's not a good idea, Ms. Brown."

Anne looked Phil directly in the eyes. "We should go to Hemet. We should go to Hemet right now."

"Why?"

"Because if Cliff's alive..."

Water had seeped down the back of his neck and soaked Phil's shirt collar. He loosened his tie and unbuttoned his collar button and rubbed the back of his neck. "Let me tell you why we're not going. First, I'd need a warrant. Second, we've gone from an overdose to a cover-up, possibly a murder, and now we have a missing person and in all likelihood a pretty large conspiracy. And you, you've... And, besides, how in the world do you think I'd take you on police business?" He shook his head in frustration.

Anne opened the car door and stepped out. "You should go to Hemet." The rain continued to pour. Anne's hair was plastered to her skull. Another basic premise drained away. All this time she had been operating under the assumption that Cliff's death was accidental. Nobody disappeared by accident.

The detective exited the car. "Right now I'm taking you inside."

They splashed through the storm to the house. Anne opened the front door. She could hear the television in what her father called the den and what everybody else referred to as the media room. "Anne?" called Bob.

"It's me, Dad!" she responded and then turned to the detective. "Possible murder. You said possibly a murder. Was Ryan Simms murdered?"

"No."

"No? You mean, no, he *wasn't* murdered?"

"I mean, no, as in I'm not discussing this with you."

"Huh. Not discussing...as in the evidence you weren't at liberty to discuss. The evidence you found at The Buccaneers? That was dipped in Clorox? That showed up in infrared? Oh! And I wonder why you went looking at The Buccaneers again? Maybe with a warrant? Maybe because I told you James and/or Ben were kicked out for doing drugs? Maybe because I told you the church bought The Buccaneers? And, I don't know, what've I come up with recently? Anything useful?"

"Before you get too carried away with yourself, did you ever wonder why I asked you if Clifford White was gay?"

A frown was all Anne could manage.

"Because when the coroner examined the cadaver she found lubricant and traces of latex in the rectum. Unfortunately there wasn't any ejaculate or..."

Anne rounded on Phil Vasquez and took hold of him by the lapels. It should have appeared absurd but the febrility of Anne's anguish made it anything but. "Why aren't you looking? Why aren't you looking for Cliff? That wasn't him! That wasn't him! And the funeral! And the... Right now they're back at his house! Looking for, for, blood or, or fingerprints, or... Where's my... Where is he?!"

Phil closed his eyes to shut out her face.

Bob stepped into the foyer and stood at the bottom of the stairs, witnessing the whole weird tableau. He saw the detective standing with his eyes closed while his bold but small daughter, wailing like Fury, threatened a man who carried a gun. They were both soaked with rain.

Anne shook Phil, her eyes wide and filmed with tears, her speech illogical and shrill. "No, Cliff's dead! He really is dead and you're not telling me! Tell me the truth!"

The detective cautiously—like he was subduing a delirious child—took hold of her wrists and loosened her grip on his coat, then held her fists tight in his large, scarred, hands.

"Hey! What the hell?" shouted Bob. "Annie? What the hell's going on?"

Chapter 31

I WILL SURVIVE

A couple of hours later Anne lay in her bed, her bedroom door open to the landing. The light flicked on in the hallway and her father passed by, putting on a hat and pulling on a coat. It was nearly midnight. She couldn't sleep and she couldn't take anything to knock herself out because she was wary of doping the fetus. "Dad?" She sat up.

Bob paused with his hand on the banister. "Hey, pumpkin."

"I forgot to tell Detective Vasquez that James Johnson is in France."

"How do you know that?"

"I saw Shamari at Barneys. She told me." Bob nodded thoughtfully. Anne asked, "Where you going?"

"Over to Cole's," he answered.

"But—" Anne didn't say anything more. She didn't need to. Phil Vasquez had, in the end, given Anne the information on Cliff White and Ryan Simms that she had desperately needed, and Bob had heard it too. In fact, it was the combination of Anne's distressed state and Bob's forceful yet concerned presence that had formed the double spur that resulted in Phil divulging the information. However, the admonition for silence and the need for secrecy, which Phil had delivered to both of them, had seemed to Anne's ears less like a warning when given to her father than the transfer of a protectorate. Phil and Bob had shaken on it but there seemed to be a shadow agreement between them regarding her. She could have done without the condescension, yet hadn't said a thing about it, before or after the detective left the house. After all, she thought, *maybe I'm mistaken.*

When she had suggested to her father, following Phil's departure, that they drive out to the desert, he said, "Sweetheart, I want you to get out of those wet clothes and take a warm bath and try to relax." Anne felt the frustration and anger rise again. "None of that Nancy Drew stuff now, Anne. How do you think you're going to get the answers you need that way? I'm eighty and you're five feet tall. C'mon, take a step back and leave it to the cops. I know that's hard for you, what with thinking you're invincible and my brother egging you on. But I want you to concentrate, right here in this house, on staying safe. Okay? I want you in this house. You and the baby. Safe."

Bob tightened his grip at the top of the banister. "I know what the detective said. But I have obligations, Anne. And one of them is to Cliff's father."

"Daddy." She got out of bed. "It'll take me two seconds to get dressed." Anne understood that he thought he was doing what was best for her. Despite not being able to say anything, she felt queasy at being patronized, and despairing at the greater sense of powerlessness. She wanted to spit out a venomous retort in reply to Bob's assertion about his "obligation," something about him still indulging in macho bullshit *even though he was eighty*, but it remained burning, unsaid in her throat.

Bob walked to Anne and gave her a hug. "Chipmunk. You need rest."

Anne was brittle with anxiety and fatigue, and being treated like a little girl did not in any way contribute to her sense of well-being. In truth, her father's infuriatingly primitive paternalistic attitude caused her to behave even more childlike. "I can't sleep!"

"What are you? Four? Go downstairs and watch some TV and I'll be home in a while. I know. Give me your phone." Anne took her cell phone off the nightstand and handed it to Bob. He pocketed it and brushed her hair away from her cheek. "If you need me, call me on your phone." Bob Brown thought cell phones were tethers and was adamant that if someone wanted to talk to him it would be at his leisure and always on his landline.

"I'm coming with you."

"Sorry, Charlie. Nothing doing."

Having won the battle, Bob left, brandishing an umbrella in front of him like a sword. Anne, agitated and irritated, padded downstairs. She felt like calling her sister, but Los Angeles, unlike New York, shut up and went to bed well before eleven.

In the den she opened the liquor cabinet and looked at an assortment of bottles she could have sworn had been at the same levels since 1987. She sat on the couch where she had read while her father watched the Academy Awards. There was an ashtray on the side table. Nobody, as far as she could remember, had ever smoked in the house, not even Bob's big brother, Manny. Next to the ashtray were a lamp, a phone (not wireless), and a Rolodex. A Rolodex.

Anne flipped through the cards. She remembered catching hell on one of her preteen visits for calling, in quick succession, a bunch of luminary "B's"; Bacall, Beatty, Brooks (Albert and Mel), and someone only noted as Billy with a German accent who had picked up and chatted affably until asking to speak to her father. She looked for Billy's card. It was still there. In her father's hand and in various inks it noted a birthday, included a quote, *If you're going to tell people the truth, be funny or they'll kill you*, and finished with the date March 27, 2002. Billy must have been Billy Wilder.

Her eyes stung. She crossed her arms over her stomach and thought about Cliff. She thought about the police at his house. She thought about the mobile labs. She thought about what Phil Vasquez had said. And how he had said it. Finally, she had to conclude that Cliff, though he had come alive in her thoughts off and on throughout the evening, was likely dead. Still dead, just as he had been assumed to be. She began to cry, to weep and shudder, to shiver as if exposed to extreme cold. It might seem hysterical but she didn't care; she felt storm-wracked with sorrow; she felt as if her soul had cracked open and all the misery in the baleful world had entered it, an abject, breathing, nightmare.

Chapter 32

MUSIC WHEN THE LIGHTS GO OUT

A day passed by. Sunny, bland, ordinary, and quiet. Her father let the machine pick up his calls and only responded after reviewing the messages. Anne turned off her cell phone. She didn't check her email. They walked. They cooked. Her father insisted she eat. They discussed her grandfather's birth in White Chapel, a cockney slum in London, and her grandmother's father, Raphael, who had emigrated from Austria in 1860 and joined Lincoln's army. Bob told Anne about a great-grandmother who had had twelve children, how his mother earned a Phi Beta Kappa key and tutored her husband-to-be and his father-to-be in mathematics. The distance of history left her struggling to feel a connection to her ancestors. Bob unearthed a trunk full of family photographs. And it was while looking at these images that she felt the jolt of recognition; it was there in the curve of a smile and the certain familiar way someone held their head; it was there when she saw the Phi Beta Kappa at sixteen laughing at the beach, dressed in a bathing costume that included tights—the Phi Beta Kappa with her own flyaway hair; it was there in photographs of her uncle as a teenager and her father as a little boy, both offering versions of the same laugh to the sky. Anne lingered over the picture of her father as a child standing holding a toy boat beside his mother sometime in the 1930s, his face aglow with unaffected delight. She found herself wondering if her child would have her grandmother's chin. The photographs, those captured moments, allowed her to feel that connection with the past and to perceive how the bloodline would go on. As dusk came, Anne turned on her computer and stared at a roster of electronic messages and then turned the computer back off. She turned on her phone and cleared her texts without looking, her voice mail without listening. None of those things meant anything to her at the moment. Had they ever? Her thoughts were full of her baby's other bloodline. Cliff's bloodline: would it bestow warm blue eyes and an easy grin?

The following morning she was looking at her cell phone screen, distracting herself with the Internet, when it trilled into life in her hand. It was Cole. She answered. She could hear the rush of the road as Cole had her on speaker from the car, "Annie, love?"

"Yes, sir."

"Annie! I want you and your father to meet me at Cedars in five minutes."

"What? Where?"

"Emergency room. And notify Dawn. No, she swore out a restraining order against me, no; well, you better had, hadn't you!"

"Cole?"

"Five minutes!" and then he hung up.

Anne called, "Dad!"

She walked into the foyer calling out to her father, hearing footsteps above on the upstairs landing. "Dad! That was Mr. Starkey on the phone," she said, as Bob bustled down the stairs. "He wants us to meet him at Cedars."

"Fine."

"Fine?"

"You know something, honey? There's something I've gotta tell you about Cole." Anne would ordinarily have thought it an odd time to bring something like that up, even for her father, who didn't play by the usual rules, but there was something about the way he said it that told her this was truly important. So she simply listened.

Chapter 33

LUCY IN THE SKY WITH DIAMONDS

On the way back to Los Angeles from Tokyo in 1981, Cole Starkey and his fourth wife were detained at the airport, their passports seized, after a small quantity of pot was found in the inner pocket of Cole's overcoat. Before it hit the press and swelled into a small-scale scandal or became the subject of jokes on the then-flailing *Saturday Night Live*, a not inconsiderable amount of the green changed hands, and Cole (harangued by his spouse) and his wife (enraged by her husband) were home within eighteen hours. At the time he thought it an unfortunate incident, and later the memory of it still rankled. Bob Brown, his close friend, had used his own funds for the wire transfer to Clariden Leu (a Swiss bank), but although Cole had paid him back promptly, their relationship had become, at best, highly strained. Cole felt beholden. Bob's patience was frayed by years of his younger friend's erratic drug-induced follies. By the turn of the millennium they were no longer speaking. They knew of each other's children, but the children never knew about each other.

When Cliff had called his father about a certain Anne Brown he had met over the weekend in Palm Springs and informed him of his honorable intentions, Cole couldn't help but cackle "Karma's a bitch!" of course to himself, never to his love-struck, eager-to-tell-all son. He waited for nightfall then slipped away from watchful Fal Loa's gaze, walked to Bob Brown's home, and stood looking up at the darkened windows of the house like a rejected, moony teenager. After several minutes he went home, all the while contemplating how truly weird life was, before taking a handful of pills and falling, as a stone would plummet to the bottom of a lake, into a deep, dreamless sleep.

Weeks later, in the wake of his son's death, the unheralded arrival of Bob Brown at his home, in the midst of an L.A. downpour, didn't, at that point, strike him as strange. The return of his years-estranged friend was no cause for surprise in comparison to recent events. The first words from Bob, unknown in Cole's house for at least twenty years, were, "Are you sober?"

"I haven't had a drop since you tossed my drink."

"Pills, weed?"

"Don't be tedious." Bob tried to make out Cole's pupil size—easy with blue eyes—and there didn't appear to be anything suspect about them. No unnatural dilation, and besides his naturally dramatic flourishes, his gesturing, his breathing, either stentorian or silent, besides these—his eyes were tracking just fine. "May I take your coat?" Bob shrugged out of his coat and handed his hat and umbrella to Cole. Cole placed the armful of wet things on an antique wooden bench without a thought and invited his old compatriot into the cavernous living room.

"Christ! You've let the place go," muttered Bob as Cole maneuvered two armchairs in front of a blazing fireplace, kicking aside a pile of dog-eared books and seven discarded shoes, not seven *pairs* of shoes, just seven *shoes*—in order to do so. After much straining, Cole got the chairs in place, and he and Bob sat. "What happened to your housekeeper?"

"Housekeepers. I got tired of them putting things where I couldn't find them."

"Like your shoes?"

"Exactly." Cole shifted in his seat, pulled a crumpled piece of paper from under his leg, smoothed it out, read it, and then tossed it into the flames. "AT&T, so sweet, they want to bundle me." The fire cast a warming glow across the emaciated sixty-year-old and the hale eighty-year-old. Bob brought Cole up to date. Tersely, he cut to the chase, with no elaboration, only saying, without inflection or comment, that he knew Cole's son was missing and the dead boy, who had been buried in the box in his place, was a stranger from Canada. Cole pitched up and out of his chair and hissed, "All these years and I never thought you were a vicious fucking bastard, but clearly I was wrong. Fucking vicious. Get out!"

"That wasn't exactly the response I expected," Bob said. After he had quieted Cole and assured him of the legitimacy of his information, from the police, his daughter, they talked until dawn. At six a.m. they shared a pot of coffee. Bob walked home in the cool, clear blue light of morning. Cole woke Fal Loa. He and the driver jockeyed cars in and out of the carriage house until they had moved a Rolls-Royce Phantom into position and, then the big Samoan drove Cole into the high desert.

Not far from Hemet they noticed several garish mansions dotting the small hills and then gated acreage that looked like an industrial park with some interesting additions; a church with a "C" on the steeple, a building that resembled a hybrid of prison and castle—big, gray, and blocky, with crenellations and slit windows from which it was easy to imagine either a sniper or an archer aiming—and around the entire perimeter a barbed-topped electric fence.

Fal Loa pointed out cameras mounted on speed limit signs to record passing license plates. Cole instructed him to circle slowly and give everybody a good look until they reached the main entrance to the acreage. Behind the entrance there was a stone guard post. The guard opened the heavy, black, electronically operated gate and waved the Rolls in. Fal, wearing his black suit and a chauffeur's cap, stopped on the drive as the gate closed behind the car and Cole opened his window and beckoned to the guard. The guard approached the car. "There's a good soul! I'm here for my drug rehab. Could you direct me?"

The guard removed his hat and looked confused. "I'm sorry, sir, but—"

"Isn't this Clientology headquarters?"

"Wh—Yes, sir. This is home to 'C' Org. and the OCA."

Cole lifted his palm, "And?"

"Ah," the guard was clearly flustered. "Yes, sir. Please proceed and take the first right, at the Bold Era building, if you park there someone in the office can direct you."

"Of course they will. Thank you!" Cole closed his window and Fal drove on.

In the office, Fal Loa walked to the empty receptionist's desk and set a large locked case on it. He opened the case and adjusted it so the ever-present cameras could see the contents. It contained sealed bricks of hundred-dollar bills. Cole stood in the doorway looking bored and imperious.

Very shortly a man stepped into the front office. He was not the receptionist. He was "C" Org. middle management. He looked like an undernourished real estate broker, hungry and highly motivated and slightly off. "Gentlemen. Welcome. How can I help you?" Fal could see curious staff gathering behind Middle Management to catch a glimpse at the visitors through the doorway.

Cole compressed his lips and raised his brow. "I must say, this is not what I was led to believe. Fal, obviously this office is not capable of taking payment for my treatment, is it?" Fal Loa shut the case shut with a snap. "Jimmy Johnson and the Habers told me it was taken care of!" He squinted in the light. "Well, I'm not going to stand here for naught at this ungodly hour. Take me home." Fal lifted the case and got the door for Cole.

Middle Management scurried forward, "Sir, I'm sure we can work something out. Just give me a second. I can make a call and," Cole sneered at Middle Management and kept walking.

"Please, sir! Help me help you."

Cole paused. "Are you even aware of my name?"

Middle Management was stymied.

"Well, there I can help you. Cole. Cole Starkey. Golden Oldies to Grunge, Hard Rock to Heavy Metal, Stadium Rock to AOR, half of what you listen to on those inferior speakers in that atrocious little music-mangling iPod of yours is mine. Mine!" Cole was making quite a scene. A few of the less cowed and more curious office workers were quietly huddled in the doorway bearing witness to the Great Cole Starkey's verbal rampage. He looked them all individually in the eye. "Infinitely wealthy, renowned addict in search of rehab from what James Johnson said was the finest facility in the nation. Bells? Ringing? Anything? Anything?" Fal Loa turned to whisper something to Cole. Cole pinched the bridge of his nose wearily. "Surely, there's someone here who knows."

The staff in the doorway began to mutter and murmur, then parted as if at some unheard command. The woman who entered the office was tall and thin with oddly attenuated arms; she had something of the aspect of a praying mantis. She took in the sight of Cole Starkey in full self-aggrandizing mode and seemed unperturbed; she smiled as if she'd recently been taught how to, and said, "There is, Mr. Starkey. Dominic. Dominic Semyon. And he would very much like to see you, sir."

Dominic Semyon received Cole Starkey in his home, a large-scale grotesquerie of onyx and gold plate, hardwoods and garish overstatement. Obviously being top guy in a religious hierarchy paid well. When Dominic, surrounded by flunkies, entered one of the reception rooms—one of many—Cole briefly mistook him for a suit-clad fourteen-year-old. On second glance, Clientology's guiding light was obviously much older but stood only five feet five inches tall.

Cole extended his hand and introduced himself with a mellifluous, "Cole." Dominic's attendants made way as their leader stepped forward to shake hands.

"Pleased to meet you. I'm Dom—" he didn't have time to finish before Cole made a power move and, instead of taking Dominic's hand, wrapped his scarecrow arms around him in a hug like that of a bony boa constrictor that nearly pushed the much smaller man's breath from his body.

The attendants appeared agitated and unsure. Cole, arm still draped around Dominic Semyon purred, "Let's do send our peeps away. Fal, wait for me in the car; there's a good man." He smiled beneficently and then continued. "I feel we have so much to discuss, man to man, brother to brother, as it were, yes? Some good old-fashioned *raison d'être* and all that, or did I sign them? Band, yes? Swiss? Swedish? Possibly Norwegian. No matter! I can't remember. Oh, and Fal, leave my briefcase here." Fal exited the room leaving the case of cash on the floor. The flunkies stood their ground. Cole looked at Dominic expectantly. "Well?"

Dominic excused his entourage. Cole let go his hold and the two sat in facing chairs. "That's quite a grip you've got there, Mr. Starkey," said Dominic. His vowels were as flat as the prairie. The unpleasant adenoidal twang made Cole's ears ache.

"Better living through chemistry! But seriously, that's what I'm here to discuss. It is so inconvenient when one's Dr. Feelgood passes into the great beyond. But then again, one reaches a certain age and, well, you know. And that's where you come in, Mr. Semyon."

Dominic's palms were pressed together, in a prayerlike attitude; his head was canted forward at a strange angle that was meant to convey sincere engagement. "I want you to know I am here for you, for you, personally. I will see you through this; only we can make a difference. To be *in the know* is to make the world a *yes*."

"Quite," said Cole. He shifted in his seat as if trying to place something. "You'll find I have a multitude of tics, by-product of pills, I'm afraid. And, lord! Is my skin dry?! But perhaps that's just my advancing age." He took a Sharpie he'd unearthed from some pocket of his apparel and tapped it against the arm of his chair. "Doodling, it helps me focus. But I've no paper. You see?"

Dominic reached over to an adjacent table and handed Cole a telephone pad. Cole dragged his chair forward, ostensibly for the purpose of taking the pad. He had effectually invaded Dominic's personal space, which Dominic tried to ignore. "My addiction program is one hundred percent effective. One hundred percent. Our clinics are surpassed by no one," assured Dominic.

"So I've heard. And of course I am prepared to make a generous gift to the church as long as we keep this completely personal. Just between the two of us, you understand. As a matter of fact, I feel we're friends already. The crosses you've had to bear, hmm?" Cole continued to extemporize. "You know, my dear departed doctor was once part of your fold. Devout and generous with the prescription pad. Good man. Good man. He spoke ever so highly of your devotion to J. Paul Stoddard." Dominic straightened his suit jacket. Cole continued spontaneously, "I mean in the end the great man was stark, staring, staggering mad, wasn't he? And there you were, a tender twenty-two, holding it all together, keeping those prying eyes away on that funny little yacht of his, more like a toy than a seagoing vessel, nursing him as he raved and ranted and God all knows what else? Brutal. Absolutely brutal. I wonder? Did he hit you?" Dominic colored. "Do you mind if I smoke?"

"As a matter of fact—" Dominic rejoined.

"Forgive me. Where was I?" asked Cole, slipping his cigarette into his breast pocket.

"Ranting and raving."

"He was very clever though, wasn't he, J. Paul Stoddard? And this assessing, what? Just like classical analysis. Nothing I'm too fond of, I can rightly say. But instead of your practitioner being informed by years and years of professional training, all the assessor needs is the slimmest pamphlet written by the über-prescient J. Paul. I heard he penned it immediately after he was slapped with a dishonorable discharge from the Navy, a scathing thumbs-down from a board of military psychiatrists. Ouch! Right in the old ego! Clientologists are fond of saying psychiatry kills, aren't they? But in the case of our Mister Stoddard, well, look at all this! That's what I call a catalyst—a little spark that sets off an unstoppable chain reaction." He stretched out his hands, the Sharpie held like a conductor's baton, "A life of wealth, influence, and control. Funny, isn't it? And by that, I mean peculiar, not ha-ha. Apparently a sense of irony isn't significant among the faithful." Cole sighed deeply and relaxed back in his chair. "Aren't we comfy?" He scratched at the top of his thigh. "I know the church forbids pharmaceuticals and treats those who, ah, have overindulged, helps them find the True Path— in fact, that's why I'm here, in a manner of speaking. But who could blame you if you sought to give ol' Stodd a little push along the way to the hereafter…a little encouragement? Stoddard positively lived on antipsychotics; add a couple of sleeping pills, a few antidepressants, and a Godhead turned troublesome slap-happy old man quietly drifts off to a paradise of his own making. Bye-bye! Isn't that what you Americans say? Gone, and the world at your young feet. Let's just leave it at that. What?"

A vein beat in Dominic's temple. "Those are old rumors, Mr. Starkey. Old rumors, which have no proof, no validity—"

Cole signaled Dominic to halt with his palm, and then folded his long, slender hands in his lap. "No validity, no proof? Come now, Mr. Semyon. If someone with enough money and enough influence digs deep enough or kicks up enough of a stink, you'd be surprised at what people can turn up. And I wouldn't try using any of your—do you really call this a church? Anyway, I wouldn't try any of your bullyboy tactics against me."

"What do you want, Mr. Starkey?"

"Oh my dear, dear, man, with your Napoleonic grasp of reality, I'm sure you can guess. You have children?"

"Yes."

"As do I. Lovely boy. Took his mother's name. Can you imagine?"

"I'm sure it was a disappointment. I'm sorry," said Dominic impatiently, tired of the cat-and-mouse game, the slights, the sudden slippery nature of the conversation, and the sudden intimacies. He needed to find solid ground.

"Are you? I suppose so, well, as I said, that's why I'm here. To find another way to cope, yes?" said Cole.

Dominic calculated. "And what can I expect in exchange?"

Cole dropped his voice so Dominic had to lean forward to hear. "Silence."

Chapter 34

SAVE THE LAST DANCE FOR ME

"Aw, hell!" Bob said. "We're late! I'll tell you the rest later on." He hustled Anne, who had been hanging on to every word of his like a lifeline despite not knowing where he was going with his story, out the front door. They arrived at the Cedars-Sinai Hospital emergency room at half past six and the first person they saw was a huge man in a black uniform and shiny-brimmed cap, sitting upright and aloof amid the feverish, the wounded, and the dangerously intoxicated. Fal Loa saw them, arose like a walking statue, and joined them at admissions as Bob stated, "This is Mr. Starkey's daughter-in-law and I'm her father."

A Filipina woman in blue scrubs looked at a computer screen while a security guard, as burly as Fal, stood behind her with arms crossed. "Treatment room three, family only." She pushed a clipboard in front of them. "Sign in, please." Anne tried to discipline her thoughts. Had Cole really fallen dangerously ill? No. That was unlikely. Was he checking into rehab? Obviously something serious was up, but who knew what it was? Perhaps he'd called his private physician and arranged to be met at the hospital. Cole was wealthy, so people tended to dance to his tune.

Anne and Bob walked down the corridor. All the treatment rooms had glass walls revealing hydraulic examining tables and locked crash carts and blinking monitors. The light was very bright and fluorescent. Some extremely ill people lay covered with layers of cotton blankets. When they reached treatment room number three, a drape had been drawn against the glass. A uniformed police officer was sitting outside the room in a plastic chair carrying a sidearm. Anne stopped and stared. Did she have the wrong room number? All they could see through the door was the back of a stool, a bent leg, and someone's feet at the edge of the examination table under a blanket. "Officer, I'm Bob Brown and this is my daughter Anne."

"Go in."

Inside, Cole Starkey sat on a wheeled stool, but he was not the focus of Anne's attention. No, there was someone else in the room—someone lying asleep on the examination table. Someone whom the mere sight of made Anne exult…as if the world was turning in an instant from monochrome to spectacular Technicolor, as if she was bathed and basking in sunlight…as if every breath…There he was… Cliff.

Bob Brown and Cole Starkey embraced in a fashion peculiar to men—as little body contact as possible and a lot of silent thumping on the back. Anne found herself by the examination table looking down and etching what she saw into her mind as if it would have been possible for her to forget: Cliff, his skin flushed, hair cropped, chest rising and falling in regular rhythm. His chin and cheeks were shadowed with stubble, his cheekbones decidedly more pronounced than they were weeks ago. His face was perfectly relaxed. He was in complete repose. There was an IV stand next to the table with a line from a saline drip in Cliff's hand. That hand was curled and resting on his sternum and the other was spread out on the blanket near his hip. She closed her hand over his. He opened his eyes. On seeing her, he murmured groggily, "Mm. My Annie. C'mere," and pulled her close. She buried her face in his neck, inhaling against his warm flesh, felt his pulse beat, and all that had puzzled and distressed and confounded her faded away. "Annie, you knucklehead, it's only been a couple of hours," and then his deep indigo eyes fluttered closed and he drifted back to sleep. Anne straightened up and pressed her hand against this chest to feel his heart beating and turned to Cole.

"He was pumped full of benzos, Benzodiazepines. Spent six weeks in twilight—last thing he remembers is a hysterical call from Ben Haber and walking into a place called The Buccaneers. Six weeks! With that much shit in his bloodstream I'm surprised he could remember how to breathe. That's my boy!"

"But how?" asked Anne.

"Oh, Annie, there'll be plenty of time for that later. Plenty. I'm just glad to have him back."

Ten hours later, as Cliff was being transported to an intensive care ward, Anne found her father in a waiting room working on the *New York Times* crossword puzzle with the paper propped six inches away from his face, eyes squinting behind his reading glasses, and a look of grim determination on his face. He glanced up at Anne and said, "When's the last time you had something to eat?" Anne shrugged, her mind went curiously blank, and she started to escape somewhere in her head, a synaptic path that led straight back to Cliff. "Come on, Anne. You're eating for two."

"Where's Cole?"

"He went home to get some rest," her father answered.

Eight o'clock at the Mandarette Café, a few blocks from the hospital. Anne was poking at a plate of chicken sautéed with asparagus and black bean sauce. "Dad, this tastes like animal-infused dust."

"Anne, I've been taking you here since you were eight years old. It does *not* taste like animal-infused dust." Bob caught the waiter's eye and when he arrived tableside asked, "Could you bring us a glass of milk, a cup of coffee, and two slices of almond cake?"

"Of course, Mr. Brown. Everything all right?"

"Thank you. Everything's swell," said Bob. Anne smiled her agreement and popped a piece of asparagus into her mouth for emphasis.

"Sorry. I'm just tired."

"Sure you are."

"Dad? What were you telling me about Cole?"

"Oh. Yeah. That's right. I didn't finish. So, where was I?"

"Cole was telling Dominic Semyon he'd keep his mouth shut." Bob half-nodded, grimaced, then continued with his story.

Chapter 35

YOU CAN'T GET A MAN WITH A GUN

Dominic Semyon scowled for a microsecond and tried to sit tall in his chair. "Frankly, Mr. Starkey, I really have no idea what you're talking about. Silence? About what? All I've heard so far is a rehash of a highly fictionalized Wikipedia article, which I consider, uh, personally offensive and a-a-absurd." He clenched his jaw to keep from frowning. "I've been trying for years to have it taken down. You're not here for rehab at all. And your motives? I have no idea."

Cole touched his hand to heart, "I couldn't be more sincere. But, I know, I do have a tendency to prattle on, don't I? My, my, now where is it?" He looked around and found his attaché case on the floor. He picked it up, placed it on his knees, popped open the latches, and upended the contents, fat bricks of cash, directly into Dominic's lap.

The little man stretched out his arms involuntarily as the money tumbled over and over. "Jesus!" he gasped.

"Shouldn't that be J. Paul?" Cole couldn't help but respond. He set the case back in his lap and reached inside. While he did this, Dominic, his expression suffused with intense joy, laid his hands on the blocks of bills nestled around his groin. Cole murmured to himself in apparent absentmindedness, "Really. Ah. There we go." He cocked both wrists out of his case and in each fist was a steel and silver Sig Sauer P226

9mm semiautomatic pistol. "That's better. Now do you catch my drift?" Dominic froze in place. "I never carry these on my person. As I mentioned, my skin is so delicate these days. The holsters just chafe and chafe." He leveled the pistols at Dominic's chest. Dominic shriveled up against the upholstery like a sheet of plastic set on fire. Money fell to the floor with a soft thud.

"Now, now, I don't mean to alarm you, but I'd have to be a piss-poor marksman not to make a shot like this, and I can assure you I'm bloody not. Especially with a weapon so fine, yes, very close range, this." Dominic opened and closed his mouth. "I adjusted the trigger on the gun on the left to compensate for a slightly weaker pull, but I also want to assure you I don't believe in hair triggers, just tomfoolery, stuff it into your belt and then what do you get? Nothing but a bullet in the balls. Oh, dear. I've lost my train of thought. Where was I?"

"I, I have armed guards," managed Dominic.

"Yes. But they're out there," Cole gestured with the gun in his left hand, "and I'm in here. I kill you or I kill myself; either way it's a dreadful, dreadful, mess from which there is no extrication."

"What, what," Dominic's teeth began to chatter and his skin had turned an alarming shade of green.

"Calm yourself, Mr. Semyon."

"I..."

"Oh, yes!" exclaimed Cole. "I remember now!" He sighted along the barrel of one pistol so that it was pointed at

Dominic's head. "I can't be any blunter than this: you have my son. I do hope for your sake that he's alive."

Dominic gave an animal yelp, "He's alive!"

"Good," said Cole. "Then I'd be obliged if you took me to him." He wrinkled his nose. "After, of course, you change your trousers."

Chapter 36

DEAD SOUND

Does fate rest? Or is it relentless? Of course, some who don't believe in any kind of mystical, mythical anything say destiny is shaped; by genetics, by society, by circumstance. Often events in life are stacked, and fall with the precision and inevitability of dominoes—why that is—we can only ponder. After twenty years of faith, and a complete lack of curiosity, Crystal and Henry Haber, Ben's parents, had risen through the ranks of Clientology under the detail-oriented eye of Dominic Semyon. When their son became a tween idol and weekly feature on television, Dominic was pleased. Exposure on that level was good for the church. What wasn't good for the church was Ben's sexual orientation and adolescent drive. Dominic appointed Clientology handlers to guide the young star and then fired and rehired a PR firm to control the Hollywood spin. When a network executive hinted broadly that Ben should marry, and Ben, at his urging, did—Dominic thought his problem was solved. Penny, the wife (child actress and never quite college material), adapted cheerfully to the church and spent hundreds of thousands training for Religious Technical Affirmation.

However, nothing and nobody seemed to get through to the hormone-besotted boy, and he happily went from one liaison to another. When it came to Dominic's attention that Ben was trawling for a very big fish in the industry pond, he had two thoughts; the first was that Ben's attraction to older men could possibly be a stabilizing influence, while the second came into being because of the first: particularly if that older man was, or could be convinced to become, a Clientologist.

On a night in mid-February, after he had popped some pills meant to treat afflictions from which no twenty-year-old ever suffered, he and a scorching-hot guy at an exclusive club did the wild thing. It was mind-blowing, and also, for the scorching hot guy who had downed the same pills as Ben, life-blowing. The combination of swallowed Viagra and snorted Ritalin pitched his heart into a fatal arrhythmia. Had there been a defibrillator stocked among the condoms and edible lubricants in the room it wouldn't have done the unfortunate hottie any good. Ben, watching Ryan Simms die, could do only one thing—call.

He called on the house phone. He called his agent, his handlers, and his current boyfriend and whispered an incoherent and plaintive string of syllables that sounded like language but that none of them could decipher. All of the calls' recipients had the aptitude to use a reverse directory, and one after the other they arrived at The Buccaneers in Palm Springs.

James Johnson arrived first. He got Ben to unlock the door of his room, and he slipped inside, past a clucking and infuriated and unknowing Jan Prins, and locked the door behind him. On seeing dead Ryan Simms on the floor, James exclaimed, "Shit! What did you do?"

"Don't swear," Ben whimpered, remembering at this strange time another of Clientology's prohibitions.

"What did you do?"

"Your Viagra and your kid's Ritalin."

James restrained himself from throwing a punch and said, "Step back, boy! So help me, God. And, for Christ's sake, put some clothes on. I need to think." He sat down by the body and felt for a pulse, "I need to think."

A commotion erupted in the hallway, where three of Ben's handlers were trying to muscle their way past the club's proprietor, followed by a small man in an expensive suit. "Don't worry, I know the coroner," were the placating words of Dominic Semyon, a message that caused Jan Prins to scream like a girl.

James could hear the attenuated Scandinavian vowel sounds of Mr. Prins' crescendo, "I do not know you! You are not welcome here!"

"Did you call anyone else, Ben?" asked James.

"Uh, just Cliff, and some people…"

A scuffle was going on in the hall. Jan Prins was insisting that everyone leave, including James and Ben, and then a body hit the floor and James no longer heard Jan shouting.

"Some people?"

"They're from church!"

"Great. Did you think of calling an ambulance?"

Cliff was the last to arrive. When James Johnson ushered him into the club, a grave expression scarring his ordinarily handsome face, what he saw beyond the foyer was a cluster of people in the reception room: three tallish men in darkly expensive suits, a greatly shorter man in a suit tailored to make it appear that he had broad shoulders, Jan Prins out cold on the couch, Ben Haber, and, slouched unnaturally in a wing chair by the sliding glass doors, a man with a slightly blue tinge to his waxy lifeless skin. A man who not only had a build identical to his own but who was, in other ways, too, strangely familiar.

Cliff felt a chill shiver through his body. It was as if he were beholding his own corpse or seeing himself, dead, in a reflection. Even if the dead man was, on closer inspection, not identical to him, he was still near enough, Cliff's doppelgänger. He felt like he had entered *The Twilight Zone*. His throat went dry, he asked someone for a glass of water, and that, according to his deposition and his court testimony, was the last thing he remembered before pulling up at the hospital emergency room six weeks later, a passenger in his father's Phantom.

The bizarre reality was that he had been housed in a makeshift Clientology infirmary in Hemet, a purported "John Doe" under the care of an alcoholic anesthesiologist whose license was revoked by three states, including the one he was practicing in. Cliff had a steady stream of Versed pumped into his bloodstream, while his fate rested with, well, let's just say it rested.

Even the longest sleep usually ends. And so it was that consciousness came back to Cliff. Six weeks later, without a clue how he had gotten from Palm Springs to Los Angeles seemingly instantaneously, nodding in and out of sleep, slipping back and forth between blackout and the city of illusion.

Chapter 37

DON'T FENCE ME IN

In the weeks that followed Cliff's recovery (and certain legal matters having to do with misfiled death certificates), there was a shuffling of domiciles both earthly and celestial. James Johnson, after meeting with a cardinal in Paris, converted yet again, this time to Catholicism. He left Hollywood and renounced the pursuit of fame. His fortune he gave to his family. He annulled his marriage and, with Shamari's blessing, committed his body to holy orders at an undisclosed location in Northern California—a brotherhood of Franciscans who supported their monastery by refilling ink cartridges and baking fruitcake, available on Amazon.com.

Young Ben Haber, after receiving critical raves in Bill Aagard's film, spent a long evening celebrating on the Sunset Strip and then, while speeding home, missed the turnoff from twisting Mulholland, to his hillside aerie. Slamming through a guardrail and plummeting down to his death, his last thoughts went something like this, *Whoa, I wonder how fast this sucker's going?* and then he was gone. He was lauded, to many an insider's disgust, in a manner not unlike James Dean, and his parents immediately negotiated a deal to sell his digital likeness so he could act, and earn, in perpetuity.

Uncle Manny, after twenty-five years in a tower at Park La Brea, moved on—to his brother's in Beverly Hills. Bob had the heater replaced in his frigid and algae-covered pool, and after a chlorine shock it was suitable for Uncle Manny to receive physical therapy in its cleansed and balmy waters. He bestowed his Jaguar on his physical therapist, overjoyed by a return of body mass. Whether this was due to exercise or Bob Brown's hot fudge sundaes, no one can say.

Cole Starkey sojourned briefly in Switzerland, where it was rumored he went through several blood transfusions to avoid the withdrawal symptoms of an assortment of drugs too numerous to list. On returning home he was counseled to relinquish his guns to the LAPD under an amnesty program. He and Bob Brown continued to bicker relentlessly, and Cole was invited to join the retired moguls' weekly bridge game. "Bob, I love you, man, but really, surely you're joking, right?"

Anne emptied her apartment in Manhattan and moved into Cliff's on Deronda Drive. When pressed, Cliff remembered very little of the night previous to his weeks of sedation, but he knew if it hadn't been for his inquisitive Anne he would have never returned from the desert. Surprisingly, Cliff was informed by a crack team of doctors that his drug-induced coma would have no lasting physical effects; the psychological effects of the kidnapping, of course, would have to be reconciled. Bob Brown counseled hard work as a curative for Cliff's sense of betrayal. Cole Starkey offered the couple ownership of a small island somewhere near Tahiti, a benevolent gesture they declined. And as it came to pass, they settled in together, if intimacy engendered by danger, conspiracy, zealotry, and pregnancy can be referred to as settling.

Considering the circumstances, Anne and Cliff got along. Of course, being in love certainly helped color their perceptions. Instead of finding each other's domestic habits jarring and new, they found them charming and unique. Due to his

organizational skills, nothing ever went missing. Due to
her doggedness, a small office was converted into a nursery
in eleven days. Cliff found himself laughing at what many
would find obstinate in Anne's character and exclaiming,
"No! Tell me what you really think!" Anne found herself
constantly delighted by what others would find controlling in
Cliff's character and would exclaim, "You really do think of
everything." Then she'd go all misty and wonder again if the
baby would have blue eyes. As Bob Brown often commented,
"Ain't love grand?"

The birth of their daughter coincided with their decision
to marry. Three months after the appearance of Ava White, a
realization rose up like a storm bank: with the addition of a
child, their lives would never, ever be the same. When they
asked their parents why nobody had mentioned this shocking
fact, they received myriad replies. Dawn White said, "It's a
transformative mystery no one can prepare you for," followed
by Jill Shayes' "Ha! Welcome to my world, babe"; Cole's
response was simply, "Does it? I hadn't noticed," and all Bob
Brown said was, "Yup. How about I take the baby Tuesdays
and Thursdays?"

At ten months Ava could be seen around town strapped
to her grandfather's chest, peering out at the world while
Bob Brown explained the view. The Los Angeles County
Museum of Art was a frequent stop on their circuit. In a
gallery that housed works by Helen Frankenthaler, Mark
Rothko, and Sam Francis, Bob Brown would rumble on
about the distinctly American post–WWII school of Abstract
Expressionism while baby Ava crooned in reply. Color fields
excited the sensory cells in her young eyes and she would
stretch her body back against Bob's ribs and raise her arms in
front of Sam Francis' ten-foot-by-fourteen-foot canvas, *Toward
Disappearance*, a cool white expanse punctuated by a trail of

blue images floating like water lilies with one vivid blossom of red, and her grandfather would say, "See that, kiddo? That's a masterpiece. You see it. I see it. Some paintings entertain you, and some make you mad, but a masterpiece makes you see everything that's come before you, and everything that comes after. One stream, and we're all in it, and it's all good."

And with that, he kissed the top of her head and strolled off toward the cafeteria thinking about egg salad sandwiches.

14712071R00165

Made in the USA
San Bernardino, CA
02 September 2014